The Song of Pentecost

W. J. CORBETT

Illustrated by Martin Ursell

MAMMOTH

First published in Great Britain 1982
by Methuen Children's Books Ltd
Published 1992 by Mammoth
an imprint of Reed Consumer Books Ltd
Michelin House, 81 Fulham Road, London SW3 6RB
and Auckland, Melbourne, Singapore and Toronto

Reprinted 1995

Text copyright © 1982 W. J. Corbett
Illustrations copyright © 1982 Methuen Children's Books Ltd

ISBN 0 7497 0926 X

A CIP catalogue record for this title
is available from the British Library

Printed and bound in Great Britain
by Cox & Wyman Ltd, Reading, Berkshire

Contents

1 Snake Dries His Eyes

Young Snake's troubles began at home on Lickey Top. The accidental death of his father was the first cruel blow.

The two had been enjoying a game of puzzles, a popular pastime amongst snakes. The game involved the tying of knots in the tail and the solving of them by the other party. Sadly the old snake had tried a clever but dangerous knot too near his throat and had choked to death. Frantically his only son had attempted to solve the knot, but in vain. He was too young and inexperienced to tackle such an intricate puzzle. Suddenly the young snake was an orphan in a harsh, uncaring world.

He had never been alone before. Always, in the past, his father had been near to advise and comfort when the need arose. And worse, he had no mother to turn to: she having left home after a bitter quarrel.

For many generations the Oily Green Pool had been home for the snake family. It was oval-shaped, with rushes and weeping willows all around. The waters were deep, and the young snake had spent many happy hours diving to the bottom to see how long he could hold his breath without dying, or coming to the top. It was a dangerous game but very exciting.

The surface of the pool had an oily sheen that glowed a cool green when the sun shone upon it. Long ago the branch of an oak, severed by a bolt of lightning, had fallen across from shore to shore, making a superb platform for water-sports. The young snake enjoyed lying upon it, his head in the water, blowing bubbles.

Now all had changed. Snake's grief over the loss of his father was intense. For one whole day he sobbed his heart out, the tears falling like raindrops into the still, green pool. He was quite inconsolable, or would have been had anyone called with words of comfort. But no-one did. No-one cared. Not one friend had the decency to drop by with a consoling pat, or a word of sympathy. But then Snake had no friends. His father and their pool had been his whole world. Now his father had gone, and if that wasn't enough, Fate struck him a second savage blow. He was to lose the only thing left to him: the pool.

The morning after his father's death he pulled himself together. He knew life had to go on. The old snake would have wished it.

It was that afternoon just as the sun was sinking behind the Lickey Hills when the stranger snake paid him a call. The visitor insisted that he was Snake's long-lost cousin. The 'cousin' had bad news.

'Get off my property,' he snapped. 'I've come for what's mine, so start making tracks.'

Snake was flabbergasted. He began to stutter and stammer but the cousin was having none of it.

'For a start I'll thin those rushes out,' he mused, glancing about the pool. 'One needs plenty of room to throw wild parties. But on the whole it's not a bad little property, as properties go. It'll feel a bit strange at first, but I expect I'll soon get settled in. Are you still here?'

'Of course I'm still here,' cried the bewildered snake. 'What do you mean, "you'll soon get settled in"? This is my pool.'

'It was your pool,' corrected Cousin. 'And now gather up your things and let's see the back of you, eh?'

'But I've got no things,' Snake whispered, his head in a whirl. 'I'm an orphan. I've been an orphan since yesterday. And father never mentioned a cousin. My only relative is an aunt who travels the world on banana boats, but she's never visited us.'

'Well, you've got a cousin now,' said the intruder briskly. 'And are you going to get off my property or not?'

Snake's head began to swim. He found he couldn't control the shaking of his tail. He was confused, frightened, and felt terribly alone.

'This is some awful mistake,' he insisted. 'I'm sure you must have the wrong pool.'

'It's the right pool all right,' said Cousin, looking about admiringly. 'Uncle kindly left all his property to me in his last will. That includes the Oily Green Pool and all its pleasant surroundings. But it doesn't include you. So would you mind hopping it? I've friends coming along for the pool-warming later, and I don't want you around when they arrive. Got it?'

'You mean you want me to leave?' said Snake disbelievingly.

'Now you're getting the idea,' replied Cousin. 'And don't get the notion that you can swindle me out of what's rightfully mine. Uncle didn't mention you in his will. And if you're thinking of making trouble I've got proof, haven't I?'

This last remark was addressed to the small creature who stood shivering near the tip of his tail, half-hidden by the tall rushes. For the first time Snake noticed the frog. It resembled a quivering green jelly. Two large and bloodshot eyes bulged with fright, as its knees knocked together.

Cousin continued, 'Luckily this small friend of mine heard every word that passed between your late father and myself. He's called an eavesdropper. A cunning green eavesdropper. Aren't you?' Cousin's glittering lemon-flecked eyes trans-

3

fixed the quaking frog. The poor creature hung its head and muttered something inaudible.

'But let the honest little creature tell the story in his own words,' Cousin went on. He slapped the terrified witness with the tip of his tail, causing the frog to stumble forward.

'Well, it was last March,' the frog gabbled. 'Or was it April? I know I was feeling poorly at the time. Anyway, I was standing on a stone near Leaping Pond, doing my deep breathing exercises ... as I said I was feeling poorly at the time...'

'And you'll feel even poorlier in a minute,' said Cousin, interrupting. 'This young snake has just lost his inheritance. Don't you think he's upset enough without you rambling on about your aches and pains? It was last April, get on with it.'

The unhappy frog rushed on, 'Well, I'd just finished my stretching and bending – it eases my shooting pains down this one side, you know – when I heard voices. Hello, I can hear voices, I said ...'

Cousin butted in again, 'To cut a long story short, the voices he heard were those of your late father and myself.' He paused to allow a tear to slide down his triangular face. At the same time he gave a choking sob. 'Uncle had such a kind and caring voice,' he explained. 'Who would have thought he had so little time left. Please excuse my breakdown. It's just that when I remember ...'

'I understand,' said the young snake kindly. His dimness was really amazing, for he went on, 'If the memories are too painful perhaps we could play puzzles for a while? It might cheer you up.'

'No,' said Cousin controlling himself. 'I'd sooner get it off my chest.' He was instantly business-like again. The tale unfolded. 'Well young fella-me-lad,' Uncle had said, 'I'm not long for this world, and before I go, I want to feel that my pool will fall into safe management. Now my son is a pleasant enough youngster, but he's as thick as two planks. I'm afraid that if I left the pool to him he'd let the place go to rack and ruin, or allow some swindler to cheat him out of it. I've decided, therefore, to leave all my property in your sole charge for ever. Are you getting the picture?'

Snake's eyes filled with scalding tears as he nodded.

'It's word for word correct,' said Frog. 'As I live and breathe. Honest.' And he began to nod his head and seemed unable to stop until Cousin rapped him across the nose with his tail-end.

'But what am I to do?' cried Snake. 'Where will I go? I haven't a friend in the world to turn to.'

'Don't look at me,' said Cousin airily. 'It's not my fault. Why blame me?'

'I'm not blaming you,' wept Snake. 'But the pool is the only home I've ever known.'

'Was the only home,' corrected Cousin. 'Let's get our legal facts right, eh? I'm sorry, but I must respect Uncle's wishes in this matter. For myself, I don't particularly want this beautiful pool, set in such perfect surroundings, but it's what Uncle wished. So are you going to sling your hook, or would you rather be thrown out bodily? Remember, the law is on my side.'

'Perhaps you would allow me to stay?' said Snake hopefully. 'I promise I'd be no trouble. I'd keep to the far side of the pool, out of your way.'

'It wouldn't work out,' said Cousin. He looked sad. 'I intend to have friends up for wild parties and a goody-goody like you would spoil things. So come on, slide off my water-sports branch and be on your way. I wonder if I'd have time to thin out those rushes before nightfall?' he murmured to himself.

The young snake, his heart and spirit broken, slid from

5

the branch. His distress was such that he began to slither about in aimless circles, watched by the still trembling frog and a contemptuous Cousin.

'Which way shall I go?' he cried in despair. 'I've never been away from home before.'

'So you keep saying,' Cousin replied irritably. 'But if you want my advice, wise up, and quick. Learn to live by your wits, as I have. And here's a valuable bit of wisdom for you: never give a sucker an even break.'

'Never,' said Frog firmly. 'Not even if he's poorly.'

'And now hop it, both of you,' said Cousin, his patience at an end. 'I'm throwing a wild party tonight and I have arrangements to make. And never let me set eyes on either one of you again.'

'I do so hope the party is a success,' said Snake, wriggling sadly away.

'Thick as two planks,' murmured Cousin when the poor lost soul was out of earshot. 'They never learn. And now, what was I about to do? Ah yes, those rushes . . .'

All that night Snake wandered the Lickey Hills. The morning found him shivering under a bush, hungry and with his nerves in a terrible state. For two more days he lived the life of a vagabond, sliding from this point to that with no sense of direction at all. So sick at heart was he, all thoughts of personal cleanliness left him. His once sleek olive skin grew wrinkled. His eyes, so bright before, quickly lost their lemon sparkle and became empty and dull. His tongue sprouted a coating of fur, caused by worry and lack of sleep. He was going rapidly downhill. How could it be that he, a once loved and pampered son, was now an outcast, homeless and shunned by all? Once he had had a warm hollow log to sleep in, a cool pool to plunge into. Now he had nothing. But he was learning fast. He had been tricked. He realised this now. And by an expert. By probably the most skilful con-merchant in the world.

The third day of misery forged a new snake. A snake filled with a burning desire for justice and revenge. But he realised he could never take back his pool by force. Hadn't the cousin mentioned friends, a luxury he himself had never known? The solution to his problems was clear now. The lying frog was the key. Find him, force a confession and he would be almost home and dry. He would confront the cousin with a reformed frog, and the truth would out. Then the imposter, deserted, naturally by his friends, would admit to his pack of lies and leave. This was the young snake's simple reasoning.

'Never give a sucker an even break,' he mused. 'Well, two can play at that game. One day I'll give that cousin enough of his own medicine to choke on. I'll get my pool back if its the last thing I ever do.' So saying, Snake set his stony face in the direction of Leaping Pond and slid off to flush out the lying frog.

The frogs of Leaping Pond were crushed together beneath a rocky overhang as Snake approached. They had been warned only just in time by one of their look-outs. The little frogs were packed in the centre out of harm's way.

'I'm looking for a frog with bad nerves,' snapped Snake. 'He'll be feeling poorly too, as likely as not. Send him out. I wish to ask him a few questions concerning my inheritance.'

An elder, who appeared to be their leader, hopped forward. Nervously he cleared his throat. 'We all suffer with nerves here,' he said in a harsh croak. 'It's a common complaint amongst frogs. And now, Snake do your worst. We are quite prepared.'

'Is this where we get swallowed?' piped a tiny frog from the centre. His mother shushed him.

'The lying frog, that's all I'm interested in,' said Snake. 'And I warn you, my patience is wearing thin.'

The leader, braver now, took another hop forward. 'Does the one you seek suffer with shooting pains down the one side? If he does, I'm pleased to inform you he's gone. No, I'm not. I'm sorry to inform you he's gone. I was forgetting my manners for a bit. It's my nervousness, you'll understand.'

'And where has he gone?' asked Snake. 'And no lies, mind.'

'There I can help you,' said the leader, relieved. 'You'll find him at Pentecost Farm. He went there for health reasons, so he said. We all used to live there once. Before the City spilled over, of course.'

'Pentecost Farm being exactly where?' asked Snake evenly. 'As the crow flies, if you don't mind. I'm in a hurry.'

'Certainly, Snake,' said the leader frog. He closed his eyes and thought for a while.

Suddenly the tiny frog in the centre spoke. In a piping voice he chanted, 'Swim up the stream till you come to the mighty river. Cross the river to Ambush Path. Follow the path until you come to a small clearing. Once across the clearing you'll be entering Woodpecker Wood. Hurry through the wood as fast as you can to the beautiful Lake of the Lilies. Swim or skirt the lake as your whim takes you and you'll stand at the foot of World's End Hill. Climb it, turn left, and a small pond will meet your astonished gaze. It will have crocuses all around it in the Springtime. Bluebells in the Summertime. And purple blackberries in the Autumn.'

Snake looked puzzled. The frogs began to fidget and giggle. The tiny spokesfrog had an expression of triumph upon his face.

The leader cleared his throat. He spoke, his voice full of apology, 'A slight problem, Snake. The directions should be followed from the end back to the beginning. To follow them from the beginning to the end would merely lead you...'

'Back here, tail first,' sang the tiny frog. 'And extremely astonished, I'll bet!'

'Shush,' said the leader, his expression anxious. He addressed Snake once more. 'We do so hope you catch him,' he said. 'A born liar and troublemaker is that one.'

'Traitor!' yelled the tiny frog.

'His suffering is all in the mind, you see,' explained the leader, hopping alongside Snake. 'He wouldn't feel half so poorly if he told the truth from time to time. Frankly, we're glad to see the back of him.'

'I'm not,' shouted the gallant little frog. 'For the born liar is my dad, whom I love dearly, warts and all.'

But Snake was out of earshot. He was already on his way to Pentecost Farm. And like the shrewd snake he had become, he was following the directions from the end to the beginning. He wasn't half the fool he once was.

2 Meetings at the Stream

It was dawn. Already the sun was rising over Pentecost Farm. But with the coming of the light the place was revealed to be a farm in name only. Now it was just another housing estate with a polluted stream seeping through its middle. A row of overgrown back-gardens ended at the hawthorn hedge that grew alongside the stream. Over on the other bank was a small piece of wasteland, in the centre of which smouldered a rubbish dump. An old footbridge spanned the waters, its handrail broken, its planking dangerously rotten.

The hunted frog sat on a rusting dustbin lid in the middle of the stream. Even though quite alone, he lied. He had convinced himself that this place was a little paradise. The bin lid was a beautiful pea-green lily pad. The stagnant waters flowed by, crystal-clear. The rotting vegetable peel, the piles of battered tin cans, all were ignored. He chose not to notice his webbed feet lapped by detergent scums. The unsightliness of Pentecost Farm was hidden away beneath a carefully-woven skein of lies.

He had almost blotted the snake affair from his mind. This was not too hard a task, for he still suffered his dreadful shooting pains. From morning till night they nagged away at his tender body. And as he sat, so he groaned out loud from time to time. It was this that the avenging snake heard as he slithered along the bank of the stream.

'So,' he mused. He smiled bitterly. 'Could it be our green friend is actually welcoming us to Pentecost Farm? Perhaps he's waiting to give himself up? No doubt he's realised I'm prepared to follow him to the end of the world?' He grimaced. 'And this surely must be that place.' He paused to listen awhile, his slim head poking up through the grasses for a quick look around.

'It is him,' he hissed excitedly. 'Quietly, Snake, quietly.' He began to edge his way towards the moaning frog.

The frog was a liar, but he was no fool. He quickly noticed the parting grasses, and put two and two together. With a strangled cry of fear, he leapt from the dustbin-lid, and vanished into the reeds of the stream.

Snake had already hit the water in a desperate attempt to capture the quarry. The end of his tail, hissing through the

11

air, and aimed to knock the frog cold, struck nothing. 'You just wait, you home-breaker,' yelled Snake in frustration. 'I'll find you, never fear. Your lying body will never be safe so long as there's breath in my body.' There was no reply. Just the sigh of the wind through the reeds.

'And now, somewhere to rest up,' said Snake, looking around. 'I'll need to be good and fit before I start tracking him down.'

Finding nothing better, he crawled inside an old dolls' pram that lay on its side near the water. Curling up into a neat pile of coils he was soon fast asleep.

Some time later he awoke and poked his sleepy head outside the old pram. The bright sunshine hurt his eyes and he blinked against the glare. It was at that moment he saw, away in the distance, the Lickey Hills, sparkling in the sun. He could have wept. Instead he quickly drew his head back inside his shelter. A sudden movement had caught his eye. Snake swallowed hard and fixed his gaze upon the old mattress that lay beside the rubbish dump. There, the movement was repeated. Could it be the frog? Snake held his breath and waited.

About halfway up the rubbish dump a tuft of horse-hair stuffing was pulled aside and a biscuit-coloured head poked out. A quick glance about and out tumbled a brown Harvest mouse with a white chest and paws to match. Pentecost, for that was the mouse's name, hurried to the bank of the stream and slid down. The rusty tin cans and the discarded plastic knick-knacks seemed not to bother him. Pentecost had become used to living in squalor. Not that he enjoyed it at all; it was a question of having to.

Once this part of the world had been rich farming lands. But one day the City spilled over. For the Harvest mice in particular, it was the end to a way of life. Through countless generations they had waited, safe in their grass-spun nests, for the golden crops to ripen. The thought that perhaps one day the City would spill over never occurred to them. After all, why should it? It had never done so before. Part curious, part afraid, they had watched as the trees were felled, the hedgerows ripped out, the fields scraped and scarred by the lumbering bulldozers. And they wondered why, for they saw no sense in it at all. Wasn't Pentecost Farm their own land? Then why were the Humans destroying it, and with what right? But they had yet to learn that might was right. Eventually, only the stream with its strip of green along either side remained to remind them of a world nearly totally destroyed. They were soon hurrying to hide in what little cover it gave, and trying to rebuild their lives as best they could. But it was hard, and there would be harder days ahead.

The more fortunate creatures fled. The stronger, the fleeter ones, made their way into the Clent and Lickey Hills, but the Harvest mice were well aware of the dangers that awaited them if they attempted the same. So they stayed close to the stream and learned to survive in a changing world.

The mouse had no idea he was being watched. Although the dolls' pram was a mere few yards away, Snake was keeping very still and quiet.

Pentecost often came down to the stream to think. But it was a worried mouse who stared into those murky waters. On the bottom of the stream lay a sliver of wall mirror. Mouse stared at reflected mouse. Pentecost noted the sad eyes, the sparse grey whiskers. There was no doubt about it: he was getting old. He felt it was high time he gave up the title of Pentecost and passed it on to a younger mouse. A

13

mouse who could lead the family more vigorously through these hard times. Looking up at him was a face that clearly said life was becoming too much to cope with.

These visits to the stream gave him time to talk with the inner mouse undisturbed. The inner mouse was wise and Pentecost always listened carefully when it spoke. Plop! Pentecost took a quick dip in the stream and clambered on to the bank once more. It was amazing what a little cold water could do for a clouded brain. The mornings were still rather cool despite it being early summer. Pentecost shivered. As his fur steamed and dried in the sun, so he continued to converse with his inner voice. Meanwhile the world began to awaken. The air began to fill with tendrils of blue smoke as a breeze arose to kindle the smouldering rubbish dump. Pentecost eyed it warily. But it was a tired old fire, without sufficient energy to leap into flame. The breeze died and the smoke subsided. It would smoulder gently all day, nothing more. Thankfully, Pentecost relaxed. His family would be quite safe for the time being. So long as the fire wasn't prodded and excited it would keep to its side of the dump.

In some respects it was a useful fire. Its steady heat kept the family warm on chilly nights. Some mice, especially old Uncle, complained that the smoke got on their chests, but that was the least of the family's worries. Nevertheless, thought Pentecost, it would be foolish to look upon the dump as a permanent home. This set him thinking and worrying even more.

'Go. Leave this place. There's nothing here for you any-more.' The inner mouse again. What else could Pentecost do but agree? But it wasn't as simple as that. There were so many things to consider. For a start there were the little ones. Was it fair to uproot them from the only home they had ever known and drag them across country in search of a new one? And then there was the question of the old ones, himself

14

included. The perils of a long and dangerous trek would surely prove too much for them. Pentecost was thinking of Uncle in particular.

Old Uncle had terrible paws. Apart from being smelly they were riddled with gout. Or so he insisted. Every morning he bound them tightly with sweet-smelling herbs and hobbled around, complaining about anything and everything.

Pentecost shook his head sadly. He stood up and began to pace along the bank of the stream. Often he would stop and shake an angry paw in the direction of the new houses. There were rows and rows of them, all with a green door and a concrete path leading up to it. Each house cast an ugly square shadow where once the shade of oaks had fallen. Humans were very strange, thought Pentecost. They seemed to have a hatred for natural beauty. They had a passion for neat rows. All their vegetables they planted in straight rows like so many soldiers. They had quickly torn up the carpets of pea-green chickweed, the buttercups, the clover patches, for their beauty seemed to infuriate them for some reason. As far as Pentecost could gather, their favourite hobby was to stand on their crazy-paving paths and watch the caterpillars gnawing away at the cabbages. Yes, Humans were strange creatures.

A sudden movement and a rustling sound distracted him. Pentecost peered towards a clump of tired-looking bulrushes growing on the farther bank. It was at that moment Pentecost saw the face push out to stare at him. It was a battered face covered with ugly-looking warts. It was the face of an extremely sad frog.

'Excuse me,' said the frog in a low whisper. 'If you promise not to give me away, nod your head.'

Mystified, Pentecost nodded his head. 'I wouldn't dream of it,' he replied solemnly.

15

'Keep your voice down,' implored the frog. 'He's about somewhere.'

'Is he?' said the mouse.

'And I feel so poorly all the time,' the frog said sadly. 'I keep getting this shooting pain all down the one side. I've never felt so miserable in all my life.'

'With shooting pains like that, I'm not surprised,' the mouse replied. 'But who's he? I mean, how will I know who not to give you away to? "He" isn't much to go on, is it?'

The frog shuddered. 'He's all long and thin and olive green with orange ear muffs,' he said. 'You couldn't mistake him for anything else.'

'Anything else than what?' asked Pentecost politely.

'Than Snake of Oily Green Pool,' yelled the frog. 'Who else would I be talking about, you thick mouse?'

'Don't you take that tone with me,' Pentecost warned. 'Don't forget I haven't crossed my heart yet. Just keep a civil tongue in your head while you're on Harvest mouse land.'

'You're just a sneaky twit like the rest of 'em,' said the frog bitterly. Suddenly he ducked his head back into the rushes.

'Now what?' said Pentecost.

'Over there,' whispered the frog. A webbed foot pointed in the direction of the old pram. 'There's something moving inside. It's him. It's Snake. Look, you can see him breathing. For Heaven's sake don't wake him up.'

Pentecost looked behind at the pram. 'It's just a bit of old rope,' he said. 'Fancy mistaking a bit of old rope for a snake. Don't be such a silly frog. You'll ruin your health going on like that.'

'It's ruined already,' the frog replied.

Pentecost was glad that the frog was now only a voice, for his ugliness was very off-putting.

16

'Whatever have you done to make you so afraid?' he asked.

'It was because I wasn't well,' said the frog. 'I always tell lies when I'm not well. Or is it that I always feel unwell when I tell lies? I just don't know any more.'

'What a pickle,' said Pentecost. 'Never mind. If I see this snake, I promise I won't tell him I saw you. It's the least I can do, even though you did call me a thick mouse.'

'I did not,' said the frog indignantly.

'Yes you did,' replied the mouse. 'And you called me a twit.'

'I did not,' said the frog stoutly.

Pentecost began to get angry. 'And I suppose a snake with orange ear muffs isn't chasing you at all?'

'What snake?' said the frog. His head emerged once more. Pentecost recoiled from such ugliness.

'Do you always lie like this?' asked the mouse. 'You distinctly said that a snake with orange ear muffs was chasing you.'

'I said no such thing,' repeated the frog. 'It's all in your imagination. All I said was good morning. Can't one say good morning without having one's words twisted?'

'And I suppose you don't feel poorly at at all?' said Pentecost, his temper at boiling point.

'I've never felt better in my life,' said the frog. 'Snakes chasing me indeed! Wherever do you get these stories from?'

'In that case,' said Pentecost, 'you won't mind company. Because a certain piece of rope with orange ear muffs is on its way over.'

The frog gave a strangled croak and vanished. The mouse wasn't lying. The pile of old rope had stirred, stretched and was at this very moment sliding over to investigate.

3 The Bargain

'You are a snake, after all!' said the surprised mouse.

'And what did you think I was?' asked the other, curling up in the sun a yard or two away.

'A bit of old rope, actually,' said Pentecost. 'But I see now you're not.'

'Thank you,' said Snake. 'By the way, who was that you were talking to just now?'

Pentecost was studying Snake's ear muffs. 'They're not orange at all,' he said. 'That was another lie he told me. They're buttercup yellow.'

'Let's forget about my distinctive markings for the time being,' said Snake. 'You just said that that was another lie he told you. Who told you?'

'I'm not allowed to say,' said Pentecost. 'I made a promise.'

'Would this liar be a muddy green colour and would he have a sharp pain down the one side?' demanded Snake.

'My snout is sealed,' said Pentecost firmly.

'I have ways of making you talk,' Snake warned. 'I've come a long way to find that frog and I've suffered, God, how I've suffered. So come on, talk before I get tough.'

'You'll just have to get tough then,' said Pentecost bravely. 'I won't break my promise, even though he did call me a thick mouse.'

'Very well,' said Snake. 'I have other means. Stare deeply into my eyes. I'm going to break your will to resist.'

Pentecost obligingly stared into Snake's lemon-flecked

eyes. 'You are feeling sleepy,' droned Snake. 'You are drift-ing into a deep, deep sleep. You feel all rubbery and you can't wait to begin telling the truth, am I right?'

Pentecost agreed that his symptoms were just as snake described.

'In a few seconds you'll begin to answer every question I ask, truthfully. I told you I had other means, didn't I? We snakes are no fools.'

'I'm ready for the questions, Snake,' said Pentecost. 'But could you make them easy ones at first, until I get into the swing of it?'

'Very well,' was the reply. 'Question number one! what kind of water thingamybob would you be?'

'No kind at all,' said Pentecost. 'I'm a Harvest mouse.'

'That sounded truthful enough,' said Snake. 'I think we can skip the next few questions and get on to number seven. Question number seven; who were you talking to a while ago?'

'I think I'd prefer question number two, please, Snake,' said Pentecost. 'My honour is involved in number seven.'

Snake looked both disgusted and fed up. 'Never mind,' he said. 'We'll try something else. The sob story, I think, that should do the trick. Now listen carefully. Once upon a time there was a happy young snake who lived with his kind father in the family's Oily Green Pool. One day...' And Snake poured out his heart. He told about his father's death. He told how he had learned to live alone with his grief and loneliness. He described the coming of the 'cousin' and the frog who had witnessed the promising-away of his pool. With tear-filled eyes he recalled how the cousin had banished him from his home so that he could throw wild parties for his friends. The wide-eyed mouse listened to the happenings that went on at Leaping Pond and how the sympathetic frogs had set Snake on the trail of their lying companion. And here he was, said Snake, and all he wanted was to ask the frog a few questions concerning his inheritance.

Pentecost had listened intently to all this. Almost immediately he gave Snake his firm opinion. 'I think you've been cheated,' he said. 'It's a known fact that fathers always leave their property to their sons. Never to cousins. And, if as you say, you haven't even got a cousin, it all sounds very suspicious to me.'

'If I could only find that frog,' said Snake sadly. 'I'm sure with a little persuading I could get him to admit his lies. It's my belief that Cousin forced him to tell a pack of lies under pain of death.'

'I don't think that frog would need much forcing,' said Pentecost. 'I've never met such a liar in all my life.'

'So you have seen him?' cried Snake. 'Quick, show me where he is. I'll give him lying and making folks' lives a misery. He'll wish he'd never been born when I get through with him.'

'Stop!' shouted Pentecost. 'Isn't there enough violence in the world? If you go on like that I won't help you to find him. I agree you've been badly treated. It's a pity you hadn't been born a little smarter, then none of this would have happened. But then, you can't help being thick, can you?'

Snake swallowed the insult in his eagerness to enlist the mouse's help. 'You will, then? You'll tell me where he is?' he said. But Pentecost wasn't listening. He was thinking. An idea was forming in his mind. A crazy idea but yet . . .

'Lickey Top, Snake,' he said slowly. 'You said you came from Lickey Top? You see, I've been listening to the inner mouse this morning and he kept saying that we mice should leave this place. I wonder . . .'

Snake was suddenly suspicious. 'What's on your mind?' he asked.

'Well, if we mice find the frog for you and you prove that

he had told lies, what would you do then?' asked the mouse.

'That's easy,' Snake replied. 'I'll take him back to Lickey Top and force him to confess in front of that cousin. When his friends hear what a cruel snake he is they'll turn against him and I'll get my pool back.'

'You hope,' said Pentecost. 'What if the cousin who isn't a cousin refuses to leave? He sounds a very worldly snake to me. And tough. A lot tougher than you, I'll bet.'

'I hadn't thought about that,' Snake admitted. 'I was hoping the truth would be enough.'

'Don't bank on it,' said the mouse. 'You'd find yourself in a fight, without a doubt. And after losing it you'd be back where you started. Have you any friends who would help you?'

Snake had to admit that friendship was an experience he'd never known.

The mouse rushed on. 'But what if you had lots of friends to help you regain your pool? Friends who would never desert you, no matter what?'

'Are you making me an offer, by any chance?' said Snake warily.

'An offer you can't refuse,' said the mouse promptly.

'Oh yes I can,' said Snake. 'If you think I'm having a bunch of mice trailing after me, you can forget it. That is your idea, I take it?'

'Think about it, Snake,' said Pentecost urgently. 'In my opinion you need all the help you can get. And another thing...'

'What other thing?' said Snake wearily.

'Well,' said the mouse triumphantly. 'Do you really think you could find that frog all on your own? You could search for days, weeks, months, and still not find him. Now we Harvest mice know every inch of Pentecost Farm. We could find him in a twinkling.'

21

'Blackmail,' sighed Snake.

'Common sense,' corrected the mouse. 'And now my plan is this: if we find the frog for you to question and he admits his deceit, you in return will do us mice a small favour.'

'What favour?' Snake asked. 'As if I didn't know.'

'Well,' continued Pentecost, warming to his brilliant plan. 'Would you know of a small vacant property in the Lickey Hills? Just a small plot where a family of well-behaved Harvest mice could settle and make a new life for themselves? If you knew of such a place, would you agree to lead us there if we found the frog for you? I think that's a very fair offer.'

'I still say it's blackmail,' said Snake. He wasn't at all keen on the idea, but he was beginning to realise he had no choice.

Pentecost, seeing that Snake was weakening, pressed on. 'A small plot by your pool would suit us perfectly. It sounds the ideal place. Of course, we would settle somewhere out of your sight. In that way, you wouldn't be disturbed by the din of the little ones.'

'I'd be prepared to consider just one or two of you coming along,' said Snake reluctantly. 'I'd hate to think of my property becoming cluttered up. Oh, I don't know . . .'

'I'm sorry, Snake, it's all of us or none. I'm the leader of the family, you see. I couldn't possibly desert any of them.' Pentecost squared his snout and looked Snake straight in the eye.

'And I suppose you mice hold noisy Harvest Festivals and Spring celebrations?' said Snake moodily. 'And I expect there'd be a lot of singing and dancing and making thorough nuisances of yourselves? I've heard that Harvest mice make an incredible fuss about such things.'

'Sometimes we can't help it,' said Pentecost. 'It's the joy of being alive, you see.'

Snake pondered gloomily. 'And how widespread would this joy be?' he asked.

'Don't be such a misery,' the mouse replied. 'But when you think about it, you've really no choice, have you?'

'How many are there in this family of yours? Although I dread to ask.'

'At one time there were hundreds of us,' said Pentecost soberly. Snake winced. 'But that was before the houses were built,' the mouse went on. 'Before the City spilled over. That was a terrible time for us. Some of the older mice got bulldozed into the ground. They couldn't run fast, you see. A great many of us died of starvation. And, of course, others died of broken hearts. We mice are very sensitive, as you may have gathered, Snake.'

'You also drive a hard bargain,' said Snake. 'But do go on.'

Pentecost did. 'So you see, we must leave this place. You are our only hope. We need your guidance and protection on the journey to the new home; you need our help in capturing the frog.'

He waited patiently for Snake's reply. Then suddenly a thought struck him. He voiced his fear. 'By the way, Snake, if and when we capture the frog, don't think you can carry him off quietly and leave us in the lurch. You'll need help in escorting him back to Lickey Top. You couldn't possibly keep an eye on him every inch of the way. You'd need to sleep and he could easily hop off and disappear for ever. Now with us mice along that could never happen. We could take it in turns to stand guard over him. So you see we need each other, don't you agree?'

Snake, despite his reluctance, was forced to agree. Then suddenly, out of the blue, he had the answer. The mice wanted a new home. Snake wanted that new home to be as far away from his pool as possible. It was a brainwave of the first order.

'Of course,' he said. 'I've got the perfect solution. As

it happens, I do know of a plot of vacant land. It's a small knoll on the tip-most top of the Lickey Hills. And it's quite deserted, except for a kindly owl who lives in an old oak tree. I'm certain he wouldn't mind you moving in there.'

At the mention of the word owl, Pentecost shivered. Snake hurried on, 'You'd have nothing to fear from him. He's a recluse, you see. He likes solitude, and, provided you didn't make too much noise, I'm sure he wouldn't mind you setting up house there.'

'Yes, but even recluses have to eat,' said Pentecost uneasily. 'I don't think much of your idea, Snake. We'd much prefer to settle elsewhere.'

'What a silly suspicious mouse you are,' Snake chided. 'Didn't I say Owl was a kindly bird?' He looked reproachful, 'You're doubting my word already. You must learn to trust me. If you don't, there's no point us discussing this business any further.'

Pentecost tussled with his inner mouse. The mouse inside urged caution but the desperate mouse outside finally won. 'It's a bargain,' he said at last.

'A bargain, it is,' Snake replied. 'And you won't regret it, I promise. And now, how soon can you begin tracking that lying frog down? I'm anxious to get back to my pool as soon as possible. Heaven knows what damage that cousin and his friends are wreaking in my absence.'

'I'll call a family meeting this very minute,' said Pentecost excitedly. 'And we'll meet again at sunset, Snake.'

'With the frog?' enquired Snake. 'The deal's off if you don't produce the frog.'

'With the frog,' promised Pentecost. Then, much to Snake's embarrassment, he flung his paws about those yellow ear muffs and hugged him. 'You won't regret it,' he said. 'You'll soon have your Oily Green Pool back, and we mice will have a new home where we can live in peace and quiet for ever.'

'I'm so glad for us both,' said Snake softly. 'By the way, what's the fishing like around here?'

But Pentecost was already hurrying for home to break the glad tidings, and to make known to the family a decision he had arrived at. He was an old mouse and he had wisely realized that this new venture called for new and youthful leadership.

Meanwhile Snake scoured the banks of the stream for a likely-looking fishing spot. After a long and fruitless search he gave up. Sighing, he slid back inside the old pram and settled down to sleep away the hours until sunset. Before he drifted off to sleep he allowed himself a wry smile. He was imagining Owl's face when a family of noisy Harvest mice burst upon his privacy. 'But, of course, I won't be there to see it,' he thought. 'By that time I'll have my pool back and what happens to the mice after that . . .'

Contentedly, he fell into a deep slumber.

4 Pentecosts Old and New

There were three small families living inside the rubbish dump. Although separate units, they were all related in some way. Harvest mice tended to get mixed up in matters of who belonged to which family and who didn't. Each family had cousins, nieces and nephews in other groups. Often grandmothers were shared, and even great-aunts several times removed. It wasn't unusual for a mouse to be the cousin of a niece four times removed from a great uncle who was the grandfather of one's mother's youngest sister. Some relationships were even more complicated and to try to unravel them, even with all the time in the world, would be folly, not to mention impossible.

The small mice, given a choice, would have voted the ancients their particular favourites. It was fun to tie their tails together and learn new swear words. The old mice rarely used the same oath twice. They also thought that Great Aunts were the strangest of lady mice. Great Aunts liked to twist grass stems into interesting shapes with their nimble paws. 'Busyness is next to Godliness,' they were fond of saying. At other times they would shout, spying a young mouse with grubby ears, 'Cleanliness is next to Godliness,' causing the offender to run away as fast as his filthy paws could carry him.

But the prime source of the family's amusement was old Uncle. Not that he made jokes, he rarely did. He was fun because he took himself so seriously. He was also the craftiest mouse in the Midlands, not to mention the most idle. He too had a favourite saying. 'Soft living makes idle bundles of bones,' he would declare, after he had steered the conversation back to the old days, the days of his youth. And he knew what he was talking about for he owned a set of his own.

Most of the small mice had been forced to run an errand for Uncle at some time or other. He would pretend to be very ill and speak in a cracked, pain-filled voice. 'Run and get me something tasty for my lunch,' he would wheedle. 'Something sweet and soft. A succulent root will do nicely. But nothing hard, mind, for my old teeth are wobbly in their sockets. There's a good little mouse,' he would add cunningly.

It was hard to resist his heartrending appeal, especially when he turned to the subject of his painful knee joints. 'I would go myself, but my joints are giving me gyp today. I cannot put one paw before the other without stumbling on my nose,' and his eyes would mist up as he explained how dearly he would like to scurry off and search for his own as the others did. It was nothing of the kind, but Harvest mice are kindly creatures and will forgive the boldest of liars. 'No mouse is perfect,' they would say. Anyhow, the family had a soft spot for him, a fact Uncle exploited to the full.

The family paid little attention as Pentecost scrambled back inside the mattress home. It was well-known that he liked to go down to the stream bank to think. Only Uncle realised that something was in the air. He alone had noticed Pentecost talking to what the old mouse took to be a pile of rope. Thinking his leader had finally lapsed into madness he followed hot on Pentecost's heels to hear the good news. There was no love lost between the two mice, chiefly because they were brothers and thus rivals.

'Gather the family together,' shouted Pentecost. 'I have something important to tell them.'

'Quick, wake up,' said Uncle, hobbling about amongst the sleeping mice. 'Our leader is about to admit his mad mind. I saw everything, and I feel nothing but pity for him.'

'You can save your pity,' said Pentecost. 'As a matter of fact I bring good news.' By this time all the mice were awake and listening. 'I have the honour to inform you that all our troubles are over.'

Immediately a mighty cheer went up from the family. Pentecost held up his paw for attention. 'If I may continue,' he said. But once more Uncle interrupted.

'Is this good news anything to do with the pile of old rope you were talking to?' he said.

'I won't tell you again,' warned an angry Pentecost. He addressed the other mice. 'Am I to be allowed to speak or not?'

'Be quiet, Uncle,' cried the little ones. 'We wish to hear the good news even if you don't.'

'More hair-brained ideas, I suppose,' muttered Uncle, but the angry buzz from the family warned him to say no more.

There was a deathly hush as Pentecost cleared his throat and began his story. 'I have gathered you together to tell of a wonderful stroke of luck,' he began. In the meantime the family's attention began to wander as smoke filtered in through the walls of the home.

'It's that boy with the ginger hair back from school,' said an old mouse. He had been peering outside. 'He's just poked the ashes with a stick, I saw him. How much longer must we endure this miserable life? It is worse for us elderly mice with our chesty coughs.'

'Why do we allow ourselves to be bamboozled by that Pentecost mouse,' gasped Uncle. 'We are about to be scorched alive and what does he do? He calls us together to tell of a wonderful stroke of luck that exists only in his wild imagination. In my opinion the only stroke of luck he had was not to be gulped.'

'Gulped,' cried old Mother clutching at her heart.

'Gulped,' said Uncle firmly. 'For didn't I see that fool-hardy leader arguing with a snake with orange ear muffs?'

'Silence!' cried Pentecost. 'This bickering is getting us nowhere. Now, listen to me for time is short and we have a lot to do before the sun goes down.'

And so the family, seated in a semi-circle, listened to Pentecost's tale of his meeting with Snake and the bargain they had made. But first, Pentecost, following the tradition of leaders down the ages, recapped upon times past.

'For many generations the family has lived in this once-peaceful spot. In the old days life was good and the wheat, the wild fruits and the sweet roots were plentiful. Then the

28

'hiding' was a game much enjoyed by our little ones, but alas, they do it now in fear.'

'Pentecost speaks for us all,' said old Mother. 'For such thoughts lie unspoken in my heart.'

'And in my heart lies a terrible boredom,' sighed Uncle. 'If my paws were strong enough I would go for a long stroll until this recapping was over. That Pentecost just likes to hear himself speak. I would much sooner use this meeting for the singing of songs and enjoyment. In fact, if an obedient little mouse would run and dig me up a sweet root I would gladly sing an old-fashioned song.'

'The sweet roots are still bitter, Uncle,' cried the small mice. 'And even if they were sweet we would not go. We wish to hear of Pentecost's good news and the bargain he made with Snake of the orange ear muffs.'

'So do I,' said a tiny mouse with oddly-coloured eyes. 'But I am in favour of listening to the recap first. I'm extremely interested in wisdom.'

For a moment the family were taken aback. This particular mouse rarely spoke. His mother had often expressed her dismay that her only son showed all the signs of thickness. Also, since his birth, his eyes had been the subject of much comment. The left one was inky black, the other was as blue as a cornflower. This oddity, added to his apparent lack of brainpower, had caused his parents to hide him at the back during the family's social gatherings. And now here he was, speaking in a firm and even tone about his interest in wisdom, of all things.

After a short but embarrassing silence Pentecost continued. The elders sighed as they listened and remembered. The young ones, who had known only this present miserable existence, were entranced to hear that life long ago had been so happy. The Great Aunts shook their heads and tut-tutted, nimble paws ever weaving. At long last Pentecost's recap was brought up to date: 'But now we can no longer sit in the sun's brightness, for the shadows of the houses fall across the golden mornings like black sorrows.'

'And the birds sing less sweetly,' said old Mother. 'And now only sad songs.'

'And now,' said Pentecost, 'I come to the stroke of luck. It is a strange and sad tale. It concerns a snake with an inheritance problem, a frog who is unable to tell the truth and a brand new home for the family.'

The mice listened with bated breath, for this promised to be an exciting story with such a rare mixture of ingredients.

'And also a cousin who isn't a cousin,' Pentecost continued. Suddenly he frowned. Then he began to gesture with a paw as if sorting thoughts into their correct order. The family watched uneasily. It wasn't the first time Pentecost had shown signs of advancing years. They sympathized deeply. They knew that he had a story inside him bursting to come out, but at this critical moment his memory was playing tricks. The mice suddenly realized what Pentecost had realized down by the stream. It was time for a change of leadership.

It took a long time and a great deal of effort for Pentecost finally to put the family in the picture. His garbled tale began to make more sense as, with the utmost tact the mice asked a question here and a question there, but gently, so as not to destroy his confidence. The suddenness of their leader's breakdown was shocking. Only Uncle was pleased to see this tragic ending of a fine and wise leadership.

'Notice how my brother rambles?' he said evilly. 'How does he expect us to understand such rubbish? Why does he talk a lot of poppycock about Oily Green Pools and ugly frogs and back-to-front journeys? It's all quite beyond me, and you too, I'm sure.'

'No, it isn't,' said the young mouse with oddly-coloured

eyes. 'Pentecost's story made perfect sense to me. One simply needed to gather the confused sentences together and put them in their correct order.'

'He spoke again,' said Uncle, looking bewildered. 'And since when have little ones been allowed to butt into the wise talk of grown-ups?'

'Since now,' said the strange little mouse. He glanced at Pentecost. 'May I explain what you were trying to say?' Pentecost, visibly relieved, nodded.

And out of the mouth of the youngster came the story that Pentecost had tried so hard to pass on to his comrades. The other mice marvelled at his clarity of vision and speech. They gazed earnestly into his odd eyes that seemed to possess some hypnotic power all of their own. Despite his youth his every word was hung upon, for the mice recognized greatness when they saw it. His parents watched proudly as their son displayed his sudden gift of speech.

It was uncanny the way his young mind grasped at the garbled account of Pentecost's meeting with Snake and made sense of it. As the old leader listened, he realised how true was the saying, 'the world belongs to the young'. It was as if this confident little mouse saw clearly the future of the family in his mind's eye. As he spoke on, so he appeared to grow in stature. It was with regret, and not a little relief, that Pentecost felt his authority slipping away. Now he knew he had never been destined to lead the family to the new home on Lickey Top. Quietly and unnoticed, he took his place amongst the rapt audience. His work was finished, his heavy responsibilities laid down. There was a new leader for a new beginning, accepted without question from the moment he took the floor and spoke.

'This is the position then,' the tiny mouse was saying. 'Snake needs our help to capture the frog who can prove the cousin lied. Now, make no mistake, snakes are no friends of

31

ours. If he didn't need our help we'd soon find that out. Now, according to Pentecost, this snake is prepared to lead and protect us on the journey to the new home. He says that the sole occupant of that place is a kindly recluse owl who won't mind in the least us settling there. That could be true, but maybe it isn't. That is a bridge we'll have to cross when we come to it. But, returning to the question of Snake, we must face the fact that he is offering to help us for purely selfish reasons. We must be on our guard at all times if we undertake this journey. However, one thing is certain. Snake won't dare to trick us until the frog has been safely escorted back to the Lickey Hills. Even snakes need to sleep, and a journey of many days would present the frog with many opportunities to escape if he wasn't constantly watched. I think that, though the risks are great, we should accept Snake's offer. I think we should take our chances and go, for you all know there is nothing for us here any more.'

For a while there was total silence. Then suddenly Uncle, who had been listening with his mouth agape, scrambled to his paws.

'Nonsense,' he said. 'Why are we listening to this young mouse, who has barely opened his eyes upon this terrible world? And why is my brother, the old Pentecost, sitting quietly in a corner like an ordinary mouse?'

'Because there is a new leader amongst us,' he was told. 'You heard the small mouse speak, Uncle?'

Uncle glared at the grave-faced youngster. One black eye and one blue eye returned the angry mouse's stare unflinchingly. 'But I myself have a plan,' spluttered Uncle. 'Why am I never listened to quietly? What has this ugly mouse said to make you pay attention so?'

'Don't you speak about my clever son like that,' said the mother of the prodigy.

Uncle was almost speechless with rage. 'But only yester-

32

day you were weeping and wailing because of his backwardness,' he cried.

'That was yesterday,' was the smug reply. 'We realise now that he was deeply thinking about the problems of the world.'

'And what do you think I've been doing all my life?' demanded Uncle.

The young mouse, who had sat down after his speech, rose again. 'We are prepared to listen to anyone who can help us get to Lickey Top in safety. We are a democratic family and, if Uncle's plan is better than the one Pentecost put forward, we will hear it by all means.' He sat down again.

'I can't understand where he came from,' said Uncle in a bewildered voice. 'I've never heard him say more than two words. All he ever did was sit staring at things with those creepy odd eyes. And now, all of a sudden, he's making Pentecost look the fool he is; which isn't difficult, for I always said he was the worst leader ever.'

'Tell us your plan or sit down, Uncle,' said old Mother, 'and have a little respect for our Pentecost who isn't himself today.'

'Well,' said Uncle, his eyes gleaming, 'My idea is to wait until Snake falls fast asleep and then fall upon him and choke his neck . . .'

Again the young mouse rose. Patiently he said, 'Don't you all think this is a waste of valuable time? We have to meet Snake at sunset with the frog captured and ready to travel.'

'I knew I wouldn't get a fair hearing,' said Uncle bitterly.

'Let Uncle describe his choking plan,' shouted the little ones. 'We were enjoying it.'

Uncle beamed and glanced triumphantly at the young mouse who spoke again. 'I take it Uncle is prepared to do the actual choking. It's his idea, after all?'

Uncle ignored the remark. 'My idea is that all the able-bodied mice fall upon Snake's throat in the dead of night. Then, when all the breath has petered from his mouth, I, who will be standing guard on the other side of the stream, will shout, "Have you had enough, Snake?" If he gasps, "No," the Great Aunts will rush forward with their strong grass stems and weave Snake into a neat bundle.' All this was described with great relish.

'Then what?' said the odd-eyed mouse. 'We've got Snake tightly bundled. What do we do then?'

'Am I talking to a bunch of idiots?' cried Uncle. 'Why, we then force him to take us to Lickey Top.'

'He would hardly be able to travel, all tied up,' said one of the mice. He stroked his ginger whiskers. 'Unless, of course, we rolled him. But the trouble with that idea is mud. He would be bound to collect a lot of mud on his body. He would almost certainly grow larger as the days passed, which means, and this is my telling point, heavier and heavier.'

Uncle lost his temper completely. His idea was being criticized and he hated that.

'It's impractical,' insisted the ginger mouse. 'And how would Snake be able to lead the way with mud in his eyes? It would be a good idea but for the mud.'

'It would be a better idea if we began the search for the frog immediately,' said the odd-eyed mouse.

Suddenly old Pentecost got to his paws. He motioned for silence. 'I have been your leader for a long time now,' he began. 'But I am no longer young. I believe this great adventure calls for new leadership. Perhaps this is the right moment to step down in favour of a younger mouse. I propose that, before we go any farther we choose a new Pentecost. How say you all?'

'I accept the leadership,' said Uncle quickly. 'And now that that business is over, paws up the volunteers to fall upon

Snake's neck. We will worry about the problem of him gathering mud later. Perhaps we can plunge him into the stream now and then to soften up the mud? But, on a more personal note, I would like to say how honoured I am to be chosen as leader. However, as you all know, my paws aren't too strong so I shall expect a few willing young mice to carry me to Lickey Top.'

Once again Pentecost spoke. Insultingly he turned his back on Uncle and addressed the family. 'I propose that the little mouse who spoke so wisely should take my place. All in favour, say aye.'

'Aye,' chorused the family. 'It is the wish of us all.'

'It isn't mine,' said Uncle stoutly. 'I can see only disaster ahead if you make this insane mistake.'

The odd-eyed mouse stood up. 'I accept,' he said simply. 'And now there is work to be done. In a few hours it will be sunset and, before that time, the frog must be found.'

'I always said that small mouse would go far,' fawned Uncle. He ignored the giggles. 'I was only joking about myself, of course. You all know my wry sense of humour. In my opinion that striking little mouse will make a perfect leader. We must obey his orders immediately. I will set an example and hurry to do his bidding, for I am a law-abiding old mouse.'

'You are an old sinner, Uncle,' cried the little ones. 'You never run errands and you never help about the home as the rest of the family do.'

The new Pentecost interrupted. For one so small and young he possessed an amazing amount of authority in his voice.

'Uncle is a member of this family and, as such, will be treated with respect,' he said quietly. 'We know he has many cunning ways, but when one is as old as he, it's to be expected.'

35

'One's paws suffer also,' said Uncle. 'But this is a loyal family. I daresay many mice will offer to carry me over the bumpy bits during the journey. One thing is certain, the new Pentecost will never forsake me.'

'More's the pity,' muttered a mouse from the back.

'All right,' said the new leader briskly. 'Let's cut out the chattering. I want all able-bodied mice to split up into small search parties. Scour the banks of the stream, search every bed of rushes, look behind the rocks and beneath the hedge-row. We are seeking an extremely ugly frog with sharp shooting pains. He must be found. And now to work . . .'

It was as if the old Pentecost had never existed. Now there was a new leader to be obeyed and the old Pentecost merged into the general throng, receiving no special attention and expecting none. Such are the ways of Harvest mice.

5   The Questioning of Frog

The hunted frog quaked in his makeshift hide. It was an old water-vole's hole dug into the bank of the stream and cunningly hidden. By craning his head he could see quite a way downstream. What he saw caused him to tremble even more. He could see small groups of Harvest mice searching every nook and cranny along the banks of the stream. They could only be looking for him, he was certain of it. It all fell into place. The mouse he had spoken to this morning had given him away to Snake. But why had the mouse done such a thing? He hadn't seemed the sneaky type. The only motive the frog could think of was gain. But what could the mouse hope to gain from his betrayal? It was a fact that Snake would swallow a mouse with the same ease and relish as he would a frog. So what had the mouse and the snake agreed upon to cause them to become allies?

The frog knew quite well why Snake wanted to see him. But the mice? Why should they also be eager to seek him out? Was it something he had said? He remembered calling the mouse a twit, and didn't he call him thick, too? Had the mouse taken it so much to heart that he would organize search parties to flush him out? That was carrying things a little too far, thought the worried frog.

'If only my tongue would behave itself,' he moaned, 'but the lies just slip out of their own accord. If only folk could understand how difficult it is to tell the truth. And me so poorly too.'

Although Frog would never know it, the root of his problem had been sown at birth. His father at that time had been a happy-go-lucky type, fond of travel and, more especially, travelling alone. Fearing that his lady-love of the moment would tie him down, he had strenuously denied being the father of the tiny frog who gazed so adoringly up at him. Callously he had left to continue his aimless wanderings, leaving behind a weeping sweetheart and a bewildered son. It was then that the tiny frog's lying began. He had got a father, he insisted, when other young frogs, with secure families, mocked him. His dad had only gone away for a day or two, he maintained. Soon the lies became second nature to him. And with the lies began the aches and pains that would plague him throughout his life. If he had stopped to think, he would have seen that the more he lied, the more poorly he felt. He would finally have understood that his pains were purely imaginary and simply his body protesting against the suppressed guilt. But he wasn't a bright frog, just a wicked liar who wouldn't have recognized the truth if he fell over it.

The search parties were coming closer. The mice were painstakingly thorough in their task. Nothing escaped their attention. Soon they would discover the frog's hiding place, and then the game would be up. The desperate creature pressed closer to the muddy sides of the smelly hole. But his pathetic attempts to avoid detection were in vain. A movement outside, a cry of triumph, and it was all over. A pair of bright eyes peered inside at the frog.

'Lie yourself out of this one,' said the mouse with satisfaction. He turned and called to the others, 'Quick, over here, before he gives me the slip with a cock-and-bull story.'

The poor frog hopped to the entrance of the hole. Deep pain was etched across his ugly face. He opened his mouth to speak, to say anything. A pair of black suspicious eyes regarded him warily. 'Whatever you say I won't believe,' said the mouse. 'Just keep your trap shut.' The frog tried to protest but the mouse quickly covered his ears with his paws.

The keen-eyed mouse was soon joined by his comrades. They clustered about the entrance of the hole and whispered excitedly amongst themselves. Then suddenly a shout went up. 'Here comes our new Pentecost. He'll know what to do.' They parted to allow an even tinier mouse to peer inside the hole. Despite his anguish, the frog couldn't help but notice the mouse's strange eyes.

The odd eyes scrutinized him. 'Are you prepared to give yourself up and become our prisoner?' said the Pentecost mouse. 'And if you say yes, can we take that for the honest truth?'

'Yes,' said the frog in a limp voice.

'Seize him,' snapped Pentecost.

'But he's just agreed to come quietly,' said the mouse who had made the find.

Pentecost sighed. 'You haven't listened to a word of Snake's tale, have you? The frog is probably the greatest liar on earth. "Yes" in his poor twisted mind means no. Do as I say and make him fast.'

The frog was dragged from the hole and pinioned. His slimy skin caused a few mice to recoil but the prospect of a new safe home was worth a little queasiness in the stomach.

'Are you prepared to be frog-marched to see Snake and there to answer any questions he may care to put to you?' said Pentecost.

'Yes,' said the frog once more. 'But, please, I ask you to take into consideration my poor state of health. My poorliness hasn't improved and my side is throbbing with shooting pains. I only beg that you frog-march me with care.'

'Are you sure these pains don't shoot down the right side?' asked Pentecost.

'Yes, the right side,' said the frog, indicating his left. 'All down here.'

'He is the frog we seek,' said Pentecost. 'A born liar, if ever I heard one. He won't even admit to the true position of his illness. Bring him along, but be as gentle as possible for we don't want to increase his suffering.'

The mice led the frog back downstream, hurrying him along for the sun was rapidly disappearing. Frog-marching wasn't as easy as the mice thought. Only the captive seemed to get the hang of it properly. At last the mice allowed the frog to frog-march himself while they fell in on either side to make sure he made no attempt to escape. All in all, it was the perfect solution. The party reached the old pram a few minutes before sunset. Snake was waiting. His agitation quickly changed to relief as he saw the frog in the centre of his escort.

He had spent a rotten day. Extreme hunger had forced him to root about in the piles of refuse that littered the banks

39

of the stream. His haul had amounted to a smelly cod's head, a couple of half-eaten fish fingers and a stale currant bun with the currants prised out. Not unnaturally, he wished to be gone from this awful place. He was anxious to reach the Great River again, a mile or so down stream. There he knew the fishing to be good for the water flowed cleanly and swift, unlike this polluted trickle. He was still peeved at the thought of having to shepherd a bunch of mice all the way home to Lickey Top. But, if it resulted in the return of his pool, so be it. He would hide his distaste and go along with the idea. His only concern was for his lost inheritance, and when that matter was resolved ... well, who was bothered about a family of homeless Harvest mice?

He advanced to meet the party and prisoner. Concealing his boredom he listened as it was explained to him that a new Pentecost had been chosen. He was introduced to the odd-eyed mouse who surveyed him coolly as if measuring him up. Snake was annoyed to find himself feeling uncomfortable in the mouse's presence. And then the moment came when Snake stood face to face with the hated frog. For a while Snake just stared, savouring this bitter moment. The frog avoided his piercing gaze and squirmed miserably. There was no pity in Snake; he had learned that such emotions softened one. He had received a short sharp schooling from his 'Cousin', a lesson he would never forget.

It was now a little after sunset. All the family were gathered about the old pram. They were highly excited. They had left their rubbish dump home, hopefully for the last time. Now they were impatient to start the journey to the Lickey Hills. Pentecost realised that their future hopes depended on what the frog said. Or what he didn't say. Somehow or other the truth had to be extracted from him. It wasn't going to be an easy task. But the little mouse enjoyed a challenge. His busy brain was working furiously upon the problem. How to make a liar tell the truth? Just how?

A head count was being taken in the failing light. The Great Aunts had lined up all the young mice and each was given a number. They were then required to shout it out aloud, much to Snake's annoyance. Uncle had bound his paws with soothing herbs so they would not become too hot and swollen during the long march. Not that he intended doing much marching. The young Pentecost had kindly arranged for two sturdy mice to assist him if the going became too rough.

It was the first time the majority of the mice had seen a snake close to. They took care not to approach him too closely. But they were proud to note that Pentecost showed no fear of him at all. Snake was an imposing sight in the fading light. His triangular head swayed, and his lemon-flecked eyes seemed to bore like gimlets into the soul of any mouse who dared meet his gaze. Few did. His mouth was quirked into an expression of contempt and bitter amusement, despite his attempt to appear amiable. The dullest Harvest mouse could see that they weren't Snake's favourite people.

Suddenly the surroundings were illuminated by a ruddy glow. Showers of sparks and crackling twigs were dashed into the air as a gust of wind whipped the smouldering rubbish dump into an inferno of flame. It was an omen. Now, with or without the help of Snake, the family would have to leave. They had burned their boats behind them, or rather the ginger haired boy from the houses had.

For a while the fire burned fiercely and the mice sadly watched as their home was consumed. With a whoosh the old mattress burst into a sea of cherry-red flame before subsiding into a heap of glowing cinders. The flickering glow lit up the faces of the mice. The little ones wore expressions of awe and excitement. The elders looked solemn. Mothers were heard to murmur 'dear, dear,' while the Great Aunts, grass stems twirling busily between their nervous paws, tut-tutted and wondered aloud, whatever was the world coming to?

'Are you going to stare at that fire all night?' asked Snake, trying to hide his irritation. 'Bring our green friend into the light where we can see him.'

The frog was hastened forward to where Snake sat in a neat bundle of coils, his majestic head rearing skyward. His icy-cold eyes peered down at the shivering creature. The frog, unable to control his limbs, fell into a crumpled heap upon the ground. Pentecost, his heart moved to pity, stepped up to him and patted him kindly.

'Don't be afraid,' he said. 'Snake just wants to ask you a few questions. If you answer truthfully I'm sure he won't deal too severely with you.'

'Thank you,' said Snake. 'And now, question number one.' He eyed the frog with distaste. 'Did you or did you not eavesdrop upon a conversation between my late father and a snake calling himself a cousin?'

'Yes,' said the frog earnestly. 'I certainly didn't.'

Snake controlled his temper with an effort. 'We'll try again. Just answer yes or no.'

'Yes or no,' said the frog promptly. He looked to see if his answer had pleased Snake. It hadn't.

Pentecost beckoned to Snake, who lowered his head to listen. 'I don't think we are going to get far this way,' he said. 'I'm afraid the frog couldn't tell the truth, even if he wanted to. But I have an idea. The only way to get at the truth is to turn the frog's answers back to front. For example, if I were a wicked liar and you asked me who was the cleverest mouse in the Midlands, I would reply, "not me". Do you see what I mean, Snake? Now, my truthful reply would be, "I am".

So all we have to do is to turn the frog's answers back to front. It's quite simple really.'

'It has the simplicity of genius,' said Snake admiringly. 'No wonder they chose you as leader. By the way, who *is* the cleverest mouse in the Midlands?'

'Modesty forbids,' said Pentecost shyly.

'Well, I think you are,' Snake said. 'Without a doubt.'

'I shall be even cleverer when I'm grown up,' Pentecost's odd eyes lowered humbly. 'I believe I was chosen by Providence to lead the family to the new home on Lickey Top.'

'Do you indeed?' said Snake, raising his heavy eyelids. He cast the mouse a deep unfathomable look, a half-smile playing about his triangular jaws. But his mood quickly changed. He turned once more to the frog, who began to tremble again.

'Remember, all I require is a yes or no to my questions.' he said. 'In that way we can get this unpleasant business over with quickly. Now then, did you hear this Cousin snake threaten my late father in any way?'

'Yes,' said the frog.

'According to my clever idea, that means no,' said Pentecost.

Snake glared at him. 'I've got the point,' he said. 'Would you mind if I conducted my own cross-examination?'

'What a way to talk to our leader!' said old Mother in a shocked tone. 'Whatever are things coming to?'

'That new Pentecost asked for it,' snorted Uncle.

'You'll get yourself forsaken if you aren't careful,' warned a Great Aunt. 'That tongue of yours is far too long. It needs snipping.' Uncle swallowed hard and closed his snout firmly. Pentecost forgivingly patted the old mouse on top of his greying head.

Snake put his next question. 'After my father's death you visited my pool with this so-called cousin, did you not?'

'No, definitely not,' said the frog. He was pleased with

43

the way the interrogation was going. Smooth as silk, he thought. Already he was confident enough to begin planning for the future. The word 'scot-free' was whirling about in his mind. He'd need treatment for his various illnesses, of course, but afterwards ... a cosy little home ... a plump hard-working wife perhaps ... but then he already had one, he'd quite forgotten. And his son ... he wondered how the little scamp was getting on? It had been a long time ... He awaited the next question with confidence.

'It was a put-up job, was it not?' snapped Snake.

'No,' the frog replied happily.

'You were forced to say what you did under the pain of death, is that not true?'

'Negative,' said Frog.

'In fact you backed up this cousin's story in the most callous manner, even when you saw how upset I was?' said Snake, holding back his tears.

'That's a downright lie,' said the frog stoutly. He proceeded to do a few knee-bends to keep his stiffening joints supple. The mice, who by this time were thoroughly bored by this question-and-answer game, began to ape him. Uncle managed one knee-bend before having to be laid flat on his back and straightened out.

Snake was becoming used to these extraordinary bouts of behaviour, but the frog's casualness made him very angry indeed. The creature had the bare-faced impudence to exercise in his presence as if the disinheriting, which he had helped bring about, was a trifling matter. 'Stop that at once,' he said in a soft deadly voice. The frog froze, as if turned to stone.

'And now, the most hurtful question of all,' said the Snake, steeling himself. 'This cousin alleged that my father said I was thick as a plank. What is your reply to this terrible slur on my character?'

Something quite amazing happened at this point. Afterwards the frog would declare that this moment was the turning point in his unsavoury career. 'He said no such thing,' the frog replied. 'The imposter snake said you were thick as two planks. That's twice as thick according to my sums.' Then the frog appeared to stagger with shock. He looked confused for a while. Then a strange cleansing light filled his eyes. 'What did I say?' he whispered. 'I feel so strange. I feel ... I'm not quite sure how I feel, but it's ...'

'Do you feel as if a great weight has been lifted from you?' asked Pentecost quickly. 'Do you feel whole and clean and good inside?'

'All that and more,' said the frog dreamily. 'I have a lovely giddiness. It's all floaty and nice, I can't quite describe it.'

'And what about your shooting pains down the one side?' asked the mouse.

'All gone,' breathed the frog. He looked wistful. 'If only I could feel this well for ever and ever.'

'You can and you will,' said Pentecost. 'Because do you know what you just did? You told the truth for the first time in your life, that's what you did! You called the cousin snake an imposter, and you admitted this snake was twice as thick as he thought. It took great courage to say what you did for, mark my words, Snake won't like you any more for it.'

'You can say that again,' snapped Snake. 'But at least the truth is coming out.'

'I never knew telling the truth could feel so good,' yelled the frog. 'Could I tell some more, please? Ask me any question you like. I don't believe I can ever lie again.'

'Are you quite sure?' asked Pentecost. 'Because, after a lifetime of lying, it's quite easy to slip back into a relapse. I think we'd better give you a little test first. I want you to state your honest opinion of Snake here. The truth, mind.'

45

'I think Snake is the most selfish bonk-eyed bully that ever slithered across the face of the earth,' said the frog, delighting in his new-found honesty. 'And what is more he's mean and cunning and will cast you aside the moment he gets his pool back. That's what I believe from the depths of my truthful soul.'

'He's passed the test!' cried Pentecost. 'This frog will never tell a lie again.' The mice got to their paws and cheered.

Snake was furious. He longed to do the frog a terrible injury, but he knew he daren't. The frog seemed to sense his thoughts. He had arrived at a decision. He spoke plainly and without mincing his words.

'I will return to Lickey Top and tell the truth only if Snake promises to find my Harvest mouse friends a new home. If Snake doesn't agree, I will stay here and share their miserable existence with them. And even if Snake forces me against my will to return, I will repeat my wicked lies and risk the return of my shooting pains rather than desert them. They are the first true friends I have ever known and I wish to share their destiny, if they will allow me to. I owe this glorious floaty feeling to the Pentecost mouse, who encouraged me to tell my first truth, I will be indebted to him for ever. Do your worst, Snake, truth and right will prevail!' Once again the cheers of the mice reverberated along the banks of the stream. They danced about for sheer joy and hugged Frog, their champion. 'It wasn't a lily pad at all,' cried Frog, hysterically. 'It was a dustbin lid all the time. When I think of all those years of misery! And how ashamed I feel that others have suffered because of my lying. I feel like a new frog, and most marvellous of all, I have friends.'

Snake watched moodily. It seemed everyone was happy except him. 'I agree to your terms,' he said. 'You keep your part of the bargain, I will keep mine. And now, let's away, for we have a long way to go and I wish to reach the Great

River by morning.' He glanced around at the assembled mice, the frog in their midst.

'We knew you'd see it Frog's way,' said Pentecost. 'You aren't such a bad snake, really. And now we are ready to travel.'

'I would like Snake to make me a promise too,' declared Uncle. 'As he has no choice, I insist that he travels slowly out of consideration for us elderly mice. That must be included in the bargain too.'

'It sounds more like an ultimatum to me,' said Snake bitterly.

'That's that then,' said Uncle, satisfied.

So at last the great adventure began. Snake slid off along the bank of the stream, followed by Pentecost and Frog, the two now firm friends. Just behind came the lady mice and the little ones, the Great Aunts busily weaving their grass stems. Bringing up the rear came the older mice, Uncle complaining angrily, even at this early stage of the journey. His two reluctant helpers also grumbled; they had dearly

wished to be appointed as scouts, a much sought-after role. Enviously they watched their more fortunate comrades proudly patrolling the flanks of the expedition for lurking dangers. And so the party vanished into the darkness.

6 Two Brothers

As Pentecost and the family travelled through the night, heading for the Great River, two brothers slept soundly, dreaming of times past.

The Water-vole brothers were twins and alike in every respect but temperament. Big Brother, so-called because he was the dominant one, was bad-tempered and inclined to bully. On the other hand, Little Brother was gentle, and possessed a heart filled with unused love. They lived their bachelor existence at a point where the stream entered the Great River. Here the banks of the stream were wide and the waters less polluted.

Once, long ago, they had lived a mile or so upstream in Pentecost country. Those had been idyllic days, with a doting mother and a strict but proud father to care for them. They had been born in the spring. Four sleepy eyes, opening on the world for the first time, saw the stream. It was love at first sight. Sometimes a sudden gale would whip the waters into a stinging spray, and the rushes would thrash and bend before the winds. Then would come calm days and the young voles never tired of watching the fishes leaping for a glance at the world, before falling back to a place that had rhythm and sense in its cool deeps.

The twins learned to know both worlds. The land was warmed by a sun that was pleasant to bask beneath. The banks of the stream, with its sticky mud-holes and rotting tree-roots was a treasure trove for the pottering voles, whose curiosity seemed boundless. And, high above, there were pale blue skies to gaze at when bellies were full, and young minds had time to expand and wonder.

'Our twins are of no particular colour,' their mother would say proudly, 'just like their father. It was a happy day for us when they were born. Already they are developing characters. One is so wilful, it is a joy to be vexed by him; the other so will-less it is satisfying to cajole his uncertain mind. They are twins to be proud of, and proud we are.'

In their damp, warm, sandy hole, they slept and woke and wondered. They knew how the water felt to touch and lick, but to plunge beneath? Black inquisitive eyes and sensitive whiskers explored their domain, but always it was the water that entranced them. The twins soon found to their relief and delight that swimming hardly needed to be learned. It was just a matter of getting used to it. The moment their bullet-shaped noses touched the water, swimming, floating and boring deeply to the bottom seemed as natural as can be.

It seemed as if the pattern of their lives was set. They had a fine home, kind parents, and all the tasty filling meals growing voles required. They were particularly fond of the apple cores that occasionally came floating down the stream, indeed, the twins became hopelessly addicted to them. They would lie and watch the flowing water for hours, and their hearts would thud with excitement when they spied such treasure bobbing towards them. To the twins in their innocence, the future looked sweet and serene. But one day, for the voles too, the City spilled over into their lives.

It was a pile of clumsily stacked house-bricks that put an

end to the lives of their kind parents. The area about had become a dumping ground for the building materials needed for the new houses. One moment the twins were part of a happy family, the next they were homeless orphans, with a full stop where once had been a bright future. All that dreadful day, and the next, the twins lived as if in a dream. For a long time the larger brother was inconsolable. He swam round and round in aimless circles and nothing his gentle brother said could comfort him. But, strangely, it was he who jerked them back to face reality. On the third day, abruptly recovered and practical, he said, 'Come on, we're leaving.' And that was that. Without a backward glance they swam off downstream towards the Great River, two damp heads cutting through the water perfectly in line.

Little Brother awoke. It had been a beautiful dream – except for the last part. That sad event always woke him up. He glanced at his brother. He, too, was beginning to stretch and blink his eyes. The smaller vole looked outside. It promised to be a nice day. The king cups were in bloom, and the sun's oblique rays glinted on the dewdrops that clung to their petals. The young vole adored this time of year. Early summer, the time of plenty, and the stream comfortingly close and cool when the sun paused directly above. Yet for some strange reason the morning felt somehow different. Not to look at, but to feel. As if something out of the ordinary was about to happen. The small vole's intuition rarely played him false. Today would definitely be different.

His brother was grumbling as usual. His mood never varied. Nothing aroused his interest, save for his deep hatred for trespassers. He spent most of each day patrolling their property in search of strangers who, he declared, had no business there.

50

'Come on,' he said abruptly. 'As like as not, our property will already be swarming with trespassers. Will we never be left in peace? Every day is the same. But never fear, Little Brother, we'll soon sort 'em out.'

Reluctantly the small vole set off behind his determined brother. Soon they stood upon a small hillock. From here they had a clear view of the surrounding countryside. The larger vole's keen eyes searched for the tell-tale parting of grasses, the shaking of a bush, which could mean in his mind but one thing: illegal trespassers.

Suddenly he spied what he sought, indeed hoped for. The bully in him delighted to gaze on what was probably the largest case of trespass he had ever seen. His mouth fell open in surprise. Little Brother also experienced shock as he gazed upstream. A procession of assorted creatures was wending its way along the bank towards them. In the lead slid a snake with buttercup yellow ear muffs. Close behind followed a mouse and a frog. Then came a motley bunch of Harvest mice of all ages, sizes, colours and different states of health. Some limped, some hopped, some could barely hobble along at all. Yet all wore expressions of determination upon their faces. Finally, at the rear, supported by two sturdy-looking mice, came an old mouse, his loud complaining, even at that distance away, easily heard.

The two voles stood on the bank and watched the travellers approach. As they neared, Little Brother noticed the coldness of the snake's lemon-flecked stare. The malevolence in that gaze was warning enough to proceed warily. Little Brother felt suddenly afraid. In contrast, his brother was working himself up into another rage. The gentle vole nudged his brother and attempted to pacify him.

'It is only that "passing through" cannot be classed as trespassing,' he said. 'They seem to be heading for the Great River, if my sense of direction is correct. And aren't the frog

51

and the snake familiar to us? Didn't the frog pass this way some days ago, and the snake only yesterday morning?'

'Then why are they coming back?' shouted his brother. 'Anyhow, there is no such thing as "passing through", only trespassing. It is lucky for them we took no action the first time. To trespass a second time is too much. And see, they have brought along a multitude. This is the largest case of trespass ever. We won't stand for it. They will trespass through our property over our dead bodies. Our beloved father would expect it of us. Stand close to me, Little Brother, and prepare to give your life in defence of our lands.'

'Is not life too precious to cast away so lightly?' said the small vole hesitantly. 'I fear the snake will pass through, the savage gleam in his eye leaves no doubt in my mind.'

'To show fear at such a time,' said his brother, contempt in his tone.

'I will fight for what is important,' was the reply. 'Why pick quarrels for no reason at all? Why don't we ask them to stay and rest awhile? They may be quite friendly folk, and it's a long time since we spoke civilly with visitors from the world outside our boundaries. We live too deeply within ourselves; it can't be good for our spirits.'

'Think back and grieve,' snapped his brother. 'Remember our dear parents who died beneath the fallen house-bricks. Even now their freed souls watch us. Do you wish them to see cowards for sons?'

Little Brother drew himself up. 'I will stand my ground at your side,' he said quietly. 'But take care for your temper once aroused cannot easily be controlled.'

At last the two parties stood face to face. Snake had slid to a halt, sensing trouble. He raised his head menacingly, his tongue flicking rapidly in and out of his hissing mouth. The Harvest mice were huddled together, the little ones in the centre, out of harm's way. The frog sat a little way away, an expression of serenity lighting up his battered face. After a short hesitation, Pentecost moved away from the family to take his place at Snake's side. It was a brave thing to do, for Pentecost was a very tiny mouse.

'Thank Heaven for the heavy mob,' whispered Snake, with a wry smile.

'I'm not the heavy mob, Snake, I'm just a small frightened mouse,' breathed Pentecost.

For a time neither side spoke. Then suddenly Big Brother hurled a challenge. Everyone jumped, for it was very loud and completely unexpected.

'No trespassing!' he yelled. 'Turn back at once, or face the consequences.'

'Then the consequences it shall be,' said Snake evenly.

The brothers backed away a little. Then Snake spoke, each word delivered slowly to make his meaning perfectly clear.

'Now listen closely, my fine furry friends. I and my tiresome companions have come a long way. We have an even longer way to go. No doubt we'll be meeting pests equally as bothersome as yourselves. My words to them will be the same as those I now say to you. It is advice, you understand, so don't feel hurt, or take it too personally. My words are as follows. I once had an Oily Green Pool. I no longer have an Oily Green Pool. Here you see a small ugly frog. Once this frog was a proven liar. Now he claims to have seen the light, whatever that means. Now, with his help, that Oily Green Pool will return to its rightful owner. You two chappies are standing in that rightful owner's way. My advice is to step aside, now.'

There was no doubt Snake meant every word. For a moment the big vole's courage faltered. It was the gentle brother who spoke up bravely. As usual, he trotted out the old story. 'It is only that my brother suffered a tragedy early in his life,' he said. 'And he tends to offend and defend against the slightest trifle. The harm is not in him but in the spilling over of the City which took his parent's lives so brutally. That I see good in him is proved by my loyalty and patience, for I am my brother's keeper for better or for worse.'

'All this is very sad,' snapped Snake. 'But we are not trifles, at least I'm not. I too have suffered. I too have lost my father. At this very moment wild parties are taking place on my stolen property and I mean to put a stop to it ... don't we?' This last remark was addressed to the frog who sat on his haunches, looking very fit and confident.

'We certainly do,' said Frog. 'The harm will be undone if it's the last thing I ever do.'

'I'll keep you to that,' said Snake. 'And now, is this grief-stricken little vole going to get out of my way?'

Snake's words had brought about a change in Big Brother's attitude. Tragedy was a thing he understood well, and here was a fellow sufferer. He calmed down and became more reasonable. 'As long as you don't intend to settle down,' he said, 'I am prepared to discuss the passing through.'

'Cross my heart,' said Snake solemnly.

'But then why should you want to, you being a snake with property and all?' said Big Brother.

'My thoughts exactly,' Snake replied.

'And with a father barely cold in his grave,' the vole added.

Pentecost stepped one pace forward. 'We also need to pass through,' he said. 'The spilling over of the City affected us too. We no longer have a home because of it.'

Big Brother turned to Snake. 'Is it possible that such small and unimportant creatures can know what suffering is?' he asked. 'Is their passing through really necessary?'

'I'm afraid so,' said Snake. 'I need them you see. And as for their suffering, I've heard about little else since I first teamed up with them.'

'And I too have suffered in my fashion,' said the frog. 'I've been a wicked liar for most of my life and I've been despised and persecuted because of it. But, at last, I've seen the light. Now my only wish is to make amends for all the wrongs I've done. Afterwards I intend travelling widely about the world, unmasking lies and deceits, and replacing them with the truth. It's a strange thing, but you get this glorious floaty feeling when you tell the truth, and you feel as fit as a fiddle. So if you please, master vole, to carry out my mission I, too, must pass through.'

'One of those busy days, eh?' murmured Snake eyeing the flummoxed vole.

'But what about all these others?' said Big Brother. 'All these hobbling old mice and those grass-spinning crones? Surely they don't need to pass through? In my opinion they'd be much better off beneath the ground.'

'What d'you mean?' bawled Uncle, from the rear. 'If I was a younger mouse I'd grasp your throat in a choking hold. If I had the strong gripping paws of my youth I'd soon have you beneath the ground. Mark my words, they don't last long when the air can't get down.'

'Finished?' asked Snake.

'No, I haven't,' said Uncle hotly. He hobbled about among the family, glaring first into one face then the next. Embarrassed, most of the mice averted their eyes. 'Will no-one defend us elderly mice?' Uncle shouted. 'What's happened to our brave new Pentecost? I suspect he will turn out to be a phoney, like his predecessor. It is a great pity I wasn't chosen to lead the family. I am the only mouse with guts and true grit, it seems. That fat rat is making a mockery of our family and no-one says a word.'

'That settles it,' said Big Brother grimly. 'All can pass through, except him,' he pointed at Uncle.

Snake, Frog, Pentecost and the family filed past the two brothers, leaving Uncle quite alone and beyond the pale.

'But what have I done?' asked Uncle, a picture of innocence. 'I've always admired water-voles. And no-one is more
sorry than I that the City spilled over their parents. I also
understand their suffering. Haven't I the most painful paws in
the Midlands? Is it because I am old, feeble, and easily over-
powered, that you won't let me pass through with the others?'

'No,' said Big Brother. 'It is because you have insulted my
twin and me. You will pass through over my dead body.'

'No amount of pleas will move my brother's stony heart,'
said the gentle vole. 'Only a humble apology will do that.'

The little ones hurried back to gather about Uncle, who
was fuming and stomping about on his herb-bound paws.
'If you will not let him pass, we will charge him through,'
they declared. 'We will use our old Uncle as a battering-ram
and flatten that fat rat to the ground.'

'This I must see,' grinned Snake, who was enjoying
Uncle's discomfort.

The youngsters made to lift Uncle from the ground, but
he restrained them. 'I have enough illnesses without adding
to them,' he said hastily. 'I can do without a serious headache,
thank you very much. I have decided to stay and die here
and become a small pile of rotting bones. It makes no difference anyway, for I suspect the new Pentecost meant to get
rid of me when he thought the time was right. I have heard
him muttering about how I am holding up the fast pace of
the journey to the hills. And I have had my suspicions about
that hollow worm with buttercup ear muffs for some time.
Can he deny he meant to murder me in my bed one dark
night? He never liked the way I spoke my mind.'

'On the contrary,' said Snake. 'I find your ridiculous antics
quite amusing. But you've only yourself to blame for your
present situation, for you are a stubborn, insulting old
mouse.'

Dejectedly the little ones had once more passed through,

leaving Uncle a small defiant figure, facing quite alone the unmoving vole who barred his way. 'I'm still waiting for the apology,' said Big Brother. 'And I am quite prepared to wait for ever. The memory of my dear departed parents demands this. Expect no change of heart from me.'

'So much for our close-knit family,' said Uncle bitterly. 'Didn't Pentecost promise never to forsake me? How can I survive with no little-ones to run errands for me? Am I not your fond Uncle, who sings old fashioned songs and tells you stories of the olden days?'

It was Pentecost who solved the problem. He passed back through and spoke sternly to Uncle. The leader's words couldn't be heard, but Uncle was seen to fidget a lot. Whatever was said seemed to do the trick, for Uncle stepped forward a pace and spoke.

'Very well,' he said airily. 'I take back all my untruthful remarks.'

'And the truthful ones?' said Big Brother quickly.

'The truthful ones too,' replied the old mouse.

This was too much for the frog. 'But doesn't the truth count for anything?' he cried. 'For Uncle struck the nail upon the head as regards Snake. In my opinion, he summed up Snake's treachery in a nutshell. He is quite capable of murder if it will help his selfish plans. And doesn't that fat rat need choking for his bad manners?'

'There will be plenty of time for the truth when we are all safely passed through,' said Pentecost. 'If a few small lies will enable Uncle to rejoin his family, so be it. It is a sad fact that few folk get safely through life without the help of a lie or two. Uncle has apologised, Big Brother. Is he now qualified to pass through?'

Little Brother nodded. 'My brother's honour is satisfied,' he said. And so, after all the unnecessary fuss, Uncle was allowed to pass through and rejoin his relieved family.

'But no settling, mind,' warned Big Brother. 'You can stay just a short time. We want no unwelcome pests building nests and digging unsightly holes all over the place. And there are no hollow logs on my property,' he said, casting Snake a meaningful glance. The point was taken.

'We only wish to soak our paws and find a little to eat,' said Pentecost. 'For we need to be fit and strong for the crossing of the Great River. After that, you will never see us again.'

A short while later, Pentecost and Little Brother sat together on the bank, exchanging problems. It was a fine sunny morning and, with no ugly houses to spoil the view, they gazed across the Great River at the distant Lickey Hills.

Pentecost pointed. 'You see that small grassy knoll at the top of the highest hill of all? That is Lickey Top, and it's to be our new home. Snake said it's quite deserted, except for a kindly owl who lives in an oak tree there. But there are many dangers to be faced before we reach it. You see the fringe of dark trees just below our knoll? Well, those are the Weasel Woods. We must journey through those woods before we arrive safe and sound. But, after we have helped Snake regain his pool, he has promised to guide us through them. Perhaps you think us fools to put our trust in Snake but we've really no choice. There is no turning back for us now. Our old home is burned to the ground. So we can only hope that Snake keeps his part of the bargain. But look, Little Brother, isn't it a beautiful sight?'

From this far away the green hills appeared a hazy shade of blue. At their feet sprawled the red clay foothills, above which clouds of wood pigeons soared, their sharp eyes scanning the opened earth for food. The vole and the mouse sat and drank in the beauty, neither speaking for quite some time.

The small vole broke the silence. 'It is only that perfection needs a silver stream to glide in,' he said. 'But the hills, for all their beauty, lack such a necessary item.'

'Oh, but you're wrong,' Pentecost interrupted. 'As we journeyed through the night Snake described his homeland in great detail, and many tears he shed, too. Mostly he talked about his pool, of course, but he did say that, just over the brow of Lickey Top, is a clear blue stream. I think he called it Wending Way Stream. He mentioned a certain spot where the waters flow around a great hillock. Apple Tree Bend is the name of the place, I think. He also ... whatever's the matter, Little Brother?'

The vole had buried his nose in his paws and was sobbing. Tears rolled between his drooping whiskers and Pentecost, deeply moved, hastened to comfort him. 'Did I say something to upset you, Little Brother?' He patted the vole's tummy, that being as high as he could reach.

'It was the apples,' sniffed the little vole. The mention of apples always has that effect upon me. It is only that apples are the love of my life. I have been head-over-heels in love with apples all my days. Many hours have I spent gazing into the stream waiting, hoping for an apple core to come bobbing along. And at night I dream about them.'

Pentecost was still confused. 'You must love them an awful lot to weep at the mere mention of them. Tell me, Little Brother, if an apple core came bobbing along this minute, what would you do?'

The vole's face lit up. 'I would leap into the water and guide it to a quiet place with my nose.'

'And then what?' said the mouse.

'I would gobble its sweetness down, pips and all,' said Little Brother, relishing every word. 'Then, when it was all gone, I would pretend it wasn't, and gobble it down again.'

'You know,' said Pentecost slowly, 'you would love

Apple Tree Bend. Snake said that the tree is loaded down with the most delicious rosy red apples every summer.'

Again the vole's emotions spilled over. 'Please forgive me,' he said brokenly. 'But you keep mentioning them. If you wouldn't mind, could we please change the subject?'

'By all means,' said Pentecost. 'I won't mention apples again.'

'You just did,' said Little Brother weepily.

'And for the very last time,' said Pentecost sincerely. 'For we are now going to talk about a dreadful waste. I mean your life, Little Brother. The importance of it shines brightly when compared to the dourness of your brother. The world would surely benefit from your harmless presence. Your brother's shady world is not for you.'

'I know this to be true,' the vole replied. 'I feel we should not live with only the departed souls of our parents for company. I often hear my brother talking to them. He doesn't need me. Sometimes I think he wishes to be rid of me. I also miss my parents, but in a different way. I remember the happy times we spent together, while my brother only broods on the manner of their passing. He cannot banish the picture of the falling house-bricks from his mind. He wakes in the night and weeps and, for all my concern, I cannot comfort him.'

'You are worthy of a better life than that,' said Pentecost. 'For you are a kind and optimistic vole and shouldn't be dragged down by your brother's despair. You should leave and make a new life for yourself. You cannot always be your brother's keeper. He is beyond help, you are not. What would suit you is a nice clear bit of stream, preferably with an apple-core tree close by. Perhaps, in time, you would see a pair of bright eyes regarding you with approval. You would like a family of your own?'

'It is only that such happiness will never come my way,'

said Little Brother sadly. 'But I thank you for the delightful picture you have conjured, I shall treasure and imagine it constantly.'

'Wait a moment!' Pentecost had a sudden thought. Suppose ... just suppose. 'But why should it remain a dream?' he said slowly. Little Brother gazed at him with bright hope-filled eyes. 'You see, I am thinking that one day the City will spill over this pretty place,' said the mouse. 'And what will happen to you then? Little Brother, I think I have a plan.' He called loudly. 'Snake, Snake, could you spare a moment?'

Snake was gliding lazily about the stream, the warm sun glinting on his wet olive green skin. Upon hearing his name, he ceased his bubble-blowing, raised his head, and eyed the pair suspiciously.

'Now what?' he said flatly. 'Don't you like to see others enjoying themselves? You, Small Mouse, have the unpleasant habit of spoiling things when they are at their most pleasurable. What is it? And the answer is yes, anything for a quiet life.' He swam to the bank prepared for the worse.

'Well,' said Pentecost. 'I have a request to make on behalf of Little Brother, then he will speak for himself.'

But Snake had already sized up the situation. He was nowhere near as thick as two planks, as some folk would have it. Sometimes he could display an astounding shrewdness, for one who had been bamboozled by a slick con-merchant.

'I know,' he said. 'He wishes to come with us. And with a brother like his to put up with, I'm not surprised. As I've already said, the answer is yes. Now can I get back to my fishing?'

Pentecost looked unhappy. He had wanted Snake to hear Little Brother's sad story from his own mouth.

Snake relented. 'All right, let's have it,' he said wearily. 'But make it short, eh?'

'It all began long ago,' said Little Brother. He paused as if searching for the right words.

Snake interrupted. 'And it all ends here,' he said abruptly. 'I'm sorry but your sob-story is of no interest to me. You can come with us, now let's hear no more about it.'

'What bad manners you have,' said Pentecost. 'I notice you talk a lot, but you rarely listen to others, Snake. Little Brother's story is similar to my own. I, too, wish to raise a family one day. Perhaps a son to follow in my pawsteps, even become leader and bear the proud title of Pentecost.'

Snake showed interest for the first time. 'I meant to ask you about that,' he said. 'How come the name? I mean, I'm Snake, he's Water-Vole, that cunning little beggar on the lily pad is Frog, how come you're a Pentecost?'

'It isn't really a name at all,' said Pentecost. 'It's a title. It means Spring Festival. As you know, Snake, spring is a time of rebirth and hope. I as Pentecost represent that hope. It all sounds very grand, I know, but I'm quite a humble mouse, really. I just do my duty as a leader should. But if I fail in this, the family will choose again. That is the law.'

Snake sighed. 'I promise I'll never ask again,' he said. 'The mysteries of mice are too hard to fathom on an empty stomach.'

'But I've just explained!' shouted Pentecost. 'It's simply that . . .'

But Snake, quite bored, had returned to his fishing. 'Be ready to travel in one hour, and no more talking, please. You're frightening the little fishes!'

'Snake!' called Pentecost. 'A moment more, if you please.'

Fuming, Snake swam to the shore once more. 'Yes,' he said testily.

'Thank you very much indeed,' said Pentecost sincerely. 'For letting Little Brother come with us.'

'Don't mention it. Although how I'm expected to get a

bunch of landlubber mice across the Great River is quite beyond me.'

'You must have faith, Snake,' said Pentecost. 'Faith can move mountains.'

'Maybe,' muttered Snake, slipping away. 'But can it remove cousins from Oily Green Pools? Which reminds me, keep your eye on that Frog. I don't want him giving me the slip.'

'Come share my lily pad,' cried the frog gaily. He had found a real one in this clean bit of stream and was bouncing up and down upon it.

'Not just now,' said Snake politely. He dipped his head beneath the water and blew some more bubbles, enjoying the tickling sensation as they rose and popped about his ear muffs.

'That's settled then,' said Pentecost contentedly. 'All your problems are over, Little Brother. Soon you will be swimming about in Wending Way Stream, and waiting for the you-know-what to ripen.'

'It is only that you make me so happy my voice breaks,' said the gentle vole.

'And now all that remains is for you to tell Big Brother,' said Pentecost. 'Or would you rather I break the news to him?'

'There's no need,' said a harsh voice from behind. The pair turned. The large vole stood looking down at them. He had heard every word. He spoke briefly, brutally and to the point. He appeared neither glad nor sad. In fact, he showed no emotion at all.

'So you've decided to become a passer-through, Little Brother? And you leave within the hour? Well, remember this. Don't ever return, for I have no further need of you. My parents and I will get along quite well without your company. And now I must go, for I hear them calling me.

64

Don't be here when I come back.' With that he turned and left. And that was the last anyone ever saw of Big Brother. He had finally achieved the solitude he craved.

An hour later the expedition was gathered along the bank of the Great River. The farther shore, thought Pentecost, his heart sinking, seemed an awfully long way away.

7 *Across the Great River*

The noise and the traffic along the river was shocking after the tranquillity of the camp on vole property. Huge clouds of gnats gyrated above the wind-tossed bulrushes, and dragon-flies hummed by, the sun sparkling on their transparent wings. From time to time a pleasure boat passed by, its sharp nose cutting through the green waters with a sharp hissing sound. The chug of its engines, the happy cries of its passengers, filled the mice with apprehension.

'Not this mouse,' said Uncle firmly. 'I vote we go back immediately and forget this crazy journey.' He and the family gazed at the disturbed waters surging and boiling and sending wave after wave crashing against the bank. The Great River fascinated the Harvest mice. The stream they had left behind compared in no way with this majestic sweep that lay between them and their goal.

Pentecost strained his eyes to see across it. He could just make out the thin brown strip that was the distant shore. It appeared featureless and flat. But beyond were the welcoming, beckoning Lickey Hills and that cone-shaped crest, with its crowning forests glittering in the sun. 'We'll make it, Uncle,' he said. 'Snake will get us across somehow. One day we'll look back and laugh at all our doubts and fears.'

'I notice you aren't laughing now, though,' said Uncle with a cynical grin. 'It's my belief we're all doomed. I'm waiting to see the first mouse go bobbing across that water.' He turned to the family. 'Does that Pentecost think we are all fools? I know what's going through his mind. He wants us useless old mice to go bobbing across first.'

Pentecost was thinking hard. He was becoming a very worried mouse. He glanced at the trusting faces of the family. The young, the old, the infirm, all were waiting for him to make a decision.

'Nice day for a swim,' said Snake casually.

Pentecost resented the remark. Snake was a first–class swimmer, and could afford to be jovial. Little Brother and Frog were also well–equipped for water travelling, but Harvest mice?

'It's an ideal morning for a paddle, Snake,' said Frog. 'I agree whole-heartedly.'

'There's nothing quite like water to relieve the tensions of the day,' said Little Brother. 'It is only that I relish the thought of an invigorating swim with such delightful companions.'

'In we go then,' said Snake, sliding into the water. 'Last one over is a sissy.'

He was soon at least a quarter of the way across. The frog was a short distance behind, using a slow but enduring breast stroke style. Little Brother was just about to slip into the water when a sudden thought struck him. He turned to look at the mice. They were all slumped dejectedly upon the shore. Their expressions told Little Brother everything he needed to know. Quickly he cupped his snout with his paws and hailed out across the water. 'Snake, come back,' he called. 'It is only that a problem looms large. Snake, come back, the expedition has foundered upon the shore.'

Luckily Snake was within hailing distance still. He returned, looking extremely irritable. 'There'll be another boat along in a minute,' he said angrily. 'We don't want to get caught in its wash now do we? What's the hold-up?'

'We mice can't swim,' said Pentecost miserably. 'We can paddle a little, but we need to have our toes on the bottom for confidence.'

The frog had also returned. 'Trouble?' he asked sympathetically. 'It *is* a bit deep. And that current is a real puller.'

Suddenly Little Brother had a brilliant brain wave. Excitedly he explained. 'What if Snake entered the water and allowed his tail to be gripped firmly by Pentecost?'

'This is hardly the time to be talking about revenge,' said Snake warily.

'No, no,' said the impatient vole. 'I am talking about a ferrying plan I've just had. I am thinking of a long chain of mice, all gripping the tail of the one before in his teeth. In the meantime, Frog and I could ferry the old and the infirm across on our backs.'

'What a marvellous idea!' cried Pentecost.

Snake was looking fed up. 'It wouldn't work,' he said. 'For a start, how could I squiggle through the water with a long chain of soaking wet mice hanging on to my tail? All my innards would be stretched out of shape. And I certainly don't intend to go through life with teeth marks in my tail. I'd be a laughing stock.'

'Snake's right,' said Pentecost. 'Has anyone else a better idea?'

'I have,' said a Great Aunt. 'If we spinners wove a long rope of grass stems, Frog or Little Brother could swim across with one end and make it fast on the other side of the river.

Then we mice could swim across it, without sinking to the bottom.'

'I have an even better solution,' said Frog grandly. 'We, that is, Snake, Little Brother and myself will form a ferrying service. I think Snake, with his enormous length, alone could carry many mice across without straining his back.'

'That is the best idea of all,' said Pentecost. 'I suggest we measure Snake's length immediately for his mouse capacity. Lie down and stretch yourself out, Snake.'

Not keen on the idea, but unable to come up with a better one, Snake allowed himself to be smoothed out amongst the warm pebbles of the shore. Pentecost moved along Snake's length, his paws apart, measuring out so much space for each mouse.

'Twenty,' he announced. 'Snake can ferry twenty at a pinch.'

'Nineteen,' corrected Snake. 'I'm not having a mouse sitting on my head. I must be able to see where I'm going, after all.'

'That was my place,' said Pentecost sadly. 'I was going to be captain there.'

'You'll be captain a little further down, or nowhere,' said Snake firmly. Pentecost agreed reluctantly.

'And I can manage five,' said Little Brother.

'And I three,' said Frog. 'And I shall ferry Uncle, for I am developing a soft spot for him. I will seat him in such a way that his sore paws will be kept perfectly dry.'

Uncle beamed. 'I always liked that frog,' he said. 'Even when he was a wicked liar, I could sense the goodness beneath his shifty manner. I alone realised he wasn't rotten to the core.'

The frog wept and quietly blessed Uncle for his faith. 'May the truth guide your path through life', he murmured.

'According to my counting, it will mean an extra trip for

one of us,' said Little Brother. 'And, as I am now a happy vole with good friends, I will volunteer.'

'Three cheers for the end of the problem!' cried Pentecost. 'Hip hip . . .'

The Harvest mice cheered themselves hoarse, Frog turned a backward somersault and Little Brother beamed and beamed. Snake looked up and down the river. There were no pleasure boats in sight. The river was deserted, but for a few birds soaring over the water. 'Now's the time,' he said. 'Never mind the cheering, we aren't over yet.' He slid into the shallows and waited as the nineteen passengers climbed aboard. There was much squabbling and jostling for position, but Snake bore it all with a weary resignation.

It was then that the accident occurred. Snake began to sag in the middle like a waterlogged reed. 'I don't think the problem is solved completely,' he said to Pentecost, who was clinging to his neck. 'I'm developing a list amidships. And if that isn't enough, a thought has just struck me. I'll need to lash my tail to move through the water. I'm afraid a few passengers may get swept overboard. Would it matter if we lost one or two? There's also the question of a complete capsize. We can't rule it out, you know. All hands lost and all that.'

But his worries were completely unfounded. Pentecost had also noticed the sag and he had thought of a remedy. 'You won't be doing any swimming,' he said. 'All you need to do is to fill yourself full of air. Then, if you keep your body quite still, we mice will paddle you across with our paws. Just pretend you are a hollow log and not a snake at all. And don't worry so, Snake, I'm right behind you.'

'Now I'm a hollow log,' said Snake gloomily. 'Is there no end to my suffering? Oh well, we can but try. Hold tight.' He breathed in and out a few times and then drew in a huge lungful of air and held it.

'You won't let it go, Snake?' said the mouse anxiously.

'Mmmmm,' wheezed Snake.

'He means no,' said Pentecost thankfully. 'And remember, Snake, you mustn't let your breath go until we reach the other side.'

'WHOOSH,' went Snake. The air gushed from his mouth. 'One lungful all the way across?' he gasped. 'It's impossible. I'll need to fill up at least twice.'

'Aren't you forgetting the sag?' said Pentecost. 'We'll all sink if you change breaths in mid-stream. Look on the bright side for a change. How do you know you can't do it, unless you try?'

'It's just this feeling I've got,' said Snake. But he pulled himself together and agreed to try. Once again he filled up with air.

'Now, cast off,' shouted Pentecost. The mice began to paddle furiously with their forepaws and Snake moved majestically out into the river. 'This is your captain speaking,' called Pentecost. 'Keep up a steady paddling rhythm and no shirking. All together now, in out, in out. That's the way. We'll soon be across at this rate.'

The birds wheeling over the water sheered away as the strange vessel approached. They uttered startled cries and circled warily above, all thoughts of fishing swept from their minds. Later they would be scoffed at as they told of the

weird sight they had witnessed. Frog, easily supporting his three passengers, breast stroked alongside Snake's head. Little Brother, with his five, swam along behind, his bullet-shaped nose cutting through the water like a knife through butter.

The travellers were so intent upon their dangerous voyage that they failed to notice a small orange-coloured insect, who dived and buzzed them from time to time. It was apparent the bug had more on his mind than plain curiosity. It followed their progress closely and appeared to be listening to their conversation.

'Hey ho for the new life on Lickey Top!' shouted Pentecost.

The insect seemed especially interested in that remark.

Pentecost's excitement was infectious. A small mouse on the tip of Snake's tail ceased paddling and clambered to his paws. He began to sing and shout about how happy the family would be once they arrived on Lickey Top. Only prompt orders from Pentecost saved a possible shipwreck, for Snake was threatening to turn turtle.

The pin-point of orange light continued to gather information as the crossing neared its end. Then, as if satisfied with the results gained, it soared high into the air and sped off in the direction of the Lickey Hills.

Meanwhile Snake was beginning to act in a peculiar manner. He began to emit worrying snorting sounds. Pentecost leaned forward, his face filled with concern. What he saw made him feel suddenly afraid. Snake's eyes were spinning around in his head, each in a different direction. But still he held his breath in a most heroic way.

'Not much farther, Snake,' encouraged Pentecost. 'Just hang on, the shore is quite close now.'

But rivers are deceptive. They always appear narrower than they really are. The brave snake had barely reached the shallows before the inevitable happened. 'WHOOSH!' he went. He sagged in the middle as the stored air burst from his lungs. The mice were flung violently into the water. Somehow they managed to scramble ashore, leaving Snake rolling over and over in his agony.

'Stop!' cried Pentecost. He had remained, treading water, and trying to hold Snake's drooping head above the surface. 'Get back into the water and help me drag Snake to safety. Have you no loyalty at all?'

Shamefaced, the mice waded out again, seized Snake's limp body, and somehow managed to haul him up the bank. And there he lay, completely spent, and convinced his life was ebbing away.

Frog and Little Brother disembarked their passengers and hurried to help Snake. 'It is only that he needs rest and quiet,' said Little Brother. 'And now I must return for the remainder of the expedition.' Soon he came coasting into the bank with the last load of passengers. The expedition was united once more.

Pentecost glanced at the sky. Soon the sun would be gone. Quickly he organized food-gathering parties and posted look-outs around the camp. This was unknown country and one couldn't be too careful. Frog, after a filling meal of water-boatmen and other disagreeable morsels, scraped himself a hole in the mud and went off to sleep. Little Brother, obliging as always, went fishing. In no time at all he had caught a fine fat trout which he laid temptingly before Snake's nose. Snake sniffed and groaned, and lapsed back into unconsciousness. Everyone else settled down for the approaching night, with the exception of the look-outs who scanned the countryside for lurking dangers. It had been a long and eventful day. The blue sky was beginning to darken and cloud over. There would be no moon to cast its ghostly light over the Great River that night. Already there was a spit of rain in the air. The little ones lay curled up in a soft

72

heaving bundle. Soon everyone slept, except for Pentecost, who spent most of that rainy night thinking about the morning and what it would bring.

8 A Word in the Ear

As the exhausted expedition slept, a bright orange light spiralled downwards towards a grassy knoll high on Lickey Top. An observer on the ground might have mistaken it for a shooting star, but its erratic flight would have caused him to have second thoughts.

A dull flicker of lightning lit up the horizon, followed by the faintest clap of thunder from far away. There was a storm approaching. The oak tree stood out stark against the grey sky. It bore many scars of previous storms, yet still it stood. A few bright green leaves still clung to its one remaining branch. Halfway up the trunk was an oval-shaped hole. Beside it jutted the stump of a long-fallen limb. The hole was a home; the resident; Owl of Lickey Top.

The orange glow alighted upon a slip of bark beside the black hole and peered inside. It spoke in a suppressed but excited whisper. 'Owl, wake up. Have I got news for you! An invasion, Owl, and heading this way.' The tiny bug's glow illuminated the dark interior. The sleeping fat form within was bathed in its pale lemon light. 'I can't wait to see his face when he hears my news,' said the bug gleefully. 'Oh how long have I waited for this moment? At last, one in the eye for Owl. That's right, sleep on, old buddy. Look at him, that smug fat face and those filthy claws, sticking up in the

73

air. No dignity, that's Owl's trouble. Hated and despised throughout the whole of the Clent and Lickey Hills. Just one friend in all the world who cares. Me. And now it's my sad task to break the terrible news to him. But then, what are friends for? Oh, this suspense, is killing me. Owl, Owl, for Heaven's sake, wake up!' The rain increased, the winds howled louder. Quickly the bug sought shelter beneath the slip of bark. And there it hung, upside-down, suspended by its spare leg.

The orange-backed, seven-legged cockle-snorkle was an extremely rare insect. It was a collector's item, or would be if a lucky bug-hunter could lay his hands upon one. Such people would give their right arm to pop one in a pickling jar, or have one pinned against blue velvet with a Latin tag attached. Cockle-snorkles were the unicorns of the insect world, almost mythical creatures. Always they had escaped capture. The reason for this lay in their elusiveness. They had developed the trick of concealment to a fine art. They had the clever knack of being able to dim themselves from a natural bright orange to the dullest of grey shades. A swift tucking-away of a spare leg and, hey presto, a common or garden bug, and of no interest at all. But still the bug-hunters believed the cockle-snorkle to be a reality, if only they could track one down. The search continued, the results, nil.

All these talents had enabled the bug to become a first-rate spy. Its sole reason for living was the gathering of information. But a spy needs a master. The spy needs to unburden himself, for what good are secrets if kept to oneself? Owl was this cockle-snorkle's master. Owl, whose only contact with the world outside was his willing spy. The two needed and deserved each other. It was a love-hate relationship. The cockle-snorkle shunned its own kind, for spies, notoriously shy, prefer the twilight world of secrecy and stealth. Gossip, scandal, spicy stories, nothing, however trivial, escaped the attention of the ever-prying cockle-snorkle. It would suffer physical injury and almost any discomfort, in order to listen in on someone's private conversation. Its reward, a tactless whisper, a blurted secret, was worth all the long hours of cramped waiting. But everyday gossip was mere bread and butter for the cockle-snorkle. The jam came when a big story broke. For this particular bug, the 'biggie' had broken that very afternoon.

'That's the trouble with news,' muttered the bug. 'It needs to be fresh to make an impact. And here's me with a red-hot story getting cooler and cooler by the minute.' In desperation he yelled into the hole again. This time he received a response.

'What's up?' groaned Owl. The bird heaved himself over on to his back and opened his eyes. 'What time is it? And what's it doing outside?'

'It's later than you think,' sang the bug. 'And it's a real stinker. Belting down with rain.'

'Drat!' snapped Owl. He turned his face to the light and stared at the bug through cold unblinking eyes. The bug's soft lemon light revealed the cruelly curved beak, the needle-tipped talons, the bloated stomach of his master. Owl was a sight to send shivers down the spine. But the terror he inspired in others was lost on the extremely rare bug.

'Would you like the bad news first, Owl?' he said. 'Or would you prefer to talk about the weather?'

'I sometimes wonder about you,' said Owl slowly. 'This bad news for instance. Would it concern me, by any chance?'

'It certainly would, Owl,' the bug replied. 'It isn't fair. Why won't they leave you in peace? I mean, you mind your own business and suddenly this happens.'

Owl looked suspicious. 'Why are you always so cheerful when it's bad news for me?'

'How can you say such a thing?' said the bug reproachfully. 'And us such good friends, too.'

'Very well,' Owl said, not completely convinced. 'Let's have this calamitous news of yours.'

The bug's tale unfolded. 'I am grieved to inform you that your solitary existence will soon be at an end. At this very moment, an invasion is heading this way, intent upon making your life a complete misery. We are to have neighbours. Noisy rampaging neighbours, all running amok over your property.'

A flash of lightning zig-zagged across the sky and the rest of the bug's words were drowned in a crashing roll of thunder. The steady rain became a torrent and the winds shrieked across the exposed hill top.

'That was right overhead,' said the bug ominously. 'If I were you, I'd keep my head well down, Owl.'

'What do you think I'm doing?' said Owl irritably. 'Now what were you saying? Did I hear you right? An invasion? Impossible. No-one would dare. I'd rend them to pieces, I'd rip them into tiny shreds. No, you must have heard wrong.' He snuggled deeper into his hole and cocked a moody eye at the weather outside. 'And I was going hunting tonight,' he said. 'I just fancied a nice plump fieldmouse for my supper.'

'How about Harvest mouse?' enquired the bug. 'Very tasty are Harvest mice.'

'Yes,' sighed Owl. 'But there'll be nothing about tonight, not in this weather. Pity.'

'Tell me, Owl,' said the bug. 'What if Lickey Top was swarming with Harvest mice? You must admit you'd have your supper nice and handy. There'd be no need to hover all the hours God sends over the lower fields. Just pop out, grab, and Bob's your uncle.'

'Not likely!' said Owl. 'I couldn't have that. All those noisy festivals, all the dancing and singing? My nerves wouldn't stand it. No, I like Lickey Top just the way it is. Nice and quiet.'

'Well, I'm sorry to say this, Owl, but it's a Harvest mouse invasion that's heading this way. They plan to settle on Lickey Top. Snake of Oily Green Pool has put 'em up to it. He's told 'em this place is up for grabs.'

Owl sat bolt upright. 'What!' he shouted. The cockle-snorkle turned away and winced, as a string of oaths poured from the bird's beak.

The bug waited for him to calm a little. He then explained the situation. He told of how he had listened in to the conversation as the mice had crossed the Great River. As he talked, he watched the bird closely. Owl was beginning to froth at the beak and his filthy talons clawed at the roof of his hole.

'They must be stopped!' shouted Owl above the howling winds. 'Do you hear me? They must be destroyed before they reach here. Where are they now?'

'Well, they've crossed the river,' said the bug. 'I imagine they'll have made camp for the night. But don't worry, Owl, tomorrow they'll have to travel along Ambush Path. They've no choice if they're heading for Woodpecker Wood. Snake knows there's only one way up here. That's what they'll do. And I reckon that's as far as they'll get, Ambush Path, if the Ruffians have anything to do with it.'

'Yes,' said Owl, relaxing a little. 'They'll never get past the Ruffians. But it's the devil of a cheek, don't you think? Who does Snake think he is, parcelling out other folk's land without so much as a by your leave?'

'Yes, well, Snake has lost his pool, if you remember, Owl,' said the bug. 'I think he's playing some funny game of his own. The lying frog is involved somewhere. I'll have to check.'

'You do that,' said Owl grimly.

'Who do they think you are?' said the bug indignantly. 'Some lily-livered owl who they can walk all over? Some fat slob who wouldn't recognize an invasion if he fell over one? Some saucer-eyed whining recluse with filthy claws, with . . .'

Owl frowned. 'Be careful,' he said softly. 'You've made your point.'

'Well, they can't treat my best friend like that,' said the bug vehemently. 'Not if I can help it, they can't.'

'Too true,' thundered Owl. 'If I want a mouse supper I shall hunt one down for myself. But to have the place swarming with them, it's not on.'

'That's my old buddy,' said the bug approvingly.

'Haven't I suffered enough?' said Owl. 'Didn't I come here in the first place to get away from the snide remarks and persecution?'

'Ah yes, that would be that unpleasant Clent Hills business?' said the bug. 'The egg affair. You never did tell me what really happened, did you Owl?'

The bug's question was deliberately barbed. He knew that to mention the sordid egg business was the surest way to infuriate the bird. Sure enough Owl went into a terrible rage. The memories came flooding back as the bug goaded and prodded at that raw nerve.

Owl had been born far away in the Clent Hills. The moment his beak poked from the shell, his parents fell in love with him.

'Just think, in a few days our sweetling will have a brother, the spitting image,' said Mother, gazing first at her son and then at the unhatched egg beside him. 'For a brother it will surely be, and equally adorable.'

The small owl uttered a practice hoot to please them.

'What a set of pipes he has,' remarked Father proudly. 'And now, Mother, before he jigs himself out of the nest in his eagerness – his mouse.'

The youngster's eyes brightened. A moment later he was tearing into his supper and enjoying every last scrap.

But this happiness was to remain short-lived. One night the parents returned home from a hunting trip to find the unhatched egg smashed to bits. Deeply shocked, they gazed at the yolk dripping from their son's claws. They noticed his downcast eyes, the drooping posture. Immediately they drew their own conclusions.

'This is a case of murder,' said Father quietly. 'He has struck down his brother in a fit of jealous rage. His reasons would be greed, I imagine. He probably couldn't bear the thought of sharing a mouse.'

'But we could have brought home one a-piece when the time came,' cried Mother. 'Ask him to explain his actions. Give him a chance Father.'

'What chance did he give his brother?' was the grim reply. 'But very well. Let him speak.'

Words poured from the little owl. But they were a meaningless jumble, mingled with sobs. Pathetically he began to shovel the sticky bits of shell together.

'It's too late for that!' Father shouted. 'He'll be as dead as a dodo by now. And your spluttered excuses will cut no ice with us.'

'Perhaps we could find it in us to forgive him?' said Mother hopefully. 'And who knows, it could easily have been an accident. When he stops his spluttering, the true story may come out.'

'The truth is before our eyes,' thundered Father. 'As soon as he learns to fly he can go fend for himself. In fact, I intend to start his flying lessons immediately.'

Mother watched as the miserable little owl was dragged

and pushed from the nest. He plunged earthwards to hit the ground with a sickening thud. Again and again he was forced to repeat this, his father returning him to the nest after each painful fall. There was no pity for him.

Owl learned to fly in record time. Throughout this period, Father steadfastly refused to listen to his son's stammered explanations. 'You don't remember, indeed,' he snapped. 'How can you not remember murdering your brother?'

'Perhaps if we had more eggs and taught him love and respect?' ventured Mother. 'I say he should be given another chance.'

'Another chance?' echoed Father angrily. 'Another chance to have a crack at yet another brother? And maybe at us, too, as he gets larger and more confident. Not likely. He can get out now, for he's become a beautiful little flyer, despite his black soul.'

The confused little owl flew up into a tall poplar and stayed there for two whole days. Even though in two minds about his guilt or innocence, his mother continued to feed him left-over scraps when Father wasn't watching. He was her son after all, and it was the least she could do. 'God forgive you,' she would whisper. 'Or us, if we are wrong. One day, when you stop spluttering, the truth will out. I pray with all my heart we have misjudged you.'

And so there in that tree the young owl sat and grieved. For hours he racked his brains, trying to remember what had really happened that fateful day. But his distressed young mind couldn't cope. It played him tricks. The time came when he began to believe he really had committed the dreadful deed. His despair was shared by an orange-backed bug who had been skulking about in the area for the past few days. The bug appeared to know more about the incident than the chick himself. He didn't seem bothered that the young owl had been accused of murder.

81

'Put it from your mind,' he advised. 'Your guilty past will be safe with me.' He then put to the other a proposition. He explained how his master, also an owl, and a recluse, to boot, had passed away. His property on Lickey Top was now vacant. Was the young owl interested in becoming a recluse? It was surely the best solution. And, after all, who could be sure the chick wouldn't feel the urge to kill again? Now, a recluse would have that temptation removed, would he not? The young owl agreed. That night they left for Lickey Top, one never to return, the bug only on rare spying missions.

From that time on, Owl's character changed. No longer was he the 'sweetling' of those former happier days. If his father thought him evil, so be it. He would live up to that reputation. It cost him dear. Born with a sunny outlook, he would live in shadow. It was a terrible price to pay.

The rain began to ease and the cockle-snorkle climbed from beneath his slip of bark.

'So what do we do, Owl? About the Harvest mice, I mean?'

'At the moment, nothing,' replied the bird. 'But I want them under constant surveillance. You will return to the Great River at first light.'

'I will return to the Great River at first light,' repeated the bug. 'Should I introduce myself to the clever Pentecost mouse, Owl? He's their leader. Some say he's brushed with genius, you know.'

'Genius mouse,' scoffed Owl. 'There's no such thing. There's only one genius in the Lickey Hills. Need I say more?'

'You need not, Owl. I happen to be speaking with that genius right now. Wasn't it I who realised you were one?

What with your great mind and my extreme rarity, we are an unbeatable combination.'

'Must you keep going on about this so-called rarity of yours?' snapped Owl. 'You have to get it in, don't you?'

The bug apologized. 'I know I've only a small claim to fame, compared with yours, Owl,' he said. 'Just the unimportant fact that I have an extra leg and that no human has ever set eyes on a member of my species. I mean, just because owls are common as muck doesn't mean to say they aren't special, too. In your case, it's a question of quality, not quantity.'

The bug's barbs were cleverly concealed behind a thick larding of flattery. Owl looked pleased. Then he frowned. Sometimes Owl had difficulty deciding just what the bug meant by such remarks. He had no sense of humour at all and, because of that, he was never quite sure whether the bug was flattering or insulting him. The bug, aware that his intelligence was far superior to the bird's, took advantage of the fact. His seemingly innocent remarks were a small, but deadly, weapon in his armoury. It was his cunning way of getting even with Owl without upsetting their relationship.

'Your orders are clear then?' said Owl. He glanced up at the sky. A fine drizzle had begun to fall again. He sighed. 'Might as well go back to bed. I'm not venturing out on a night like this.'

Once more the cockle-snorkle repeated his orders. He, too, decided to catch a few hours of sleep before his early morning mission. He felt a surge of excitement. He was looking forward to his meeting with the Pentecost mouse. Sleepily he crawled beneath his slip of bark and winked out his light. Presently he drifted off to sleep; to all appearances, a scrap of drab leaf-mould adhering to the hoary old oak.

9 Ambush Path and Woodpecker Wood

Pentecost awoke to a grey, overcast sky. He had managed to catch a couple of hours sleep before first light. He stretched and yawned. Glancing about, he could see the family were still sound asleep. Softly, so as not to awaken them, he crawled from the warmth of the nest and looked around. He could just make out the farther extent of the field. In the left-hand corner stood a clump of bushes. The mouse noticed that, from where he stood to the distant bushes, a track had been worn through the grass, the red soil showing through, indicating the pressure of many passing feet. 'The bushes must mark the spot where Ambush Path begins,' he thought. 'Didn't Snake say some such thing?' He shivered as a thrill of fear ran through him. He tried to think of more pleasant things. And suddenly, the sun broke through the cloud in a blaze of glory. Large fluffy clouds were drifting away over the western horizon and large blue patches of sky began to appear. It was just as the mouse turned to retrace his steps that the voice spoke.

'Would you be the genius Pentecost mouse?' sang an orange star, that couldn't possibly be, so long after first light. It buzzed the astonished mouse, before settling on top of a hedge.

'Who are you and how do you know my name?' was the reply. 'And why should you think I'm a genius?'

'I just do,' said the bug. 'It shines out of those ugly odd eyes of yours. One glance and I said to myself, there's a genius if ever I saw one.'

'Thank you very much,' said Pentecost. 'But I do wish folk would avoid saying unkind things about my eyes. Beauty is only skin deep, you know.'

'Would you say I was beautiful?' asked the bug. 'Take your time. Feast your odd eyes on my body and give me your honest opinion.'

'I think you're very unusual . . . and bright,' said Pentecost slowly. 'I must admit you've a very attractive glow.'

'Don't you mean glorious?' ventured the cockle-snorkle.

'I think you're a little too small to be called glorious,' said the mouse. 'Unless one peered closely at the details.'

'Feel free,' breezed the bug. 'And while you're peering, I'll ask you a few leading questions.'

'Leading to where?' asked Pentecost, inspecting the bug closely. 'And why should you need to ask me questions?'

'Because asking things is my trade,' the bug explained. 'It's all part of my life-style. Finding things out, flying errands for Owl, delivering messages, listening to idle gossip and unlikely tales. I've been watching you since yesterday, and I smelt a story the moment you set out across the river.'

'In other words, you're a spy,' said Pentecost scornfully.

'I am indeed,' said the bug boldly. 'I'm also an extremely rare, seven-legged, orange-backed cockle-snorkle. There's not many of us left, you know.'

'I'm not surprised,' said the mouse. 'Spies don't live long, so they say. They usually get bumped off early in life.'

The bug was tiring of the discussion. 'Can we move on now?' he said hurriedly: 'I've already stated I represent Owl of Lickey Top. Now then, where is your expedition heading, and who gave you permission to go there in the first place?'

'By sheer coincidence, we are heading for Lickey Top,' said Pentecost. 'It looks as if we're going to be neighbours, Cockle-snorkle. Owl, who you know is a kindly bird, will make us welcome. Snake said so.'

'So,' said the bug, 'that slippery character is responsible for this invasion, eh?'

'After he's got his pool back from the cousin, he is going to lead us there,' explained Pentecost.

'And who is going to lead you back?' asked the bug.

'No-one, we intend to settle.'

'Owl will be pleased,' said the bug. He flew into the air, looped the loop and returned to the hedgetop.

'Do you really think so?' the mouse smiled happily.

'Certain of it,' the bug performed his looping trick again.

'Why do you keep doing that?' said Pentecost, looking puzzled.

'Because, with a bit of luck, you just might make it and then Owl will be taken down a peg or two,' grinned the bug. 'I always loop the loop when I'm happy.'

Pentecost looked envious. 'I wish I could do that,' he said. 'When I'm happy I jump into the air and kick my back paws together ... like this.' Pentecost demonstrated his happiness kick for the amused bug. 'Of course,' he said. 'It isn't as satisfying as looping the loop, but it's the next best thing, don't you think?'

'You know, I've a mind to help you,' said the bug slowly. 'I think I'm falling in love with your winning ways. You,

86

small mouse, despite your extreme ugliness, have personality plus. You have a way with you.'

'It's usually the way with ugly folk,' the mouse agreed. 'God rewards us in other ways. You are glorious in fine detail, I am gloriously pure in soul.'

'Yes, well, enough of this trumpet-blowing,' said the bug. 'As I say, I have fallen deeply in love with you. Because of that, I intend to play both ends against the middle.'

'And how would you do that?' asked the mouse, interested.

'By becoming a double agent,' was the prompt reply. 'All spies usually end up as double agents. It's dangerous, but great fun. In years to come, this bit of business will be referred to as 'the great double-cross'. I shall go down in history as the most despicable traitor of all time.'

'Wouldn't you rather be remembered with affection?' said Pentecost. 'Surely you wouldn't wish folk to hoot and jeer whenever your name is mentioned?'

'Yes, I would,' said the bug seriously. 'It's my ultimate ambition.'

'But why do you need to become a double agent?' said Pentecost. 'And why should we need your help at all? Owl is a kindly bird and Snake has assured us a welcome awaits us on Lickey Top.'

'Snake,' said the bug dryly, 'is leading you astray. He is the most selfish creature in the Lickey Hills. He'd tell you anything, if it helped get his pool back.'

'Now isn't that strange,' said the mouse. 'Frog said much the same thing. Now look, Cockle-snorkle, there is something you aren't telling me. Something about Owl, am I right? I'm beginning to suspect he doesn't want us on Lickey Top at all.'

'I'm saying no more,' said the bug firmly. 'The plot must thicken. Folk must be kept in the dark. If I revealed everything I know, all the fun would be lost. I need you to flounder about, trapped in a web of intrigue and skulduggery. At the same time, my friend Owl, believing me to be an honest little bug, will lap up everything I tell him, like the thick bird he is. Only at the very end will I allow my mask to slip and reveal myself as the most vile of traitors.'

'I must admit, I'm still very confused,' said the mouse. 'In fact, I don't know what you are talking about. It's all double-dutch to me.'

'I know, great, ain't it?' sang the greatest turncoat of all time. 'And now, a word of advice, take care when you travel along Ambush Path. In the meantime, I shall be following your progress with the greatest interest. I shall be seeing you from time to time, but now I must be off.'

'And so must I,' said Pentecost. 'The family will be wondering what has become of me. I don't suppose you would explain a little more of this mystery before you go?'

The bug spiralled into the air, glowing fiercely. 'There'd be no point,' he called. 'Everyone knows that double agents aren't to be trusted. And now, goodbye, and remember I love you dearly.'

Pentecost watched, his head craned back, as the bug zoomed high into the air, dashed about in circles and finally sped off in the direction of the Lickey Hills. He returned to camp feeling disturbed and troubled. His conversation with the strange insect had only served to confuse what little information he had received from Snake. Could it be just possible the bug was setting some kind of trap? The more he thought about it, the more confused he became. And all this talk about double agents? Whatever could the bug mean? And his offer of help? If the bug was to be believed, the mice weren't in the least welcome on Lickey Top. So Snake was lying? Certainly the frog thought so. It was all too much for the mouse to absorb at one go. He decided to let events take their course for a while and, in the meantime, watch for danger signs. In particular, he intended to keep an extra close watch on Snake. And if the bug showed up again, he would demand a full explanation. The next time he wouldn't be fobbed off with winks and nods and veiled warnings. He would mention his meeting with the bug in a casual manner and watch for Snake's reaction. Someone was telling lies, and Pentecost was determined to get to the bottom of it. The safety of the family was his responsibility, and he intended to honour that obligation.

Snake was stirring when he arrived back in camp. He still looked wan and fragile after his ordeal of the previous day. Pentecost couldn't help but feel guilty. Snake was now under suspicion, yet no-one could deny the heroic way he had ferried the mice across the Great River. Perhaps Snake *was* playing some game? Perhaps he did intend to desert the family, once he had regained his pool? But, up until now, his behaviour was beyond reproach. And if he had lied about the goodness of Owl, he had done so very convincingly.

Snake was staring listlessly at the distant Lickey Hills. They shimmered beneath the bright sunshine, looking fresher and more beautiful after the rains. Little Brother was trying to snap Snake from his black mood.

'It is only the after-effects of your terrible ordeal,' the vole was explaining. 'It will soon pass.'

'It's my digestion,' Snake was complaining. 'The trout won't move. It's stuck halfway down. It's through being forced to hold my breath for too long.'

'That too will pass,' said Little Brother wisely. 'You will be a healthy snake in no time at all. You have had a severe shock. Just try to rest awhile.'

'How can I rest when the creature who ruined my life is staring at me with those bulging bloodshot eyes of his?' said Snake.

89

'I am praying for you,' said the frog. 'The fact that you are deceitful doesn't deter me in any way. That trout must be most painful for you. If you would permit me to lay my healing touch upon your tortured body, I am convinced the trout would move.'

'Keep that quack away from me,' shouted Snake as the frog advanced, flippers extended. The frog was restrained by Pentecost.

Meanwhile, the family were emerging from their shelters. Damp coats steaming, they scurried about in search of breakfast. At that moment the look-outs, pretending to be utterly worn out after their night's vigil, arrived back in camp. They had nothing to report. 'It was just an ordinary, quiet, starry night,' they said when questioned. 'Not one sign of danger from dawn till dusk.' Pentecost refrained from pointing out that the night had been cloudy and, indeed, a storm had raged throughout a large part of it. But he felt uneasy. The next time look-outs were appointed, he intended to lecture them on the follies of sleeping while on watch.

'Perfect weather for travelling,' said the frog cheerfully. 'If you wish, I will gladly lead the way along the dangerous Ambush Path. But first, we must file through the parted grass to the clump of bushes yonder. If you remember, I travelled this way before, but in the opposite direction, of course.'

'Yes, fleeing from justice,' said Snake bitterly. 'But you aren't the only one who knows the way. How do you think I got to Pentecost Farm?'

'Ah, but you travelled back-to-front,' said the frog. 'I remember you saying.'

'Don't bandy words with me,' snapped Snake. 'You are a prisoner under escort and don't you forget it.'

'How unforgiving you are,' sighed Frog. 'And I felt so useful yesterday. I so enjoyed ferrying my friends across the

Great River. Surely I am a little along the path to goodness?'

'Anything to do with paths is my business,' Snake interrupted. 'I am leading this expedition. You can croak about goodness all you want, but the path to home and my pool will not be discussed by lying frogs, reformed or not.'

Pentecost saw his opportunity and seized it. 'You say you are leading this expedition, Snake?'

Snake looked startled. 'Didn't I just say that?' he said.

'But how far?' said the mouse. 'Could it be you intend to desert us the moment we reach your pool?'

'Haven't I said that all along?' shouted Frog.

Snake shot him a venomous glance. 'You are a proven liar,' he said. 'So keep your nose out of it.' The frog's face fell and he lapsed into silence. 'Naturally, I intend to carry out my part of the bargain,' said Snake. 'How many more times must I say it? I will lead you to Lickey Top, after my pool is returned to me. Once there, I will deliver you into the kindly claws of Owl. Is that fair enough?' The mice seemed to think it was. Snake was applauded loudly.

'Quiet please,' said Pentecost, holding up a paw. 'Now everyone is present, I have something important to say. A short time ago I had a strange conversation with a seven-legged orange-backed . . .'

'Oh, him,' interrupted Snake. 'I might have known he wouldn't be far away. What's he been saying this time? Stirring it up, as usual?'

'He wasn't very complimentary about you, Snake,' said Pentecost, watching him closely. Snake shrugged. It was hard to tell his reaction, his face being twisted up in pain from the stuck trout.

'It is only from surprise that I fall back on my haunches,' said Little Brother. And this he promptly did.

'Would you explain what you mean?' said Pentecost curiously.

'I and my brother had many dealings with that mischievous bug,' said the vole. 'He carried many untrue tales that aroused my brother's quick temper. No doubt, at this very moment, he is informing his master of every move we make.'

'Do you mean that rare bug is not to be trusted?' said Pentecost quickly. 'For he hinted to me that Snake was the untrustworthy one.'

'I protest,' said Snake hotly. 'That bug has always had it in for me. He is the one to beware of.'

'And Owl too?' said Pentecost, baiting his trap. Snake was about to reply, when the frog joined in and spoiled it all.

'The bug and the Owl aren't to be trusted,' he cried. 'Neither is Snake, but no-one believes me.'

'Nonsense,' said Snake. 'And the mouse was asking my opinion, not yours. Owl is completely trustworthy, I'll stake my reputation on it.'

'Well, I'm completely flummoxed,' said Pentecost. 'Someone is lying, but which one? The bug, Snake, or is it Frog?'

'Never,' said Frog firmly. 'I've turned my back on that sort of thing.'

'The cockle-snorkle said something else,' said Pentecost. 'But I couldn't make head or tail of it. Can I ask you a question, Snake?' Snake nodded wearily. 'What does "playing both ends against the middle" mean?'

'I haven't a clue,' said Snake.

'Then perhaps you can tell me what a double agent is?'

'It's all gibberish to me,' Snake replied. 'Why the questions?'

'It was something the cockle-snorkle said. I thought you might know what he meant by it,' said Pentecost.

Snake was beginning to feel worried. What had the bug been saying about him? And about Owl? He knew quite well that, if the mice lost confidence in him, they might go off on their own, taking the frog with them, then where would he be? Without the frog, he had no hope of getting his pool back. Somehow, Snake had to distract Pentecost from this dangerous line of questioning. He had a sudden brainwave. 'The trout is moving!' he cried. The mice crowded around to see for themselves, the bug and his strange remarks forgotten. To Snake's complete surprise, the fish actually was. Wide-eyed, the mice watched as the untidy bulge began to sink with a gurgling sound into Snake's nether regions. 'Right, get ready to move out,' said Snake briskly. With a groan, he set off at a fast wriggle. Too fast. Somehow his tail caught up with his nose, and he fell in a heap on the ground.

'Serves you right for trying to change the subject,' said Frog.

Snake lunged at him, determined to damage some part of that tender body. It was Uncle who unwittingly saved the frog from terrible injury.

'Who does that frog think he is?' he shouted. 'He is the cause of all Snake's troubles, with his lying.' Snake nodded sadly. Uncle continued, 'These paws are proof of the frog's unchanged character. He promised to keep them as dry as bones during the ferrying. Do they look as dry as bones?'

Pentecost inspected the old mouse's paws. They were undoubtedly sopping wet. 'It was an accident,' protested Frog. 'I did my best, but a surprise wave turned my promise into a lie. It wasn't my fault, honest.'

'So the waves of the Great River are responsible for his lie?' said Uncle sarcastically.

Pentecost hesitated. He realized the frog was trying to change for the better. But the evidence of Uncle's paws was there for all to see. He decided to give Snake the benefit of the doubt. Also, he would dismiss the words of the cockle-snorkle as the ravings of a mischief-maker. The important thing was to get on with the journey. They had a long way to go and to waste time arguing amongst themselves was foolish. 'I'm sorry,' he said to the frog, as gently as he could. 'We must believe in the honour of Snake. But never mind, one day folk will begin to trust you and, when that day comes, you can take your place amongst respectable company once more. But it will take time. Just be patient.'

'The new Pentecost is learning,' said Uncle. 'Slowly, it's true, for real wisdom comes only with age and experience. We must take the word of the hollow worm with the yellow ear muffs.'

'Thank you,' snarled Snake.

'For myself, I will follow wherever my friend Pentecost leads,' said Little Brother. 'Even unto the apple core trees, for there my yearnings lie.'

'Very well,' said Pentecost, deeply moved. 'We are ready to move off whenever you give the word, Snake.'

'Off we go, then,' said Snake, moving away at a painful crawl.

And so the expedition set off for the clump of bushes that screened the entrance to Ambush Path.

Ambush Path was overhung with elderberry bushes. What little sunlight penetrated their thick foliage performed a dappled dance about the paws of the trudging mice. On either side of the path was a deep and muddy ditch. Was it imagination that scufflings and urgent whispers could be heard coming from them? The party hurried on, eager to be out in the sunshine once more.

Now the soft patter of paws could be heard, scampering along the ditches. Now and again a flitting form could be seen, stealing from one bush to the other. A muted command rang out, and the scuffling ceased.

Then suddenly the end of the dark path was in sight. The

sunlit exit beckoned the mice to the wide-open spaces and safety. With shouts of joy, they raced for that welcoming gleam, ignoring Pentecost's appeals for caution. Snake was left far behind.

Suddenly, with the exit mere yards away, the headlong dash was halted. The lead mice had skidded to a halt and were shouting warnings to their comrades behind. For a while, there was confusion, with mice milling about, not knowing quite what to do. Pentecost pushed his way to the front and peered out into the clearing. What he saw struck fear into his heart. There, in a large semi-circle, stood a group of the most rascally-looking mice he had ever seen.

'The Ruffians,' whispered Frog. He began to quake at the knees. 'I managed to avoid them last time. Now we're for it. They tear folk limb from limb for pleasure. They are utterly ruthless and fear nothing, not even God himself.'

By this time, all the expedition members had emerged from the path and stood in a petrified huddle at the clearing's edge. Snake, newly arrived, curled up a little way away, an expression of contempt upon his triangular face. Contempt for the expedition, or for the Ruffians, it was hard to tell. Whatever his feelings, he seemed intent upon keeping out of whatever was about to occur. Little Brother, on the other hand, took his stand at Pentecost's side and waited, as did everyone, for the next move.

The Ruffians were a band of renegade mice, who roamed the countryside in search of excitement and battle. They were Townie mice, who had been uprooted by the City's spill-over, and now ran wild over this part of the world. Their hard City training made them more than a match for most creatures who crossed their violent path, although they drew the line at foxes. What they lacked in size, they made up for in cold-blooded efficiency. They fought as a well-diciplined unit, having learned the use of surprise, reserves

95

in hiding and boldness in attack, from previous battles. Their watchwords were destruction, thievery and death. An occasional beating didn't deter them at all. They bore their scars with pride. They were also unkempt and smelled badly, as the down-wind family soon learned. But the expedition had more than a distasteful smell to worry about, as they appraised that cut-throat band.

For a while, the parties faced each other in silence. Then suddenly, a Ruffian limped forward. Obviously, he was the leader. Pentecost noticed he was missing an eye and a front paw. He looked all the more fearsome for it and was aware of the fact, for his limp in no way disguised his confident swagger. Indeed, his injuries gave him a sinister air. He paused, cocked his head on one side, and spoke. His voice was heavily accented and harsh.

'Slaves we want and slaves we'll get,' he said, an air of finality in his tone. As far as he was concerned, there was no argument. 'Consider yourselves lucky,' he went on. 'We've just fought a great battle and are in the process of re-forming. We are preparing a counter-attack and need slaves to do all the heavy chores. Send out all the young strong mice and the rest of you can be on your way. Come on, jump to it.'

'You'll enslave our young ones over our dead bodies,' said Pentecost bravely.

'You leave my body out of this,' called Snake. 'I've been battered about quite enough, thank you. Fighting your battles isn't part of our bargain'.

'Pity,' said the leader Ruffian. 'I was looking forward to tying a few knots in his tail. Well, what's your answer?'

'It is only that our answer has been delivered by my friend Pentecost,' said Little Brother. 'Our dead bodies, and some of yours also, will be the price paid for your callous demand.'

'I'll count to ten,' yelled the Ruffian. 'If the slaves aren't delivered up by then, we'll come and get 'em. And, while you're about it, you can throw in a few of those old spinning mice. We could do with a few watertight shelters at head-quarters. But, really, I hope I do get to ten, for we Ruffians hate peaceful solutions.' He began to count in a loud voice. 'One, two, five, seven, three, nought . . .'

'You aren't counting fairly,' shouted Uncle. 'But mark my words, when you do get to ten, you'll find yourself in a powerful choking grip. Don't let these grey whiskers fool you.' Bravely, Uncle joined the stout-hearted band of family members, who were readying themselves for the fray.

'Nine, six, ten!' yelled the Ruffian. Instantly, he and his motley crew hurled themselves upon the resisters. Battle was joined, blood flowed. Pentecost and his companions were soon fighting for their lives. Cries of pain mingled with shouts of triumph. Uncle, sizing up a weak-looking Ruffian, gallantly hurled himself upon him and seized him about the throat. Unfortunately, the Ruffian was wiry, rather than weak. He began to revolve about in circles, the old mouse clinging on grimly. Once every circuit, Uncle screamed out in pain as his tender paws were smashed against a tree stump. But now his enemy was gasping for breath, his eyes bulging alarmingly from their sockets. But youth was on his side. The old mouse's grip was beginning to slacken. Those much-vaunted paws suddenly relaxed their death-hold and Uncle went sailing through the air to land with a sickening thud against a rock. For a while, the old mouse just lay, exquisite waves of pain racking his body. But soon he was up and into the fight once more.

It was gentle Little Brother who surprised everyone. He had suddenly turned into an efficient and deadly fighting machine. He slashed and stabbed with razor-sharp teeth. Three, four, five Ruffians fell before those formidable jaws. The wounded dragged themselves clear, only to have their places taken by fresh forces. No quarter was asked for, none given. It was a fight to the finish.

Meanwhile, a small group of Ruffians had seized the Great Aunts and little ones, and were holding them captive a short distance away. But their jubilant expressions soon changed to anguish, as they saw how the fight was going.

Snake, who had wanted no part of the battle, changed his mind. Or rather he had it changed for him. The Ruffian leader had tripped over Snake's tail in the melee. Angered, he bounded to his paws and seized Snake's tail between his teeth. He bit down hard. Snake hissed in pain and rage. The leader then began to tie neat knots in Snake's injured tail. Something snapped in Snake's mind. He became a furious mass of writhing coils. Quickly unpuzzling himself, he wrapped the tip of his tail about the Ruffian's neck and hurled him a good twenty yards into a thorn bush. The maddened reptile then looked about for more victims.

The Ruffians holding the captives flung themselves into the fray. The battle wasn't turning out as they had expected. The tide was turning against them. Frog was busily drop-kicking any Ruffian who ventured too near his powerful rear legs. As an opponent fell stunned upon the ground, so Uncle seized his throat and squeezed. It was fortunate for the beaten mice that Uncle wasn't in his prime. Most crawled away, badly bruised but alive, just. Between them, Frog and Uncle did quite a bit of damage that day.

Soon, increasing numbers of Ruffians were retiring from the fight. They had had enough. Others lay, never to rise again. Finally, the Ruffians' attack broke against such formidable odds. There was no doubt in anyone's mind that Little Brother had saved the day. The fighting ceased as quickly as it had started. After all the commotion, the stillness that descended over the clearing was electrifying. Even the birds were silent. The opposing sides broke away.

The Ruffians gathered up their dead and wounded and prepared to move off.

'It was a good fight,' said the Ruffian leader. 'I don't suppose you would care for a return match at some later date?'

Pentecost looked about him. At the blood, at the wounded, at the three dead family members who had given their lives in defence of their loved ones. The little ones and the lady mice began to wail.

'We didn't wish for this to happen,' he said quietly. 'All we wanted was to be allowed to go our way in peace. And now, we have lost three of our brothers. You, too, have lost comrades. Was it all worth it? And still you talk of more fighting. Go, for the sight of you sickens our hearts. We wish to bury our dead in peace.'

'It was just a thought,' replied the Ruffian. 'I don't suppose that vole would care to join up with us? We could use a fighter like him.' He glanced at Little Brother. The vole's expression was answer enough. Little Brother's blood-smeared coat attested to his bravery, but his heart was gentle and the carnage he had inflicted grieved him deeply.

'It is only that I wish to forget this terrible happening,' he said simply.

'Suit yourself,' said the Ruffian, looking puzzled. 'But if you ever change your mind? We'll be off, then. We've set up an ambush for a certain weasel just down that hill there, and we wouldn't want to be late. Goodbye for now.' And with those parting words, he and his rascally band departed.

The funeral was held upon the field of battle. It was a short and simple affair. Snake, Frog and Little Brother moved respectfully away, for they had no wish to intrude upon the grief of the Harvest mice.

The three dead mice were carefully covered with fern fronds. Then each mouse stepped forward to lay a token spray of wild flowers upon the grave. The bright sweetly-scented mound was gazed upon for a few silent moments, then the mice turned away.

'We are ready to continue now, Snake,' said Pentecost quietly. Further words were unnecessary. The expedition moved off across the clearing and was soon swallowed by the cool sunless canopy of Woodpecker Wood.

The din inside the Wood was ear-splitting. It was aptly named. Every tree had its woodpecker, if not two.

Now, it is the aim of every self-respecting woodpecker to drill as many holes in as many trees as he can manage in one lifetime. Why, is the woodpecker's business. Of course, some birds are better at it than others. There is an old saying that 'all are equal, but some are more equal than others'. This saying applies particularly to woodpeckers. Put simply, the abler the borer, the more equal he is. And quite right, too, for drilling holes in trees is an art and best left to the expert.

The bird, who was a little more equal than the rest, was an elderly woodpecker with a blunted beak and a critical gleam in his eye. In his time, he had bored more holes than the other birds had had grub suppers. These days he had no need to prove himself. He believed his record to be safe. Now he was an instructor and spent his time passing on his skills, and basking in the admiration of his fellows.

A bird so used to respect would have been very annoyed if, say, an old mouse with herb-bound paws had come along, and told him to keep the noise down. One such mouse did, together with a snake, a frog, a water-vole and a bunch of other mice, of all shapes and sizes.

'All this hammering and chiselling,' complained Uncle.

'And all this sawdust getting up one's nose. Woodpecker Wood? Headache Wood, more like. Stop it at once, or I'll be up that tree to pull all your tail feathers out.'

'It is only Uncle's crankiness,' shouted Little Brother. 'He means no harm. He isn't to be taken seriously.'

'And, if he isn't careful, I will be down to drill a hole in his impudent grey head,' warned the old woodpecker. 'Whose wood is this, anyway? And what good are trees without holes in them? If I had my way, every tree in the world would be riddled with holes. Be off with you and leave my apprentices in peace.'

'It's a wonder the trees still stand,' said Uncle, refusing to be quietened. 'You are a bunch of vandals. Haven't you anything better to do than to sit on your fat tails and hammer useless great holes in those poor trees?'

'What do you know about our customs?' said the bird indignantly. 'Who are you to come telling us what not to do? We have always drilled holes in trees.'

'Well, it's about time you packed it in,' replied Uncle.

'You shouldn't stand directly beneath,' said the bird, in a righteous tone. 'In fact, you shouldn't be standing in my wood, at all. This is my workshop and you are trespassing.'

'And what is more,' said a learner bird, 'how many holes wouldn't a woodpecker peck, if a woodpecker wouldn't peck wood?'

'You've got it the wrong way round again,' sighed the old bird. 'It's "how many holes would a woodpecker peck, if a woodpecker would peck wood"?'

'And what is the answer?' asked Pentecost interested.

'The answer is, one thousand and twenty three,' said the bird proudly. 'Which is my unbeaten record.'

'The farther I travel over the world, the madder it gets,' said Uncle.

'And the noise is a little unbearable,' said old Mother. 'The

102

little ones will develop ringing eardrums if they have to endure this terrible din all the way through the wood.'

'There I can help you,' said the old bird gallantly. 'The solution is sawdust.'

'Sawdust?' queried Pentecost.

'Pack it in your ears,' the bird replied. 'You'll be amazed how little you hear, with your ears stuffed with sawdust. Try it and see, there's lots of it about.'

'I'd like to stuff your beak full of it,' said Uncle evilly. 'This wood is full of nonsense-birds and the sooner I get out of it, the better.' He began to mutter to himself, 'How many pecks would a tree peck would if a peck tree ... utter nonsense.'

Meanwhile, the other mice were taking the bird's advice. Soon their ears were tightly packed with sawdust. 'It works,' cried Pentecost. 'I can't hear a thing.'

'Pardon?' said Little Brother, his ears also well stuffed.

'Did you speak?' said old Mother. 'I saw your snout move, but I can't hear a thing.'

'Utterly mad,' declared Uncle, but he copied the others and the sounds of the world vanished.

'Pardon,' said Pentecost. 'Did you speak, Uncle?'

'Pardon,' said Uncle blankly.

'For Heaven's sake,' cried Snake. 'Let's get out of this wood, before I also go completely mad.' He set off at a fast pace along the trail that led to the other side of the wood.

'Pardon,' chorused the mice, following his fast-vanishing form.

'Now, what were you saying before we got side-tracked?' said the senior woodpecker.

'Nothing,' said the learners humbly. 'You were!'

'You were explaining the principles of balance,' said a young bird shyly. 'You were saying that, for every action,

103

there is a reaction. Also, you were talking about fulcrums and levers.'

'Was I, indeed?' said the old bird. 'And did you understand what I was saying?'

'Not quite,' was the reply.

'Then I'll explain just once more,' said the bird impatiently. 'And listen, this time.'

'That's the trouble,' said the learners. 'We can't hear a word you're saying. It's all the noise, you see. We can't hear ourselves think.'

'It's a problem you'll get used to, as you get older,' said the old bird. 'After a time, one hardly hears it.'

'Pardon?' said the learners politely.

10   *The Lake of the Lilies*

'Isn't it a beautiful sight?' cried Frog. 'And see, across the other side, that's World's End Hill. We'll be home in no time at all now.'

The mice were unable to hear his words, their ears still being packed with sawdust, but they could see for themselves the lovely view, as they emerged from the gloom of the woods. They found themselves at the edge of a small lake. The water was the most delicate shade of pea-green they had ever seen. At the centre of the lake was a tiny island upon which grew a lone weeping willow tree and clumps of snow-white lilies. Gasps of delight went up from the family. After the squalor of Pentecost Farm, this place seemed like Paradise.

Snake, Little Brother and Frog threw their water-starved bodies into the inviting depths, watched by the envious mice. A more venturesome mouse, paddling in the shallows, declared that the best way to unplug sawdusted ears was to plunge them beneath the water. 'Just dip, hold the snout closed and blow through the nose,' was his advice. Soon all the family was in the water, dipping and blowing enthusiastically.

It was a perfect afternoon for relaxing. A good part of the journey was already behind them and the tranquillity of the lake lulled and soothed their troubles away. But despite their happy mood, there were few mice who didn't spare a thought for the three fallen comrades. Pentecost said that their souls would live on in the memory of the family for ever. The mice drew comfort from that.

And now the sun was falling beyond the horizon. Pentecost was just about to consult Snake about making camp for the night when the incident arose. It appeared that the young son of one of the slain mice was having trouble with his ears. He had ducked and plunged and blown down his snout, to no avail. The sawdust in his ears refused to budge. His widowed mother approached Pentecost, wringing her paws in anguish. 'It is good that the family are happy again,' she said tearfully. 'And perhaps, one day, I shall feel happier, too. And my young son will soon forget he is half-orphaned, for the scars of the young heal quickly. But, what I find hard to bear, is the fact that my son is as deaf as a door-post, despite the water cure. Come, see for yourself, and understand why I weep.'

A Great Aunt stopped her weaving to inspect the small mouse's ears. 'Just as I thought,' she said. 'Completely jammed. And we know why, don't we? How many times have you been told, "cleanliness is next to Godliness". How often has this particular scamp ignored my warnings? Now he is suffering for ignoring my advice. The sawdust has mixed with the wax in his filthy ears and his hearing is trapped behind it.'

'He now has two wooden blocks in his ears, thanks to disobedience,' said another aunt. 'I am surprised he is the only case.'

'Can everyone else hear?' shouted Uncle. 'If anyone can't hear me put up your left paw. On the other hand if anyone can hear me, put up your right paw. Of course, if no-one is interested, forget it. I can't hear a word I'm saying anyway.'

The young scamp was looking very worried and bewildered. The family crowded around, jostling to peer inside the offending ears. Importantly, Uncle pushed them aside. 'I know how to cure those ears,' he said. 'It is an old remedy my great-grandfather passed on to me.'

Snake was watching the proceedings, with a cynical smile on his face. Frog and Little Brother had joined the mice, dripping water over everyone, as they crowded close to view the blocked ears for themselves.

At last, Uncle was the centre of attention. It was a position he had craved for many long years. 'First, we do this,' he said, giving the ear a sharp tweak. The scamp squealed with pain. His mother hid her eyes in her paws. 'Then we do that,' said Uncle, twisting the ear in the opposite direction.

'Ouch!' cried the terrified mouse.

'And finally, we . . .'

'And finally, you will not lay another paw on my son,' said the distraught mother. She snatched the abused mouse to her bosom. 'How can you treat a half-orphaned mouse in this fashion?' she cried. 'And he with his father barely cold in his grave. Just look what you've done to that ear.'

'One needs to be cruel to be kind,' said Uncle loftily. 'Anyhow, the ear is only a little inside-out. It will soon snap back, if we don't watch it. If we all turn our backs, it will snap back in a trice, you see if it doesn't.'

'But will it be cured?' asked Frog dubiously. 'If you ask me, that ear is ruined for life. There's no natural shape left to it.'

'No-one is asking for your opinion,' snapped Uncle. But he was beginning to look worried.

'Let's do as Uncle says,' said Pentecost. 'We'll turn our backs for a few moments. It can't do any harm to try.' Everyone turned their backs, except Snake, who had no faith in the idea at all.

'When we hear a sharp snapping sound, it will mean the first part of the cure is successful,' said Uncle. The mice waited and listened. Then they began to fidget, while waiting and listening.

'It's taking a long time,' said Pentecost. He turned back again. Everyone did likewise. The ear was still badly twisted inside-out.

'I think we'd better take you off the case, Uncle,' said Pentecost. 'Your remedy has only increased the poor mouse's suffering.'

'Will I ever be able to listen again?' asked the mouse, his eyes awash with tears. 'And go out to play noisy games?'

'Of course you will, my precious,' wept his mother.

'Pardon?' said the scamp faintly.

'I know what the matter is,' said Uncle briskly. 'I forgot an important part of the cure.' He took the ear between his paws and began to twiddle. 'Amazing what a good twiddle will do,' he said. 'See, already the ear is no longer inside-out.'

The weeping mother craned close. 'It looks the same to me,' she said. 'That ear is still inside-out and no-one will tell me different.'

'Wrong!' shouted Uncle. 'The ear is now outside-in, any fool can see that.'

107

A close inspection of the ear was carried out, much to Snake's amusement. It seemed things were becoming more complicated with every passing moment. The ears were still firmly blocked, the mouse was still as deaf as a door-post and, to crown it all, the one ear was turned to an outside-in position.

'He was such a handsome son,' sobbed his mother. 'Why didn't Pentecost stop Uncle's meddling?' Other mice were of the same opinion. Pentecost protested, but his reputation had sunk to an all-time low. A bitter argument began.

'Excuse me,' said Snake interrupting. 'As you mice have a lot to discuss, may I make a suggestion? You see I'm a peace-loving snake and all this argy-bargy upsets me. What if I swim across the lake and make camp for the night there? You mice can camp here for the night. That way, I will get a good kip. Perhaps my green friend would care to accompany me?'

'Not on your life,' said Frog quickly. 'I'm staying here, thank you very much.'

'Only a thought,' murmured Snake.

'You weren't thinking of kidnapping Frog and deserting us?' said Pentecost horrified.

'What a suspicious mind you have,' Snake replied. 'The thought never entered my head.' But of course it had.

'If you wish to sleep across the other side of the lake alone, you are quite entitled to do so,' said Pentecost. 'We will see you in the morning, Snake.'

'Goodnight then,' said Snake, sliding into the water. He was soon lost to sight.

'And I shall camp here too,' said Little Brother. 'For I love discussions. My former life was such a lonely one. It is only that I adore friendly voices.'

'You will hear no friendly voice from me,' said the mother mouse sharply. 'What about my son's ears?'

'Perhaps if we banged his head against a tree?' suggested Uncle.

'Another old-fashioned remedy, I suppose?' said a sarcastic Pentecost. 'We've had enough of your cures, thank you, Uncle.' He sat down and thought long and deeply. His agile brain leapt from solution to solution, but the correct one escaped him for a long time.

'I'm afraid our leader is bankrupt of ideas,' said Uncle slyly.

As he said it, so a smile spread across Pentecost's face. 'Of course!' he shouted and leapt to his paws. The mice watched open-mouthed as he vanished into the trees of Woodpecker Wood.

'And that's the last we'll see of him,' said Uncle. 'He's gone round the bend.'

'I have faith in my friend Pentecost,' said Little Brother firmly. 'He will return, never fear.'

The family waited with mounting unease. The moon came out. It was a near full moon and its light filled the lakeside camp with a ghostly glow. Then, suddenly, Pentecost came running out of the trees, a large shadowy form hovering over his head. Thinking the worst, the family fled in all directions, diving for cover beneath hummocks of turf and handy boulders. Their fears were unfounded. Pentecost was merely returning with a cure for the deaf mouse.

'Why it's the old woodpecker,' cried the little ones. 'Perhaps he's come to peck a hole in Uncle's head, as he promised?'

Breathing hard after his dash through the woods, Pentecost ordered the unfortunate mouse to turn his left ear into the moonlight. The woodpecker, who had landed nearby, advanced and cocked a beady eye down the moonlit ear. 'I thought you said this was a big job?' he asked, disappointed. 'An apprentice could have dealt with this little matter. And there was me, thinking at last I'd got something to test my beak on. Hard as stone, you say? Oh well, now I'm here . . .'

'There's two ears to cure,' consoled Pentecost. 'Perhaps the right one will prove more of a challenge?'

'We'll see,' said the bird. 'Now, hold the little fellow still. We don't want to drill out his brains, do we?'

The family had caught on to the idea. A few stronger mice held the scamp firmly, as the woodpecker judged the angle, the depth of penetration and other scientific details. 'Brrrrrrr, Brrrrrr,' his beak stuttered like a road drill inside the troublesome ear. Bits of hardened sawdust flew about, as that wondrous tool did its work.

'Can you hear me, son?' cried the mother. The young mouse's eyes had lost that dull disinterested look. He nodded, causing the woodpecker to miss a stroke and plunge, beak first, into the ground.

The bird rose, its beak filled with earth. 'Just let's get the job finished,' it said grimly. 'Now turn the young fellow around, and let's have a look at the right ear.'

'Brrrr, Brrrr,' the second ear was unblocked as quickly as the first. 'Thank you, Woodpecker,' said Pentecost. 'We can't thank you enough for your kind help.' The bluff bird nodded politely, shot Uncle a venomous glance and departed.

'I can hear clearly again,' cried the young scamp. 'Now I shall be able to play at taunting Uncle and listen to his angry replies.'

Uncle remained silent. For a while he had feared the woodpecker was about to attack him. He was still trembling slightly.

'Now you can hear again, perhaps in future you will listen to the advice of your Great Aunts,' said his mother. With those words, she boxed his ears and packed him off to bed.

110

Uncle broke his silence. He was anxious to get back in Pentecost's good books. As usual, he was at his two-faced best. 'On behalf of the family, I would like to congratulate our leader for his bit of quick thinking. It is a pity I alone had faith in his mad scheme. How that conscientious mouse was run down in his absence. How glad I am, I refused to believe the tales spread about him.'

'You wicked old mouse,' murmured old Mother. 'Do you feel no shame at all?'

Uncle looked hurt. 'Only shame that I couldn't have helped more,' he said piously.

It must have been a little after midnight. Pentecost lay un-sleeping. He had been lying awake, listening to the most dreadful howling, that seemed to be coming from the brow of a small hillock a short distance away. He rose and glanced about at the sleeping family. Their tired bodies rose and fell from their steady breathing. It seemed a pity to disturb them. Instead Pentecost decided to investigate the matter himself. And while he was about it, he would find out why none of the look-outs had reported in. Surely they would have heard those spine-tingling howls? Pentecost came to the obvious conclusion that they hadn't. Undoubtedly, he would find them all sound asleep. It wasn't good enough, he fumed.

'Who was asleep?' said the first look-out indignantly. 'I was just narrowing my eyes to see more clearly. What howling? I assure you it's as quiet as the grave tonight.'

'So it would be, if you were fast asleep,' replied Pentecost. He gave the humbled mouse a stern lecture and passed on to the next. He, too, was asleep. And the next. All had similar excuses to offer. They had heard nothing. Pentecost must be imagining things. Grimly, Pentecost suppressed his anger

111

and set off in the direction of the small hillock, from where the sounds had appeared to come.

'If you want a job doing properly, do it yourself,' called the north-east look-out after him. It was sound advice.

Pentecost's anger soon gave way to apprehension, as he neared his objective. His heart beating wildly, he peered over the brow of the hillock. There, with the moon balanced upon his left ear, sat a fox. 'Oh, my poor paw,' sighed the fearsome creature. He gave another long mournful howl and craftily glanced in Pentecost's direction.

If the mouse had been at all observant, he would have noticed that cunning movement of the eye. In fact, if he had known anything at all about foxes, he wouldn't have tried to creep up on one. He would have known that to be an impossibility. 'This is what comes of being friendless and generally disliked,' moaned Fox, loud enough for the mouse to hear.

Still thinking himself unobserved, Pentecost glanced down at the fox's paw. The moonlight glittered upon a steel object. The paw was firmly imprisoned between its cruel jaws. 'If I had just one friend in all the world, he would have me out of this mess in the twinkling of an eye,' wailed the trapped animal. Tears of self-pity coursed down his jowls and, from time to time, he would give his trapped paw a tender lick. 'All alone and near to death,' he sighed cunningly. 'Oh, what I would give for a friend in my hour of need?'

Pentecost's heart melted as Fox reasoned it would. Bravely, the mouse stepped forward into the moonlight and approached the friendless stranger. 'Oh what a shock you gave me,' lied Fox. Slowly, he looked the mouse up and down. All trace of sadness had gone from that expressive face. Now Fox was smiling curiously. 'Can it be true?' said Fox in astonishment. 'Has God actually answered the prayers of a sinful fox?'

'I'm not sure what you mean,' said Pentecost cautiously. 'But it is true God moves in mysterious ways.'

'And he's sent a friend, in the form of a sweet little mouse,' said Fox.

'If you're going to talk sloppy, I'll go,' said Pentecost sharply. 'And as for being a friend, it all depends.'

'Upon what?' asked Fox.

'Upon how long the friendship lasts.'

'But why shouldn't it last for ever?' Fox said. 'They say friendships based on firm foundations usually do. Why shouldn't ours?'

'Because, after I'd helped you, you might remember you haven't had supper,' replied the mouse.

'If you think that, I'd sooner you left me here to die,' said Fox, in a shocked tone. He also *looked* shocked, for he was a talented creature and could switch his mood with great

113

rapidity to suit the situation. 'Anyhow, I've had supper. Chicken actually. I'm partial to chicken. I like mice only as chums.'

'In that case I'll help,' Pentecost said. 'For I feel I can trust you, despite your crafty appearance.'

'Thanks,' said Fox, deeply moved. He went on, not forgetting the flattery so essential to the egos of the small. 'And such a stealthy friend too. I couldn't have stalked up on me better myself.'

Pentecost looked pleased. 'It's my training,' he explained. 'I learned stalking when I was quite tiny.'

Fox smiled at some secret thought. Then he was suddenly serious. 'You won't be expecting a reward, or something?' he asked. 'I mean, you can't put conditions on friendship. Are you a "through thick and thin" friend, or a "fair weather" kind? The world is full of the last sort.'

'I think I'm a "through thick and thin" kind,' the mouse replied.

'I knew it,' said Fox. 'The moment I clapped eyes on you, I thought, now there's a future pal, if ever I saw one. And now, introductions are in order, I think.'

'But isn't your paw too painful for chit-chat?' asked Pentecost anxiously. 'Shouldn't we rescue it first?'

Fox seemed to have forgotten about the paw. He glanced down at it and shrugged. 'It can wait,' he said shortly. 'At the moment, I'm more interested in your life story.'

Pentecost started. 'What, all of it?'

Fox considered this. 'Well, perhaps just the interesting bits for starters. Like, what are you doing in these parts and where are you bound?'

And so, Pentecost told his new friend about the expedition and about the new home awaiting them on Lickey Top. 'I'm Pentecost, the leader,' he added proudly. 'Of course, Snake, late of Oily Green Pool, is acting as guide. And we have a frog, who has seen the light travelling with us. And Little Brother, who is my special friend.'

All this time, Fox had been nodding and murmuring, 'Really, how very interesting,' but he frowned at the mention of Owl and the cockle-snorkle. 'Steer clear of those two,' he warned. 'They aren't to be trusted.'

Pentecost was suddenly subdued. By this time, he was well aware of this fact. 'I think perhaps the bug is sometimes on our side,' he said hesitantly. 'He's quite fond of me, so he says. At this moment, he's playing both ends against the middle, which must be a good sign. And I hope to win Owl over when we reach Lickey Top. I shall put our case to him and hope that his hard heart melts.'

'And you'll do it charmingly,' comforted Fox, with a smile. 'And who knows, with a friend like me ... perhaps I can help in some small way.'

'Would you really, Fox?' cried the mouse.

'Our close friendship would demand it,' was the reply. Fox's face took on a dreamy look. 'Could we make ours a lifetime friendship, for I couldn't bear for us to drift apart.'

'I get the feeling you're pulling my paw sometimes, Fox.' The mouse stared long and hard at the grinning creature. 'Don't go thinking I'm a thick mouse, as some would have it,' he said. 'The trouble is, I can't tell whether you're being serious, or not. Foxes are supposed to be very cunning, so they say.'

'Another myth,' scoffed Fox. 'We're just slippery. There's a vast difference, you know.'

'I suppose there is,' Pentecost admitted. Then he had a sudden thought. 'It's very strange, but you haven't commented once on my odd eyes? Most folk do, at some time or other.'

'And I promise, on my honour, I never will,' said Fox

115

solemnly. 'And now, let's get this friendship off to a good start. You can start digging whenever you wish.'

'Digging?' said Pentecost.

Fox indicated his paw. 'Best friends need to be good diggers,' he explained. 'There's not much point having a friend who can't dig, is there?'

Pentecost was forced to agree. 'You're quite right, Fox. I'll start immediately.'

He began to scrabble at the earth about the trap. Fox watched for a few moments and then stopped him. 'Hang on,' he said. 'Let's have a look at those paws of yours. Hold them up to the moonlight.'

Pentecost obeyed. He was proud of his paws. They were white, to match his chest, and they were finely-shaped. Fox sighed in disgust. 'How deep do you expect to get, with those silly little things?' he said. He held up his own free forepaw. 'Now, that is what you call a real digging paw. A genuine "getting out of scrapes" paw that is.'

'In that case, you can do your own digging,' said the mouse angrily. He began to walk away. 'And you can forget the friendship. It's cancelled, as from now.'

'I see,' said Fox. 'All high and mighty, are we? Can't take a bit of criticism? I thought our relationship was too good to last.'

'If you apologise, I'm willing to forget what you said and try again,' said Pentecost, stopping and turning back. 'You've no right to insult my paws, Fox.'

'From the bottom of my heart, I'm truly sorry,' Fox replied. It was then Pentecost noticed Fox was having trouble with his jowls. He seemed to have his tongue stuck in his cheek. The mouse drew Fox's attention to it. 'I know,' said Fox, with a toothy grin. 'It's always doing that.'

Pentecost craned upwards to get a clearer view of the bulging cheek. 'I should be careful, if I were you,' he said seriously. 'You could quite easily stick like it. And now, Fox, I'm going to prove you wrong about my paws.' He attacked a small patch of soil nearby. A shower of earth and pebbles rained about Fox's head, who, being caught fast in the trap, could only duck and dive as best he could to protect his sensitive nose. Soon the hole was so deep the mouse couldn't climb back out of it. Fox obliged by lowering the tip of his tail down the hole and yanking the digger to safety.

'I take it all back,' said Fox admiringly. He explored the crater with a sharp nose. 'A proper little borer and no mistake,' he added.

'I could dig an even deeper one, if I wanted,' said the mouse, proudly. 'And at least twice as wide ... if I wanted.'

'Don't bother,' said Fox. 'Seen one hole, you've seen 'em all. The important bit of digging is here,' he indicated the trap. 'And please hurry, for I might just decide to bite this paw off. We foxes do that sometimes, you know.'

Pentecost was horrified. He began to dig furiously, quickly exposing the buried stake that tethered the trap to the ground. A little while later, Pentecost climbed from the diggings and brushed the earth from his nose. 'There,' he said, breathlessly. 'Now all we need to do is pull.' Gripping the steel stake he heaved, his rear paws slipping and sliding on the dewed grass.

'You are doing well,' said Fox encouragingly. But he didn't offer to help. 'Come on, put your back into it. One more heave should do it.'

Pentecost stopped pulling and looked at Fox. He had just realized something. 'Aren't you supposed to be helping?' he said. 'You've got another paw doing nothing in particular.'

'I thought perhaps you wanted to do it all on your own,' said Fox, surprised. He gave the stake a sharp tug and it slid easily from the soil. 'Free at last,' he said, contentedly.

117

'Not quite,' said the mouse. He pointed to the trap dangling from his friend's paw.

'Oh that,' replied fox airily. With his long fangs and his good paw, he prised the jaws of the trap apart. Pentecost watched incredulously.

'But why didn't you do that in the first place?' he asked. 'You've stood and watched me dig that hole for nothing.'

'Two holes,' said Fox. 'Don't forget the practice one.'

'But why?' said the bewildered mouse.

'I honestly don't know,' Fox replied. 'I just do these things. It's how we foxes are. But aren't you glad you stayed? If you hadn't, we wouldn't have become firm buddies, would we?'

'It's still a tricky thing to do,' said Pentecost. 'Shoddy, even. You've made a fool of me and I don't think I can forgive you for that.'

'Ah,' said Fox sadly. 'The parting of the ways so soon. I knew you'd begin to hate me after a while.'

Pentecost peered intently at the freed paw. He could see no sign of injury at all. He turned his attention to the trap itself. But it was the first time he'd seen one and he gained no clue as to whether Fox had engineered the whole affair. But one thing was certain, it was a very poor trap, for how had Fox escaped so easily from it? 'I believe you did all this deliberately,' he said. 'All the howling and the trap business was part of a plan, am I right, Fox?'

'You are,' said Fox. 'It's this curiosity of mine. I've been watching your expedition for some time now and I was intrigued to know just what you were up to.'

'So you lured me up here to pry into our business?' said the outraged mouse.

'Guilty,' Fox replied. 'But I'll make amends, I promise.'

'And how will you do that?' said Pentecost. He was toying with the idea of leaving immediately, for Fox's behaviour rankled deeply.

118

'I have decided to initiate you in the art of foxcraft,' was the reply. 'I am about to enroll you as an honorary fox. Then, when you're fully trained, we'll stalk chickens together. But first of all, I'm going to teach you how to howl . . . like this.'

Fox lifted up his head until it pointed straight up into the starry sky. Then he opened his jaws to reveal the great curved fangs gleaming in the moonlight. And Fox howled. It was a full-throated sound, filled with power, hate, contempt and malice. It was a defiant roar, yet its tailing notes were filled with strange yearnings, never to be understood by a small, unworldly, Harvest mouse. The countryside, so calm, so still before, seemed to stir from its deep slumberings. The night air became filled with nervous twitters and squeaks from the surrounding hedgerows and trees. So terrifying was the howl, that Fox himself seemed surprised by the awesomeness of it. He crouched, his eyes glowing pools of fire, and his great brush thrashed the grass as the hair rose to bristle along his back.

'Well?' said Fox breathlessly. 'What did you think of that?'

'I could never howl like that,' said the mouse enviously. 'Not in a million years.'

'Nonsense,' was the reply. 'How do you know until you try? Come on, head up, open those mighty jaws . . . and now . . . howl . . .'

And Pentecost howled. Again, the countryside stirred. But this time, it was amusement that rippled upon the breeze. Pentecost, the fox, was a dismal failure.

'Enough of that,' said Fox hurriedly. 'We'll try a bit of stalking. I think you'll find that a bit easier.'

This time, Pentecost felt more confident. He'd always been good at hiding and cowering, and stalking was much the same thing. Impatiently he watched as Fox demonstrated.

'First of all,' said Fox. 'We lie crouched up and still, so we can't be seen. Like this.' He sank into the grass, wriggled

119

about for a while and whispered, 'See, completely invisible. You, young mouse, are watching a master at work, or trying to watch one, for you can't see a thing, can you?'

'What lovely invisible ears you have,' said Pentecost wistfully.

Fox bounded to his paws in a temper. 'What ears?' he demanded. 'How can you see invisible ears?'

'Above the grass, Fox,' said Pentecost, playing the game as fairly as he could.

'If you were a true friend, you wouldn't have seen them,' said Fox. 'We'll try again, but this time remember how fond we are of each other. Friends never see friends' ears, ever.' Again he snuggled into the long grass, wriggling and grumbling about smart-alec Harvest mice. 'Well?' he said. 'Is that better?'

'Lots better,' said Pentecost. 'Not an ear in sight ... only ...'

'Only what?' asked Fox suspiciously.

'Nothing much. Only a bit of back and a whisk of tail.'

'And I suppose you can do better?' said Fox emerging from the grass.

Pentecost ran to hide behind a hummock of turf, just in case Fox forgot about their friendship. 'Not bad for a learner,' said Fox grudgingly. 'Okay, you can come out now.'

'I think I'll stay where I am for the time being,' came a muffled voice.

'Don't be a silly mouse,' said Fox. 'You've just won the contest.' Fox poked his nose in and out of a few hollows and grass clumps, but the mouse was well hidden. He sniffed the air and listened with cocked ears for a while, before finally giving up the search. 'I suppose this is the end of our perfect friendship?' he said.

'I need time to think about that,' the hidden mouse replied. 'I'll let you know later.'

'Fair enough,' said Fox. 'Time you shall have. And that reminds me . . .' He swept the surrounding countryside with a keen night eye and, as if from a catapult, was gone.

'Reminds you of what?' yelled the mouse. There was no reply.

Pentecost crept from his hiding place and started back to camp. As he hurried along he pondered upon Fox's warning. Don't trust Owl and the bug. Now, there was no doubt in his mind that Snake was a traitor. But, never mind. When the time came, Pentecost hoped to outwit that slithery creature. Thinking back, he came to the conclusion that Fox wasn't such a bad lot after all. If one accepted his cunning ways, he could be quite good company. And he could prove useful, if a crisis developed. Hadn't he offered to help the family, if the need arose?

Back in camp, Pentecost fell asleep just as the dawn was breaking. He awoke to the sound of argument. Hastily, he rose and hurried across to see what the trouble was all about. As usual, Uncle was in the thick of it. It seemed Frog was boasting about his importance to the expedition and the old mouse didn't agree.

'Snake has not run off and left us,' Frog was saying. 'He goes nowhere without me. I am an important witness in his stolen pool case.'

It was at this point Pentecost intervened. 'I had an interesting talk with a fox last night,' he remarked casually. 'As a matter of fact, we've become close friends. I wouldn't be surprised if he popped into camp to see how I'm getting on. But apart from that, it was an ordinary night. Starry, but quite ordinary.' He sat down and waited for the reaction. It came quickly. The sharp intake of many breaths from the assembled family.

'You don't mean Fox of Furrowfield?' gasped Frog.

'He didn't say from where,' replied Pentecost. 'But I

expect he will, when he has a little more time. Something reminded him and he had to leave in a hurry.'

'But Fox has no friends,' insisted Frog. His battered face wore an incredulous look. 'No-one ever talks to Fox of Furrowfield. At least, not in a friendly manner. He's despised throughout the whole of the Lickey Hills. Even more than I am.'

'Well, I talked to him,' said Pentecost, pretending to stifle a bored yawn. 'And a more interesting fox I've yet to meet.'

'You've never met a fox before,' retorted Uncle. He was still feeling savage. He was determined to take it out on someone, even his leader Pentecost. 'Such lies, and before breakfast too,' he muttered.

Pentecost ignored him. It was the best way to handle Uncle, when he was in one of his moods. He continued. 'As a matter of fact, I saved Fox's life. He was caught in a trap and was just beginning to die, when I arrived to free him. Fox said he will be in my debt forever and he has agreed to help us to reach the new home on Lickey Top.' No sooner were those last words out of his mouth, than he realized he'd said too much.

'But why should we need the help of Fox to reach the new home?' said the little ones. 'Hasn't Snake already agreed to escort us there in safety?'

'Didn't I warn you about Snake?' crowed Frog. 'The Pentecost mouse knows something and he's keeping quiet about it.'

'I meant additional help,' said Pentecost hurriedly. 'Not that we'll need it, of course. Fox was merely making a grateful gesture.'

'Well, I, for one, am not getting mixed up with a fox,' said Uncle. 'Once in my youth, I became involved in a battle to the death with one. I left him half-choked and feeling very sorry for himself. It could well be the same one. If it is, and we meet up with him, I might just finish the job. Did this fox bear terrible strangle marks about his throat?'

'Not that I noticed,' said Pentecost, relieved that the subject of Snake had been dropped.

'It could be that I finished him off then,' mused Uncle. 'I never did know my own strength in the old days. Did this fox say he had a brother who was injured mysteriously? Did this fox happen to say that he was searching the world for a murderous mouse with bright auburn fur and clear honest eyes?'

'Your fur is grey,' giggled the young mice. 'And your eyes are dull as ditch-water.'

Uncle brandished his arthritic paws. 'Well, these have lost none of their power,' he gritted. 'And if I meet up with this fox of Furrowfield, he'll tell you the same when he gets his breath back.'

'I still say the Pentecost mouse is hiding something from us,' said Frog. 'But if he says not, I'm prepared to give him the benefit of the doubt.'

'Of course I'm not,' protested Pentecost. But, being a truthful mouse, the lie cost him dear.

'What I can't understand is, if you really did meet Fox of Furrowfield, how come you're here to tell the tale?' said Frog, refusing to let the matter drop. 'I know foxes of old. They are such changeable creatures. One minute they're your best friend, the next . . .' He closed his eyes and made a cutting gesture across his throat.

'It isn't Fox that worries me,' said Uncle. 'It's the skirting of the lake. In my opinion, this expedition is doomed. It was doomed from the first pawstep, if you ask me. What I want to know is, how are these tender paws of mine going to manage the long trudge around the lake on their own?'

The little ones dissolved in mirth. 'They won't be on their

123

own, Uncle, you'll be with them.' All the family began to laugh.

'I am always made to be a figure of fun,' said Uncle bitterly. 'Ever since the start of the journey I have suffered from the wise-cracks and giggles of the young. And the two mice, who were supposed to help me over the rough bits of ground, keep running off, saying they intend to become scouts in search of adventure. It's not much fun having to hobble over the uneven bits of world on paws like mine. Why don't you just leave me here to die? I am no longer any use to the family. I try to be helpful and cheerful, if I can. And, if I don't feel too well, still I try to keep the suffering to myself. Just cover me with a few bright flowers and be on your way. I won't last long in this scorching sunshine, so there's no need to feel guilty about anything.' By this time Uncle was weeping openly, as were most of the other mice.

'We won't leave you, Uncle,' cried the little ones between sobs. 'We will also be covered with bright flowers and left to die. We shall be proud to share the fate of such a brave phoney.'

Pentecost held up a paw. 'Uncle will not be left behind,' he declared. 'He will be carried around the skirt of the lake. The Great Aunts will weave a hammock to carry him in.'

The family agreed that only a genuine leader could have thought of such a clever plan. The Great Aunts began collecting the strongest grass stems they could find. But they sniffed a lot as they wove Uncle's hammock, for they still had a low opinion of him and his wily ways.

While this was going on, Uncle basked in the attention he received. Waiting impatiently for his hammock to be completed, he told the little ones many lies about his part in the battle with the Ruffians.

At last the hammock was finished. Uncle, eager to try it out, ordered it spread upon the ground. He then lay down

124

on it. 'It's too lumpy,' he complained. 'And I suspect the Great Aunts have woven stinging nettles into its design. All the grudges they bear me have gone into its making. I refuse to travel in such an uncomfortable hammock.'

'It hasn't been lifted from the ground yet,' said Pentecost patiently. 'The bumps you feel are from the ground beneath.'

'It was lined with the softest mosses we could find,' protested the Aunts. 'The hammock is a work of art and we resent such accusations. If that old mouse isn't careful, we will weave him a strong muzzle to stifle such remarks.'

'And I will fit it on,' said Pentecost grimly. 'So let's have no more of your unpleasantness, Uncle. We have a long way to go and it's midday already. And now, as there are no volunteers to carry the hammock, I will detail carrying parties. Each will take turns and I will tolerate no argument, is that clear?'

Silence greeted his words. Immediately, Pentecost detailed four mice to each take a corner of the hammock. They did so, reluctantly.

'And no swaying and jolting,' warned Uncle. 'I expect to feel only a smooth soothing motion.' He glanced at Pentecost. 'And now, what are we waiting for?'

'For you to shut up,' Pentecost replied. He gave Uncle a look that was as effective as any muzzle the Great Aunts could fashion. 'And now, forward,' he commanded. Obediently the expedition set off around the skirts of the lake.

'It is only that a thought has struck me,' said Little Brother, falling into step beside Pentecost. 'The reason why Snake chose to camp alone on the other side of the lake.'

Pentecost smiled. 'Could it be he feared another ferrying short cut?'

'Your words are my own,' replied the vole, with a smile to match the mouse's.

11 Fox

It was late afternoon when the huntsmen turned their lathered mounts for home. The brisk high-stepping gait of first light was now a dejected plod. Slowly the party wended its weary way down through the foothills towards the farm-houses scattered about the valley below. Behind loped the sullen hounds, their excited yappings quieted. Heads down, as if to hide their shame, they resembled a flock of docile sheep on their way to slaughter.

Of their number, three dogs seemed reluctant to leave the scene of their disgrace. Spot, Flannel-ears and Fat Billy stayed awhile to snuffle about in complete bewilderment. How could a trail suddenly stop in the middle of a field? And a hot fresh trail at that? It was puzzling. It was masterly. It was the work of Fox of Furrowfield.

A sharp command and two of them sloped off to join their fellows. Now only Fat Billy remained to lurch about in a fruitless figure-of-eight pattern, his wet stubborn nose thrust deep into the grass. Each time he returned to his starting place, he threw back his heavily-jowled muzzle to howl his hatred. He was beaten and he knew it. Another shouted command and he, too, turned to lumber off in pursuit of the distancing blur of pink-coated riders.

Now the dismal group was plodding across the furrow-fields. The frustrated pack began to snap and snarl at each other. The horses, tired and hungry, lashed out with steel-shod hooves at a hound who ventured too close. Riders, hounds and horses alike, were of a mind; the day had ended in complete and utter failure. The confidence of the morning had been destroyed. There would be other mornings, but the hunt was too dispirited to think that far ahead. Soon the riders would be comforting themselves in the taverns. The horses, groomed and freshly hayed, would languish in their stalls. The hounds, a hunk of meat a-piece, would slink away to their private corners to brood and stoke their hatred for the enemy of enemies. Fox.

Nimbly, Fox leapt for an outcrop of rock and howled triumphantly as his pursuers departed. It had been a close-run thing, but he was pleased with his day's work. Once again, he had proved his superiority.

Fox enjoyed such days. He had been caught completely unawares. If he had known beforehand that a hunt was being planned, it would have spoiled the thrill of the chase. He had been forced to think whilst on the run, having to make split-second decisions with a pack of hounds hard on his heels.

He blew sharply down his nostrils to rid himself of the chicken-down that still clung to his nose. It was a contented fox who settled down for a late afternoon nap in the warm sunshine. As he dozed, so his thoughts wandered and, out of sheer happiness, he composed a small thought-poem. Not a soul in the world knew that Fox stooped to poetry. It was his second most closely-kept secret, the first being the where-abouts of his lair. He was well aware that most folk ridiculed aspiring poets. Especially fox-poets. In the opinion of most, foxes were sly, self-centred and completely untrustworthy. They were shunned and despised. Yet, how surprised they would have been, had they known Fox's true character. Fox, a poet and with a well-hidden soft spot in his heart? Impossible.

The thought-poem was stored away in his mind. A good chase always inspired his verse. But, before he tucked it away, he thought it to himself once more:

> 'Lairs and spaces, favoured places,
> claw-raked barks, the thrills and chases.
> Spores and trails and signs and traces,
> doubled-tracks and puzzled faces.'

He flexed his russet-brown body, the sun glinting on his luxuriant brush. Sleep was very near and he was drifting, drifting ...

'Close call, Fox,' sang the cockle-snorkle. 'I thought you were a goner, that time.'

Fox sighed. Was a little peace and quiet too much to ask for? He nestled down in the long grass and pretended to be fast asleep. Perhaps the bug would take the hint and go away? But it was too much to hope for.

'And how are you this fine afternoon, old cunning-chops?' asked the persistent bug. 'A funny game you're playing, Fox, a very funny game.'

The bug hovered high overhead and proceeded to amuse himself by performing tumbles and rolls and other aerobatics. He had plenty of time. Sooner or later, Fox would have to acknowledge his presence. It was simply a matter of asking enough questions and hoping that one would strike a raw nerve. It was a technique similar to being stung repeatedly by a wasp intent upon seeking out the most tender spot.

Suddenly the bug dived and buzzed Fox's ear. The ear twitched, turned inside-out and flattened out along its owner's nape. The other ear was folded away in a like manner.

'Do you always sleep with the left eye open?' asked the bug. The eye immediately joined its fellow in repose.

The bug, in mid-air, hugged itself with glee. Its tactics were beginning to pay off. Sleeping foxes were a cinch to wake up. Its next question was carefully delivered, the bug making sure it was high enough to be out of harm's way when Fox, as he knew he would, reacted. 'How old would the cubs be now?' he asked innocently. 'I must say they seem to be in fine health, Fox. They'll be as deceitful as their old dad, before they're much older. I suppose you would think that a good thing, eh?'

Fox sprang to his paws. 'What cubs?' he demanded. 'Who said I'd got cubs?'

'No-one,' the bug replied. 'I can see 'em rolling and playing outside your secret lair. It's amazing what you can see from up here. Just look at the little scamps, spitting images of their dad.'

'You see too much for your own good,' Fox growled.

'I know everything about you, Fox,' said the bug. 'In fact, I know everything about everybody. For instance, last night . . .'

'What about last night?' was the suspicious query.

The bug enlightened him. 'Who got his poor paw caught in a nasty trap, then? And who was rescued by the Pentecost mouse? And who set the whole thing up, so he could poke his nose in things that don't concern him? And who dragged Owl's good name in the mud?'

'It was a private conversation,' snapped Fox. 'And what have you been up to? Pretending to be sympathetic and boosting the hopes of the Pentecost mouse. You know quite well Owl won't tolerate the mice setting up home on Lickey Top. Yet you lead him on by saying you will help.'

129

'I said no such thing,' retorted the bug. 'I made it quite plain I intend to play both ends against the middle.'

'You just like to see folk suffer,' said Fox. 'It's the way you get your kicks. You don't give a fig for Owl, nor the mice. You don't know the meaning of loyalty, that's your trouble. It's just as well Owl doesn't know what you're up to.'

'He won't know, unless you tell him,' said the bug. 'And you won't do that, will you, Fox? You hate Owl as much as . . .' The bug checked himself.

'As you do?' asked Fox. 'It's true I dislike Owl, but you . . . you pretend to be his loyal companion, yet plot against him behind his back. You are beneath contempt.'

'All spies are,' said the bug, in a small voice. 'I can't help being what I am. I can't help it if my style of life hurts others.' A note of defiance crept into his tone. 'Anyway, Owl's too thick to realize what I'm up to. I hope the mice do reach Lickey Top in safety. In fact, I intend to help them just to see Owl's face when they arrive.'

'Then you'll stand back and watch the fun?' said Fox in disgust. 'Pretending to be Owl's good friend, but in reality playing both parties off against the other?'

'You catch on quick, Fox,' said the bug admiringly. 'You certainly are cunning and no mistake. We two would make a fine team, do you know that?'

'Perish the thought,' Fox shuddered. He was suddenly stern. 'And if you ever mention the word "cubs" again, there'll be trouble, is that clear? Stir up as much trouble as you wish, but keep me and mine out of it.'

'I'm quite entitled to pry into the secrets of you or anyone else,' retorted the bug. 'It's a free world. And don't think I don't know about the poetry.'

'What poetry?' said Fox, taken aback. 'I don't know what you're talking about.'

130

'I've heard you're a bit of a rhymer, in your quieter moments,' said the bug slyly. 'Fancy old Fox thinking up words to rhyme with "June" and all that rubbish.'

Fox was about to retort 'moon', but bit back the word in time. The bug, tiring of the conversation, began to circle higher and higher in the sky. 'Guess what I can see,' he called down.

'Guessing games bore me,' was Fox's reply. 'And now, will you please leave me in peace?'

His words went unheeded. 'I can see a long trail of Harvest mice skirting the Lake of the Lilies,' cried the bug excitedly. 'And I can see an old mouse swinging in a hammock in the middle of 'em. That friend of ours is in the lead. You know, Fox, the Pentecost mouse. They're certainly making good progress. Now where's that lying frog? Ah, there he is. He's in the water. A nice breast-stroke style is that. Funny, I can't see the snake? Poor old Snake. Lost his pool, lost his dad, lost everything. They're taking the frog back to renounce his lies, did you know that, Fox?'

'I know I'm fed up,' Fox replied.

The bug descended once more. 'Those Hounds have really got it in for you, haven't they?' he said, examining Fox's cut paws sympathetically.

'I get by,' said Fox drily.

'Will you be coming to see the fun, Fox?' asked the bug. 'You know, the confrontation between Owl and the mice? I wouldn't miss it for the world.'

'I've got better things to do,' said Fox shortly.

'You'll mean the poetry composing?' said the bug impishly.

'I mean no such thing,' was the tired reply. 'I don't know where you got that idea from.'

'I have my contacts, Fox. I'll tell you what, we'll make a deal. You keep your nose out of the Harvest mouse affair

131

and I'll forget about the poetry. I'll also swear that you are cubless. What do you say?'

'Anything for a quiet life,' Fox replied. 'But there's no need to concern yourself about me. I won't spoil your malicious little game. Getting mixed up with a bunch of mice is the last thing I want to do.'

'It's a deal then,' said the bug, rising swiftly into the pale blue sky. 'See you, Fox!' he yelled.

'Not if I see you first,' murmured the sleepy red form. Idly, he watched the bug depart, its orange glow soon extinguished by the glare of a competing sun.

It was shortly after the bug's departure when Fox finally made up his mind. As a rule, Fox had little trouble with that peculiar emotion folk call 'conscience'. Until now, he had been unaware he had one. To his surprise, he found he had. Otherwise, why was he lying here, worrying about a small mouse called Pentecost? Why was it, every time he closed his eyes to sleep, the image of that odd-eyed creature danced about in his imagination? He was remembering the earnestness of the mouse's efforts to free him from the trap. And he, Fox, had led him on, letting him believe that the paw was truly caught fast. Fox squirmed with guilt as he pictured that scene. Why did he do these things? Was his character so firmly moulded that only deceit would satisfy his ego?

A strange thing had occurred. For the first time in his life, Fox felt genuine affection for a creature not of his own kind. All that talk last night about being 'friends and firm buddies' had seemed a good bit of leg-pull at the time. It had been a typical fox-joke and nothing more, or so he thought. But now, thinking about it, Fox realized that, deep down, he had really meant it. All his life, he had suppressed the desire to form a friendly relationship outside the circle of his own family. His instinctive secrecy had prompted this. But the courage and determination of the little mouse had impressed him more that he cared to admit. He had listened with only half an ear, as the mouse had explained why he and his family were making this dangerous journey to find a new home in the Lickey Hills. Only now was Fox beginning to appreciate just what the mice had taken on. The soft spot in Fox's heart enlarged and he glanced about to make sure no-one was watching, as a single large tear rolled down his snout.

'Now you're being silly,' he muttered aloud. 'Getting all sentimental. Why should you go out of your way to help a bunch of unimportant mice? Why should you care that Snake, Owl, the bug and, possibly, the frog are the biggest collection of scoundrels this side of the river Avon? What's it to you that the mice can't see disaster staring them in the face? If they're foolish enough to trust Snake and co., so be it. Let's get back to Furrowfield where we belong . . .'

Fox got to his paws and set off down the hill that led to Furrowfield. Then, suddenly, he stopped. Swinging around, he retraced his steps and stood awhile, shifting from one paw to the other. Then quickly, as if thrusting temptation from him, he sped off as fast as he could go, upwards in the direction of World's End Hill. One field, two fields, over the five-barred gate, tail down, ears flattened along his back, he soon left the foothills far behind and below. Minutes later, he was sitting upon the crown of a steep hill, its closely-nibbled grass evidence that he had arrived at his destination. From here, he had a clear panoramic view of the surrounding countryside. Far below, he could see the Lake of the Lilies, gleaming in the dying sun. But his sharp eyes could detect no movement down there, save for the rushes dancing in a fitful breeze. But then, mice were such tiny creatures and one could hide a multitude of them behind a hummock of turf. Nevertheless, they had to be down there somewhere, for hadn't the bug, with his even keener eyes, reported that fact?

133

Fox settled down to wait. But he still felt distinctly uncomfortable within himself. What he was doing was so out of character. He had a disturbing notion his soft spot was showing. What if someone came along and asked what he was doing here, so far from his lowland home? He could hardly say he was keeping an eye on a family of Harvest mice to see no harm came to them? After all, he had his reputation to think of. What he needed was a plausible excuse for being here. His presence on the hill would undoubtedly arouse suspicion. The more he thought about this problem, the more irritated he became. Why should he need an excuse at all? Wasn't he the mighty Fox of Furrowfield? Why not tell anyone curious enough to enquire, to go mind their own business? Yes, that's what he'd do. He felt quite angry with himself, that he had considered it necessary to invent an excuse. If he wasn't careful, that soft spot would get out of control and overwhelm him. That possibility was too awful to think about. He knew he wouldn't last five minutes in this rough and tumble world with such a handicap. He decided to indulge that soft spot very sparingly in the future. Only in cases of the gravest injustice, would he allow that hidden warmth to show through. The plight of the Harvest mice was such a cause. He would help them, while not making it too obvious that he was doing so. In that way, his basic slyness would be satisfied.

Of course, if he needed a reason, he had one. The local rabbits had named this place World's End Hill. Many had met their end here. And Fox had usually been around at the time. Not surprising then, that at this moment, there wasn't a rabbit in sight. Fox felt a stab of irritation. 'Excuse' indeed. What did they think he lived on, fresh air? He was here because he was here. Let anyone make of that what they wished.

The problem solved, Fox relaxed on the springy turf, his

long nose resting on his forepaws. But his eyes remained watchful. For a while, he gazed about him, noting the familiar lights twinkling from the farmhouse windows far below. And beyond that peaceful scene, a sight that never ceased to fascinate him, the band of multi-coloured brilliance stretching across the horizon that was the outer sprawl of the great city. But it was a dangerous beauty, and deceptive, for, close to, its mean dinginess had shocked Fox whilst on his occasional 'dustbinning' forays. He turned his attention back to the slope before him. Somewhere down there, he suspected, the expedition had made camp for the night. Now the lake sparkled diamond-bright, as the reflected moon was fragmented by the breeze-whipped wavelets. Fox, stirred by such beauty, began to compose a thought-poem in honour of it. He had barely completed a couplet before he was disturbed by the sound of voices. They were tired, irritated voices. One in particular was raised above the rest. A loud petulant voice.

'One great bruise from head to toe,' it complained. 'I've been bumped and scraped and twirled about, as though I didn't count. Don't you realize I'm a tender old mouse? I believe the carrying parties have been competing to see who could brutalize me the most. I insist you put me down by that soft bit of sand, so that I can recover from the battering I've received. I couldn't journey another bump and scrape.'

The carrying party tipped Uncle from his hammock. The old mouse fell into an exhausted sleep.

'At last!' cried Pentecost. 'World's End Hill. We will camp here for the night. It's the most perfect spot for camping I've ever seen. See how near the stars appear, the moon so bright, the sky so clear.'

'Ah ha,' thought Fox. 'The mouse never told me he stooped to poetry.' Then he spoke aloud. 'I agree, it's an ideal camping spot,' he said politely.

135

'Fox!' cried Pentecost. 'Whatever are you doing here, so far from the lowlands?'

Snake was eyeing Fox suspiciously. 'Up to no good, no doubt. There's always trouble when he's about.'

The mice and Little Brother were looking apprehensively at the huge stranger. Pentecost put their fears to rest. 'This is my friend, Fox, that I was telling you about,' he said proudly. 'I want you all to make him welcome and feel at home. Fox needs to feel he's amongst friends, he never ever having had one, before he met me.'

'Would you like to try that last sentence again?' asked Fox. 'But then, perhaps not. No doubt, you did your best.'

Pentecost looked puzzled. 'I always do my best, Fox,' he said. 'I thought everyone knew that.'

'Of course you do,' said Fox smoothly. 'Please forgive me, I was just trying to make polite conversation. No doubt, you've noticed how shy and retiring I am. It's my lonely life that's to blame. I've never had friends who think highly of me before.'

'Shy and retiring, I don't think,' scoffed Frog.

'Why if it isn't our "holier than thou" little frog!' said Fox, turning to face him. 'The last time I saw you, you were fleeing for your life. Told any good lies lately?'

'I'm a changed character,' insisted Frog. 'All that's behind me. I couldn't tell a lie, if my life depended on it now.'

'We'll see,' said Fox.

'It is only that any friend of my friend Pentecost is a friend of mine,' said Little Brother.

'And I suppose you intend to stick by every word of that sticky sentence?' sighed Fox.

'In the name of the family, we welcome Fox of Furrow-field,' chorused the little ones.

'And with those few kind words, all my anxieties melt away,' murmured Fox.

136

'Fox's kind attitude bewilders me,' said Frog, looking suitably bewildered. 'I've always known him for a hood-winker and a scoundrel. I can't understand why we aren't all at death's door.'

Pentecost interrupted. 'Which proves how little you know about him. If I'm not mistaken, he's here to explain why he left so hurriedly the night we met. Or perhaps to ask me whether I've had sufficient time to think about our friend-ship. Well, I have, Fox. We are as close as ever.'

'It being the best thing that's ever happened to me,' purred Fox. 'I've been lying awake worrying about us. We couldn't have picked a more romantic spot to make up. We and the moon and everything.'

'Beware!' continued Frog. 'That fox isn't so meek and mild as he pretends. He's up to something, mark my words. Someone should ask that fox what he's doing here, and that someone isn't going to be me. A swallowed Missionary of the Truth will be no use to anyone.'

'Could my explanation be wrong, Fox?' said Pentecost. 'How did you happen to be at this particular spot just as we arrived? It does look a little suspicious to me. We'd like the truth, please.'

'What else?' said Frog. 'Anything else but the plain honest truth would be wrong. A crime even.'

'It is only that what you are doing here interests us deeply,' said Little Brother.

'Not me, it doesn't,' said Snake. 'If no-one has any objec-tions, I'll have a kip.' He curled up into his usual tight bunch of coils and was soon fast asleep.

'I'm glad this question arose,' said Fox. 'And thank you for being so blunt and straightforward with me. I like folk who come immediately to the point.'

'Good,' said Pentecost. 'And now that question is cleared up, I suggest we prepare camp.'

'Selfish snakes, lying frogs and now cowardly foxes,' grumbled Uncle. 'This expedition is becoming a laughing-stock. There are too many members for my liking. Why should a fox from the lowlands wish to join us? It smacks of . . . of . . .'

'It smacks of suspicion,' finished Frog. 'And Fox still hasn't told us why he's hanging about our camp.'

'Yes, he did,' said Pentecost, tired of all the constant bickering. 'Now please, settle down, all of you.'

'How can we possibly settle down with Fox's huge black shadow looming over our beds?' said old Mother, clutching at her heart.

Frog shook his head stubbornly. 'Well I for one, didn't hear Fox's answer,' he insisted.

'Nor I,' agreed Uncle. In fact, no-one had, including Pentecost, after he'd given it a little thought. He approached Fox.

'I'm afraid you'll have to answer the question again,' he said apologetically.

'Certainly,' said Fox coolly. But he was having to think quickly. Whatever happened, he had no wish for anyone to notice his soft spot. He needed to appear casual, uncaring even. So he lied cleverly. 'As you all probably know,' he began, 'we foxes are cruelly-abused creatures. I came up here for a little peace and quiet. Last night too, as the Pentecost mouse can confirm.'

'But the nub is why?' cried Uncle. 'That is the nub. Ask Fox what the nub is.'

'Didn't I just explain?' asked Fox. 'Or has this old mouse got cloth ears, as well as bad manners.'

'And bad paws,' said Uncle quickly.

'Ask Fox what is the nub,' cried the little ones, not knowing nor caring what a nub was. Pentecost sighed. Fox looked uncomfortable. Uncle looked triumphant. It was Frog, with

138

his clear-eyed view of the truth, who solved the mystery of the 'nub'.

'Fox is being hounded for crimes against chickens,' he said. 'He is using our expedition as a hide-out. He is trying to mingle invisibly amongst us.'

'And making a bad job of it,' said Uncle, glancing up at Fox's impressive bulk.

'I'd hardly call pinching a chicken or two a crime,' protested Fox. 'My only "crime" is owning a beautiful orangy-red brush, which the humans would dearly love to pin on their trophy wall.'

'We don't call owning such a lovely object a crime,' said the little mice. 'We think Fox is innocent.'

'Thank you, small friends,' said Fox gratefully. 'Remind me to teach you how to howl like a mighty fox some time.'

'It is only that Uncle's nub falls flat in the face of this fresh evidence,' said Little Brother. 'But then, I'm not quite sure, because half of my mind is dreaming about the apple core tree that grows by Wending Way stream.'

'And we all have to live, each in his own way,' said Pentecost sensibly. His sense was the reason why he had been chosen as leader, so no-one was surprised to hear him say such a sensible thing. He continued, 'Although I think Fox would sleep easier and with a clearer conscience, if he tried a little wheat or a tasty root or two from time to time. And it would be much healthier, from his and the chickens' point of view, if he did that. But we must not condemn what we don't understand. Fox, with all his faults and weak character, still deserves to find a little peace and quiet in his old age.'

'What old age?' said Fox indignantly. 'I'll have you know, I'm in my prime.'

'It's all the same thing,' said Uncle, who knew about such things. 'I, too, am in my prime.'

'Heaven forbid,' murmured Fox quietly.

'I vote we allow Fox to become an honorary member of our expedition, for this one night,' said Pentecost. 'All in favour, say aye.'

'Aye,' shouted the mice and Little Brother. The exceptions were Snake and a worried-looking Frog. Pentecost asked each one why they had rejected the 'aye' vote.

'Because I dislike foxes,' said Snake bluntly. 'Snakes and foxes have nothing in common, so I dislike them generally.'

'Isn't that a little unchristian?' asked old Mother gently. 'But then, snakes are such heathen creatures, one finds, as one travels about the world. I honestly can't see you getting your pool back, if you take up such attitudes, Snake.' She would have said more, as old ladies tend to do, but Pentecost cut her short.

'And you, Frog?' he asked.

'I object because foxes are pathological liars,' he said firmly. 'Like I once was, before I saw the light.'

'We'll bear that in mind, but without the big word,' said Pentecost. 'There's no room for big words on this expedition. They just confuse everyone and make them feel nervous. You never hear me using big words. But it makes no difference. Snake and Frog are outvoted,' he went on. 'Nevertheless, as a consolation, we will ask Fox to camp on the other side of the hill. In that way, we won't be able to keep an eye on him. And then, when we get to know Fox better, perhaps we will allow him to share our camp as a fully-fledged member. What do you say, Fox?'

'I'm overwhelmed,' was the reply. 'At least it's comforting to know I'll be able to hear the merry chatter of friends, even though banished beyond the hill. Thank you so much and now, if you'll permit me, I'll slink away out of your sight.' And Fox slunk away as promised.

'Sleep tight and pleasant dreams,' called Pentecost. To make Fox feel more at home, he howled as his red friend

140

had taught him. Fox's answering howl was an echo from the other side of the hill.

Pentecost brushed away the admiring little ones, promising to teach them how to howl when he had a little more time. 'Bed,' he ordered sternly. 'Tomorrow is Snake's confrontation day. We need to be fresh and alert, in case he needs our help. Snake means to keep his side of the bargain and we intend to honour ours, isn't that so, Snake?' Snake groaned sleepily.

'I've got a funny feeling about tomorrow,' said Frog uneasily. 'I can't explain it exactly, but ...'

'You aren't having one of your shooting pains?' asked Pentecost anxiously.

'I don't know what it is,' replied Frog. 'I just feel this terrible foreboding sensation. As if something dishonourable is about to happen. But it's probably nerves. Tomorrow is the day I also prove myself. But it's strange, you know, I've suddenly got this nagging cramp in my left leg. I've had it for the last hour or so. But perhaps it'll be gone by morning.'

'It'll be the strain of the journey,' comforted Pentecost, but he was beginning to feel worried. Something told him that he would need all his wits about him tomorrow. Was the frog getting cold feet, as they neared Snake's pool? Was his love for the truth strong enough to overcome his fear of the 'cousin' snake? Only time would tell.

The frog drifted off to sleep. Everyone seemed to be asleep except Pentecost. His responsibilities came home to him as he lay tossing and turning under that full moon. Who would be a Pentecost mouse with all the worries that office entailed? After a lot of thought, he agreed that he would. He felt suddenly confident. Whatever happened the next day, he felt sure he could cope. An hour passed, then two and slowly midnight approached, passed ... and then it was morning.

141

12 Fox Trots, Owl Plots

'Are we going to get moving, or not?' complained Snake. 'You may not care, but we're only half a mile from my pool.'

A cheery voice caused everyone to turn. 'Morning,' said Fox. He trotted into camp, looking pleased with himself.

Something had caught Pentecost's eye. He approached Fox and peered intently at his nose. Fox licked his lips and yawned in a casual manner.

'What's that bit of fur doing on the tip of your nose, Fox?' asked the mouse.

'Oh that,' Fox said, squinting downwards. His eyes became crossed as he tried to focus on the offending scrap of evidence. 'I found it. I thought it might keep my nose warm during the night. It gets cold up here, as no doubt you've noticed.'

'It looks like a bit of rabbit fur to me,' said Pentecost suspiciously. 'Is there anything you wish to confess, Fox? I hope you realize this is a peaceful expedition?'

'Rabbits?' said Fox blankly. 'Do you mean to say there are rabbits up here? Well I never. You learn something new every day.'

'Didn't I warn you about him?' shouted Frog, rubbing his left leg absently. 'A tissue of lies, that's all you'll get.'

'I'm afraid I don't believe your story,' said Pentecost. 'As you refuse to come clean, I propose to banish you from the expedition as a punishment. We never want to see your furred nose again, do you understand, Fox?'

'Banished,' sighed Fox. 'Banished for sleeping soundly all night. Is there no justice in the world?'

'As I see it, you must have felt peckish in the night,' said Pentecost. 'And you woke up and rustled up a snack for yourself, am I right, Fox?'

'I can't remember,' was the reply. But it didn't sound at all convincing.

'Banished for choking rabbits,' yelled Uncle.

'It is only that goodness is sadly lacking in some folk,' commented Little Brother.

'Shut your pious mouth,' snapped Snake. 'I'm fed up to the back teeth with your constant bowing and scraping and all this "butter wouldn't melt in your mouth" act. You're too good to be true. Too good to live even. Haven't you any faults at all?'

'It is only that I am filled with sin,' said Little Brother. 'I think only of the apple core trees when I should be thinking about the welfare of others. It is only that "sin" should be my middle name.'

'Doesn't it make you sick?' shuddered Snake. 'So Fox ate a rabbit. So what? Will Fox's confession get my pool back for me? I doubt it. So you want to banish him? So banish him and let's be done with it. For Heaven's sake, let's get moving.'

'Snake's right,' said Pentecost. 'The sooner we reach his pool and get his affairs straightened out, the sooner he will be ready to lead us to the new home.'

Was that flinch a twinge of conscience, thought the mouse. He had been watching Snake from the corner of his eye. Could it be Snake was really intending to betray them, after his pool had been returned to him? Soon they would know. But in the meantime, all the mice could do was to go along with him and let fate decide the rest.

'That fox must be sent packing first,' said Uncle. 'And

afterwards, the Great Aunts must arrange my hammock more comfortably. I can't understand why they didn't line it with soft birds' down, there is plenty of it lying about.'

'We did,' the Aunts protested. 'We used the best moorhen down from the Lake of the Lilies.'

'Then what is this?' said Uncle, rummaging about in the hammock. He produced a long wickedly-pointed quill. 'If that isn't a hedgehog feather, I don't know what is,' he declared.

'Be quiet, Uncle,' said Pentecost. He turned to Fox. 'Are you going to take your banishment bravely, or are you going to tell more lies?'

Fox, wearing an expression of unconcealed amusement, turned and trotted away without a word. Suddenly he stopped, winked broadly and vanished behind the hill.

At long last, the expedition set off again. An hour or so would bring them within sight of Snake's pool. There were few mice who didn't feel a twinge of fear as they neared their objective. Each was privately wondering what awaited them upon their arrival. They were soon to find out.

Meanwhile the cockle-snorkle was winging his way homeward. He was glad to be able to exercise his wings again. He had spent the night in concealment, watching and hanging on to every word that was uttered at World's End Hill. He glowed fiercely as he went over in his mind what he intended to tell Owl. He would paint a picture as black as a beetle's back. He would have Owl frothing at the mouth with rage before he was through. He would make the expedition sound like a full-blooded attack on the bird's property and the Pentecost mouse a tyrant at the head of a ravaging horde. No matter that the mice were peace-loving gentle creatures. He, the bug, would so skilfully weave his skein of lies that Owl would come to believe he was being attacked by a pack of bloodthirsty wolves. Then the bug would sit back and gleefully watch Owl sweat. He was looking forward to that.

He was soon back on Lickey Top, clinging to his slip of bark and peering in at Owl. Surprisingly, the bird wasn't sleeping. That was unusual, for he normally shunned the bright morning sunshine. It was unfortunate that his hole faced east. Because of this, each morning, a malicious ray of sunshine pierced the gloomy interior of his home. As a rule, Owl would turn his back on it and close his eyes tightly, but this morning he had broken his habit. He lay on his back, filthy claws in the air, staring up at something the bug couldn't see.

'Dry rot again?' asked the bug sympathetically. 'Or are those wood beetles still chewing you out of house and home?'

'All is decay,' whispered the great bird.

The bug attempted to cheer him up. 'Look on the bright side, Owl,' he said. 'At least those beetles are enlarging your home. And you are putting on a bit of weight, you know. Or is all that chomping of the jaws keeping you awake?'

'You don't understand,' sighed Owl. 'I was making a profound statement.'

'Oh, one of *them*,' said the bug. 'Your head must be chock-a-block full of wise things like that. But come on, Owl, cheer up. It isn't the end of the world . . . yet.'

But Owl was suddenly irritable. 'Could we move on to something more important?' he said. 'What news of the expedition? Have they been destroyed? Did the Ruffians finish them off?'

The bug's face fell. 'Bad news there, I'm afraid,' he said. 'The Ruffians received a sound thrashing. The mice are still heading this way. It seems nothing can stop them.'

Owl flew into a rage. 'And did you make it clear, I absolutely forbid them to settle here?'

145

'I did, Owl,' said the bug sincerely.

'And?' the bird rapped. 'What did they say to that?'

'They said "Owl can go jump in the lake,"' lied the bug. 'Or was it "Owl can go suck eggs"? I know they were extremely insulting. The Pentecost mouse said that, if you so much as looked at 'em sideways, he'd pull your tail feathers out one by one. They're a tough bunch, Owl.'

'Tough, eh,' said Owl. 'We'll see who's tough. If they so much as set one paw on Lickey Top, they'll rue that day. I'll give 'em threatening my tail feathers.'

'I think one of 'em swore he'd punch you in the beak, if you got in his way,' the bug went on. He was managing to keep a straight face, but inside he was bubbling over with delight. Owl was dancing to his tune.

'I've never sucked eggs in my life and I don't intend to start now,' said Owl grimly.

'Smash 'em, yes,' said the big bug. 'But never suck 'em.' He watched closely for Owl's reaction to this clever bit of needle.

Owl's face contorted. 'What was that?' he said softly.

'How old would he have have been now, your brother, had he lived?' The bug spoke warily. He didn't want to go too far. Owl was an unpredictable bird. He could quite easily turn on the bug. The insect knew he was dicing with death, mentioning the subject of the smashed egg, but he just couldn't resist it. Luckily, Owl was anxious to change the subject.

'Where are they now?' he asked.

'At this moment, I should say they were just within sight of Snake's pool,' the bug replied. 'Oh, I almost forgot. The Frog's having problems. He's favouring his left side, I've noticed. I think he may be reverting to type.'

'Type?' said Owl. He looked mystified for one so supposedly worldly wise. A flicker of contempt passed over the bug's face, but Owl failed to notice it.

'That's what I admire about you,' the bug said. 'I begin to explain about the frog, but already you're one jump ahead. In one crisp word, you sum everything up. I don't need to tell you the frog's devotion for the truth is wearing thin. I've got the feeling he's about to change sides again. He fears that cousin more than he loves the truth, I'm thinking. If he doesn't back Snake up, there'll be a fight, make no mistake.'

'So what,' said Owl. 'Why should we care about the frog's problems?'

Patiently the bug spelled it out. 'If there's a fight, the mice could become involved. They've lost three of their number already. A fight could mean their total extinction.'

Owl's face lit up. 'Of course,' he whispered. 'And you must do everything you can to encourage that fight. This cousin, do you think he'll fight?'

'Certain of it,' said the bug promptly. 'And he's got friends. They throw wild parties up there, you know.' Owl's beak twisted in distaste. 'So what's the plan, Owl?' asked the bug. 'I'm waiting for orders, oh wise one.'

'The destruction of that expedition is vital,' said Owl, thinking aloud. 'One must be brutal, even if violence is repugnant to one.'

'And you can be as repugnant as the best of 'em, eh Owl? By the way, Fox of Furrowfield has been hanging about. I don't know what he's up to, though.'

'Well, find out,' snapped Owl impatiently. 'But I doubt if he'll upset our plans. He only thinks about himself. It'll be plain curiosity, no doubt. But watch him, nevertheless.'

'Will do, Owl,' said the bug.

'And even if the expedition doesn't come to grief at Snake's pool, they'll never get through the Weasel Woods,' said Owl. 'If they're lucky enough to get that far, it'll be the end of the road when the weasels get through with 'em.'

'But just say they did manage to survive the Weasel

147

Woods, Owl,' said the bug. Hurriedly he added, 'Not that they would, but just supposing. What then?'

'In that unlikely event, I myself would have to settle things,' said Owl ominously. He flexed his out-thrust claws and studied them.

'I get your point, Owl,' said the bug. Despite his cockiness, he shuddered as he thought of those steel-sharp claws, ripping and tearing . . .

'Any more questions?' said Owl. 'You know what to do?'

'I'm to stir things up,' the bug replied. 'And hopefully, bring you the glad tidings that the mice are no more.'

'Good,' said Owl contentedly. 'And now, leave me, for I wish to sleep.'

'Whoopee!' cried the bug, spiralling into the air and glowing fiercely.

Owl's face was a study. Bleakly, he inquired as to the reason for the bug's strange outburst. It was a long time since he had felt joy and happiness. It embarrassed him to see folk express themselves so openly.

'Just whoopee, Owl,' called the bug. 'When the excitements gets too hard to bear, I can't help it. You should try it, it gets rid of the inner tensions beautifully. It makes you feel all warm and blissful inside.' Once more he gave vent to his feelings before speeding off in the direction of Snake's pool.

For a long time Owl remained lying on his back, his claws in the air. Gloomily he watched the beetles gnawing away at his roof. Finally, unable to stand the sight any longer, he struggled to his feet and emerged from the hole. For a minute or two he stood on his perch, eyes screwed up against the glare of the sun. He was imagining Lickey Top resounding to the crisp sound of marching paws. Mousy paws. Invading paws. Never, he thought angrily. Then he relaxed, as he thought of all the dangers the mice would have to overcome

148

to reach here. His mood had changed. He now felt almost happy. It was then he did something completely out of character. It was just as well there was no-one about to see and hear. 'Whoopee,' his jubilant cry cracked about the hills. But it was a hollow-sounding 'whoopee'. There was no warmth, no joy in it. He returned to the dank hole in the oak. As he slept, so he dreamed. It was always the same dream...he is young and happy again. Excited too. For beside him nestles the companion of his future days, its warm oval beauty much cherished by the young owl...then the world seems to lurch, his senses are reeling, and he is gazing at the shattered remains about his feet. Cries are loud in his ears: murder, murder...and he is trapped in nightmare, afraid, his protests drowned in grief and sorrow...

13 The Battle of Snake's Pool

To banish a fox isn't easy. To banish a fox with a soft spot and a poetic turn of mind is nigh on impossible. As he jogged along behind the expedition, he passed the time dreaming about the great epic poem he intended to compose one day. Naturally, foxes would figure largely in it. He turned sharp left, his body obedient to the skills of his nose. At the same time, he slowed his pace, making sure the expedition was out of sight before proceeding. Now he could see the sunlight reflecting from the surface of the tree-encircled pool. Insulted and banished by the mice, his liking for them hadn't faltered. He admired courage and determination. He himself knew what it felt like to be harried and hounded. Creatures in similar circumstances could always be sure of Fox's sympathy. In this case, help also.

He chose not to dwell too long on his selfish motives. Certainly, he felt in no way ashamed of such a trait. Selfishness had helped him to survive in this harsh world. Curiosity about the outcome of this strange journey urged him onwards. One selfish motive was boredom. Fox hated to feel bored. His cubs and mate had dined on rabbit that morning, so his domestic situation was satisfactory. And he knew there would be no hunt that day. He had checked that fact before he left the lowlands early that morning. The dogs, listlessly slumped around the farmhouse yard, were evidence of that. Dogs and humans alike were licking their wounds, thought Fox with satisfaction.

As he approached the pool, his caution increased. He intended to conceal himself close enough to see and hear, without being observed himself. For Fox, this was a simple task. 'This bush,' he murmured. 'Perfect for an eavesdropping fox, I should say.' He crawled beneath its thick foliage and settled himself comfortably. His contentment spilled over into verse and the rhymes tripped over themselves, eager to find a place in the ballad of Fox of Furrowfield and immortality. He gazed in the direction of the pool. A strange, almost comical sight met his eyes . . .

After a wild party, someone has to do the clearing-up, a dreary chore at the best of times. But, if the parties go on day after day, this task becomes pointless. Why bother, after all, the place will only get messed-up again. Much better to rest up, in preparation for the next wild fling.

In the dim and distant past, great empires fell into decay because of this carefree attitude.

>   'A small, once neat and tidy, pool,
>   is no exception to this rule'

rhymed Fox, gravely surveying the chaos spread before his eyes.

The pool, once Snake's father's pride and joy, was choked with debris. The clumps of water irises, that had once so enhanced its beauty, were trampled into the mud surrounds. The log that spanned the water was strewn with bits of weed and the rotting remains of half-eaten meals. The surface of the pool was covered with a slick of stagnating filth. In short, Snake's show-piece had become a den of iniquity; its rustic charm, a rubbish dump.

Snake sat staring about him in dismay, a tear glittering on the end of his nose. By his side squatted Frog, wincing from time to time, as his newly-returned shooting pains racked his trembling body. Behind them, in a semi-circle, sat the mice and Little Brother, their eyes swivelling first to Snake and then to the log that spanned the water. Sprawled out along it were three snakes, all looking much the worse for wear. One of the snakes crawled tiredly from the log and approached the expedition. He curled up a yard or so away from the waiting crowd and looked Snake up and down through a bleary eye. It was the hated 'cousin'. Despite his debauched condition, he still found the energy to raise a cynical smile.

'What a pity,' he said. 'If you'd only come a little earlier. I'm afraid the party's over.' The two snakes on the log sniggered. The cousin continued. Indicating the pool and its surrounds with a careless flick of his tail, he said, 'Excuse the mess, you know what parties are.'

Snake was speechless. The sheer nerve of the cousin was breathtaking. In vain did he seek to remember the opening words of the speech he had prepared for this moment. His mind remained a complete blank.

151

Cousin had shifted his gaze to Frog. 'Brought your lunch, I see?' he said coolly. Then warily, 'Going on a picnic, perhaps? Just passing through?'

At long last, Snake found his voice. He shook the tear from his nose, held up his head proudly and said in ringing tones, 'This is not my lunch, as you well know. You and he have met before. Together, you plotted to cheat me out of my inheritance. Lunch indeed. This frog is about to reveal you in your true colours.'

Cousin stretched his neck, so as to bring his face inches from that of the petrified frog. 'Do I know you?' he enquired softly. There was menace in that question. The mice listened with bated breath for Frog's reply. Snake turned his head away, his face all prim and smug, as he waited for the poor creature to confirm his accusation.

'I've never seen this snake before, in all my life,' blurted Frog. 'He's a complete stranger to me.'

The mice gasped in disbelief. Snake looked thunderstruck. Little Brother interrupted his daydream about apple cores to tut-tut. Cousin drew back his head and sighed contentedly.

'What happened to the light, Frog?' called Pentecost. He got to his paws and approached, looking anxious, but also annoyed.

'It went out,' said Frog simply. 'And I'm in the most terrible pain. All down this left side.' He ran his flippered foot down the mouse's right side to indicate the spot he meant. Pentecost brushed him away. He could plainly see disaster ahead for himself and his family. Frog was going the right way to ruin all their hopes for the future.

'Think back and try to remember,' he encouraged. 'Don't be afraid, no-one will harm you for telling the truth. Didn't you, only yesterday, say how much you enjoyed being truthful?'

'That was yesterday,' said Frog, with a shiver. 'Today's today.'

'What's this stranger frog babbling about?' asked Cousin innocently. 'He looks in pain to me. I hope you aren't ill-treating him in any way. Has this snake anything to do with his condition? Been munching him, perhaps? I wouldn't be at all surprised. If he could be so unkind as to call me a cheat, he'd stoop to anything. It's a terrible thing to say. I haven't felt so upset in ages.'

Pentecost patted Snake, who was snivelling again, and spoke to Cousin. 'I think you ought to know that Snake isn't a sucker any more,' he said. 'When he dries his eyes, you'll see what I mean. And if you think you can terrify Frog into telling more lies, you can think again.'

'Who's terrifying him?' protested Cousin. He looked at Frog with those evil lemon eyes. 'Do I terrify you?' he asked.

'Not a bit,' Frog replied, his quavering voice and knocking knees clear evidence that he was lying in his teeth. Cousin grinned at his sniggering companions.

'I must warn you, we are here to see you get your just deserts,' the mouse went on. 'And don't bank on Frog's relapse to save you from justice. Snake is going to get an even break this time.'

'And a tasty dessert you'll make, too,' said Cousin, with a smile. Suddenly he was brisk and business-like. 'Very well,' he said. 'It seems I'm being accused of some foul crime. Just what, I can't imagine . . .'

'The stealing of Snake's pool,' said the mouse quickly.

'This pool was left to me by my beloved uncle, God rest his soul,' said Cousin, casting a pious glance at the sky. 'And if you've brain-washed that frog to say different, then all I can say is, you are a bunch of heartless scoundrels.'

The sheer insolence of this last remark seemed to jerk

Snake from his bout of self-pity. Once more he was in control of himself. His rage was boundless. 'Did you hear that?' he gasped in disbelief. 'Now can you see the kind of trickster we are dealing with?'

'I certainly can,' said Pentecost. 'And I hate to say it, Snake, but he must have seen you coming. He must have thought, "Ah ha, here's a thick-looking snake with a nice pool". I wouldn't be surprised if he isn't an expert at crime.'

'I was always the brightest at home,' said Cousin proudly. 'They all said I'd go far.'

Pentecost was suddenly solemn. 'I'm afraid you'll have to be put on trial. In my opinion, your story is full of holes. Are you prepared to stand trial, charged with grand theft and terrifying frogs?'

'Certainly,' said Cousin. 'Never let it be said I'm not fair. Call your first witness.'

Snake was taken aback by Cousin's reasonable attitude. 'I've only one witness,' he said. He indicated the frog.

'Well, I suppose he's better than no witnesses at all,' replied Cousin, with a toothy grin. 'Call him and let's hear what he's got to say for himself.'

'Call the lying frog,' shouted Uncle importantly.

'Be quiet, Uncle, this trial's nothing to do with you. Besides, the frog is already here,' said Pentecost.

'You seem familiar with the law,' said Cousin. 'Good, for we all wish this trial to be a fair one. By the way, has anyone ever told you how extremely ugly you are. I'm not being too personal, I hope?'

'Not at all,' replied the mouse shyly. 'I know I'm not as handsome as some.'

The watching snake squirmed with frustration. 'Can we get on with this trial?' he snapped. 'It's getting late and I want to get settled back in my pool before nightfall.'

154

'Confident, eh?' joked Cousin. 'Well, we'll see. And now, are we all agreed this mouse will act as judge?'

'Aye,' chorused the mice. Frog nodded miserably. Snake inclined his head curtly. And so the trial began.

'Begin your questioning, Snake,' said Pentecost.

'Now,' began Snake, addressing Frog. 'I want you to tell the truth in your own words. Don't be afraid to call certain cousins liars and cheats.'

Pentecost interrupted. 'I will not tolerate mud-slinging in my court. I will say who is lying, when the trial is over.'

'Whose side are you on?' asked Snake. 'We all know who's lying. This trial is a mockery.'

'Say that again and I will have you thrown from the court,' snapped Judge Pentecost. 'Now stop these delaying tactics and get on with your case, Snake.' He encouraged the frog to climb on to a fallen tree limb so that everyone could see him properly. Eyes bulging with fright, the frog obeyed.

Snake began again. 'Did you, or did you not, overhear a conversation between my late father and this so-called cousin of mine, this April last?'

'No,' said Frog firmly. There was a loud murmuring from the mice. Pentecost felt suddenly relieved. Snake flashed a pleased smile about the court.

'Your witness, Cousin,' said Pentecost.

'This conversation,' said Cousin, leaning close and frowning. 'It was in April last, was it not?'

'Yes,' Frog replied. 'I remember I was feeling poorly at the time. I was engaged in a few knee-bends and breathing exercises, if I remember rightly.'

Disappointed sighs echoed about the pool. Cousin's two friends applauded noisily.

'Did you hear my father promise to leave his pool to this cousin?' Snake demanded.

155

'I heard no such thing,' said Frog. 'I wasn't even there, so how could I possibly know that?'

Once again, the evidence seemed to be going Snake's way. He slid aside to allow Cousin access to the witness.

'And you distinctly heard my uncle will his pool to me?' insisted Cousin. 'And didn't he also say his son was too thick to manage it properly?'

'As true as I stand here,' agreed Frog. 'I remember Snake's father's voice. It was a deep kind-sounding voice.' Snake groaned loudly. Every second that passed saw his case dissolving before his eyes.

'I always said that frog was a rotten liar,' yelled Uncle. 'Isn't anyone going to spring to the defence of this poor snake? Aren't you all ashamed of yourselves?'

Wearily Snake asked another question. 'Has this cousin ever threatened you in any way? Did he promise to do terrible things to you, if you didn't go along with his dastardly plans?'

'Yes,' said Frog brokenly. 'He said he'd tie my back legs around my neck for starters. He also promised to injure me in fresh and novel ways, but just how has slipped my memory for the moment.'

Cousin looked mean. 'Do you intend to stick to that fabricated tale?' he asked. 'Haven't you already admitted you've never seen me before?'

'And I haven't,' said the Frog. 'Who are you, anyway?'

Cousin pressed him further. He pointed to Snake, who wore an expression of bewilderment on his face. 'And do you know who he is?'

'No, should I?' Frog said in surprise.

'I rest my case,' said Cousin. 'And now, will you all clear off. I'm having a wild party tonight and I've preparations to make.'

'Not so fast,' said Pentecost. 'This case smells fishy to me.

156

It appears that Frog is telling both the true story and the false one. As hard evidence, Frog's words are rubbish.'

'It is only that the truth is hidden beneath many layers,' said Little Brother. 'To get at it, we must peel off those layers.'

'But how?' asked Pentecost.

'You're the big-headed judge,' shouted Uncle. 'You think you know everything. Why does no-one ask my advice? I would know how to get at the truth.'

'Let us hear what you propose, Uncle,' said Pentecost.

A pleased Uncle hobbled from the semi-circle of mice. He glared contemptuously at Frog, who averted his eyes in shame. 'Now, if Snake will grab Frog's left rear leg and Cousin grabs the right rear leg,' he said, 'it will only require a vicious tug for the truth to come tumbling out. As we all know, Frog has a truthful side and an untruthful side. If we can separate those two sides, we'll have one snake with the truthful portion, the other with the unpleasant bit. A good hard tug will solve all our problems. It's quite simple, really.'

Cousin had eagerly seized Frog's right leg. Pentecost hastily restrained him. 'I don't think it would work,' he said. 'We would just have a split decision.'

'And a very alarmed Frog,' Uncle pointed out. 'A frog bursting to tell the truth, I'll bet.'

'All the torture in the world would be of no use,' said Frog brokenly. 'Nothing could equal the pain I'm suffering now. For the light I saw has dimmed. It was beautiful while it lasted, but now it's gone and I'm my old rotten self. In my twisted mind, both Snake and Cousin are in the right. I'm just a born liar and beg to be excused for a moment.'

'Beg to be excused?' said Pentecost suspiciously. 'For what reason?'

157

'I have the best reason in the world,' said Frog. 'But I'd prefer to explain it upon my return.'

'It's a very unusual request,' pondered Pentecost. 'But, as you tried so hard to be honest in the past, permission granted.'

Snake protested loudly at this. Cousin seemed contented by the court's decision. The mice discussed it amongst themselves and agreed Pentecost was making a grave mistake. Pentecost brushed Snake's protests aside. 'It's quite plain why Frog wishes to be excused,' he said airily. 'He wishes to be alone with his mixed feelings. He'll return with the truth separated from the lies, if I'm not mistaken. Don't fuss so, Snake, I know what I'm doing.'

In the meantime, the frog had scuttled behind a nearby bush. Quite close to Fox's actually. Neither saw the other, however. The expedition settled down to await his return. Cousin chatted quietly with his friends and appeared to be enjoying some funny joke, judging by the peals of laughter that punctuated their talk. Minutes passed. Still no Frog. More minutes and Snake was becoming increasingly impatient.

'He'll be tussling with his conscience,' said Pentecost calmly. His confidence wasn't shared by the others.

Finally Uncle could stand no more. 'What are you doing behind that bush?' he called loudly. Before anyone could stop him he had limped over to peer behind it. For a while, he remained motionless and staring. Then he turned to announce, 'Do you know what that frog is doing behind this bush?'

'No,' said the little ones. 'What is the frog doing behind the bush?'

'Nothing,' Uncle replied. 'He's gone. He'll be miles away by now. Halfway back to Pentecost Farm, I wouldn't doubt. So much for the leniency of the high and mighty Judge Pentecost.'

'I knew it,' wailed Snake. 'All the discomfort, all the ferrying which almost killed me, all the indignities I've suffered. All for nothing. I'm ruined. Now I'll never get my pool back from that swindler.'

'It's *my* pool now, plus all its pleasant surrounds,' interrupted Cousin. 'I've told you before, never give a sucker an even break. Now sling your hook and take your meddlesome friends with you.'

'That's done it,' said Pentecost hotly. 'You've insulted my family. Cheating Snake out of his pool is one thing, but insulting my family is another.'

'And about time too,' declared Uncle. 'I was wondering how long this claptrap was going to go on for.'

'It is only that I think a fight is about to take place,' said Little Brother. 'And I must warn the cousin that my skills in combat will be used in defence of my friends. I will never desert Pentecost and his adorable family.'

Hearing this, Cousin's two friends slid quietly away, like the cowards they were. Now Cousin found himself alone, facing an angry expedition. But he was no coward. He would fight. And if he lost, he would cheerfully return to his vagabond life.

Fox, still well hidden, was on his toes. The situation was getting grimmer with each passing moment. He had no doubt the mice would fight. But at the cost of how many lives? He had already sized up Snake. He had no 'true grit', as Uncle would say. Fox thought, rightly, that he would leave most of the fighting to the mice and Little Brother. The cousin, in contrast, was a fine strong supple-looking snake. He would give a good account of himself. Suddenly, to everyone's amazement, Snake spoke. From somewhere, he had found a new lease of courage.

'I challenge the cousin to mortal combat,' he said, in a loud voice. His brave decision was greeted by cheers from

159

the relieved mice. Fox relaxed again. Perhaps his help wouldn't be needed after all?

From the top of a swaying poplar, the cockle-snorkle craned his ears, every word he heard being stored away in his machine-like memory bank. His excitement was almost too much to bear. First the trial, now a fight to the finish. This was easily the biggest news story of his life and he was determined to record every detail of it for posterity.

Cousin squared up to Snake. 'Winner takes all?' he said. Snake agreed.

Suddenly Cousin lunged, feinted and threw his tail about Snake's throat. 'A perfect double loop with a half-tuck, if you're interested,' he cried. 'Get out of that, or give in.'

'Never,' Snake gasped. He wheezed, as the deadly hold tightened. With a supreme effort, he managed to swivel one eye downwards. It took only a second or two to memorize Cousin's knot. Swish, up whipped Snake's tail to enwrap his

opponent's throat with a fair copy of that painful double loop. He added a full tuck for good measure.

'Pinching my knots, eh?' gurgled Cousin sportingly. 'But it'll do you no good. Out of the way, you mice, I'm going to perform a special whip-lash throw and I'll need plenty of room.' The mice, who had gathered close to watch the fight, backed hurriedly away.

'Snap, crack,' went Cousin's supple body. Snake's hold was broken by the suddenness of it all. Cousin began to twirl Snake above his head, his powerful neck muscles bulging with the effort. Faster and faster revolved the helpless Snake. Suddenly Cousin let go. Snake went sailing through the air, to land with a loud splash in his pool.

'Well, that's where he wanted to be,' grinned Cousin. 'Just you wait till he gets out, I haven't half-started yet.'

'It's the best of three rounds, don't forget,' said Pentecost. 'Snake could easily win the next two.'

'Come now,' said Cousin. 'You don't really believe that. Are we agreed I won that round, fair and square?'

Pentecost reluctantly agreed.

'That cousin is going to win a few more rounds, if Snake doesn't buck himself up,' said Uncle. 'I can't understand why he isn't using a good old-fashioned choking hold. That Snake needs coaching, if you ask me.'

'Oh no,' said Cousin. 'He had plenty of time to train while he was in the wilderness.'

Snake was very angry. In no time at all, he was facing Cousin and waiting for the next round to start. 'What happened to the fair rules we agreed upon?' he yelled.

'Fair rules?' sneered Cousin. 'When I fight, it's no holds barred. Never send a sucker to do a snake's job, that's what I always say.'

'He's right, Snake,' said Pentecost. 'You did agree to give

161

no quarter. Have you changed your mind, now you've found out he's a better fighter than you?'

'I tripped, that's all,' said Snake sullenly. 'How did I know he was going to twirl me about his head?'

'He isn't supposed to tell you,' Pentecost pointed out. 'That's the rules of fighting.'

'Judge Pentecost has awarded the round to me, so stop whining,' snapped Cousin.

'The honourable little mouse should remember who ferried him across the Great River and who is going to guide him to Lickey Top, if I get my pool back. And only if I get it back.' There was no mistaking the blackmail in Snake's words.

Pentecost and the family huddled together. After a while, the leader mouse approached the two snakes. 'I award the round to Snake,' he announced. 'It is obvious he slipped and landed in the pool accidentally.'

'In a pig's eye,' said Cousin. 'That was a genuine whiplash throw. I dispute the decision and appeal for a reliable witness to step forward.'

Uncle did just that. 'That snake had a look of stupidity on his face,' he said in disgust. 'He hadn't a clue where he was twirling to. It was Cousin's round. He won it, fair and square.'

'Thank you, old mouse,' Cousin said.

'It is only that I think a draw would satisfy both parties,' said Little Brother. 'Would my humble opinion be of use, do you think?'

'It would indeed,' said Pentecost, vastly relieved. 'A draw, it shall be. And now, Snakes, get ready for the next ...'

But Snake had already struck. This time, he was determined to get in first. He seized Cousin's tail in a jaw lock his father had taught him and hung on like grim death. Suddenly Cousin went limp.

162

'I submit,' he gasped. Triumphantly, Snake relaxed his grip. It was a foolish mistake. Cousin immediately applied his own jaw lock and quickly closed Snake's eye, with a blow from his powerful tail.

'Foul!' bellowed Snake. 'Is there no mean trick you won't stoop to?'

'I can't think of one,' Cousin replied. Then began again the twirling. The mice were becoming a little bored with the same thing over and over again. They enjoyed a bit of variety in fighting. As if sensing this, Cousin changed his mind. Still keeping Snake humming about in dizzying circles, he crawled a little to the right, where stood the stump of a long-fallen tree.

'He'll be needing more room again, I expect,' said Pentecost, shooing the little ones away.

Deftly, Cousin flicked his head, causing Snake's spinning body to halt suddenly in mid-air. It needed only a downwards bob of the head, to bring Snake crashing down over the tree stump with a sickening crunch.

'Oh dear,' said Pentecost. He peered at Snake's inert form. 'I think you've broken him in two.'

'Nonsense,' Cousin replied. 'He's just badly bruised.' He looked eagerly at Pentecost. 'Can I start the last round before he comes round?' he asked. 'Might as well get it over with. He won't feel much, the state he's in. I fancy I'd like to try my boomerang chuck, next time.'

All the mice gathered round to view Snake. His head hung limply down over one side of the stump, his tail flickering feebly over the other. The portion in between was beginning to swell alarmingly.

'Snake should be allowed to rest before the final round,' said old Mother. 'But, if I had my way, there would be no fight at all.'

'We are hoping the final round will be even more terrible,'

163

agreed the little mice. 'We may even see blood trickling, if we keep our paws crossed.' They were chased from the scene by the irate Great Aunts.

Pentecost ordered Snake's body to be unwrapped from the stump and placed on the soft grass beneath. 'Wake up, Snake,' he called. 'If you're bluffing, nod your head. If you are really hurt, wiggle your tail.'

Snake managed a feeble tail wiggle.

'So you won't be ready for the final round just yet,' said the mouse, bending close to catch Snake's reply. The battered creature answered in a barely audible whisper.

'Who won the last round?' he enquired feebly.

Pentecost straightened. 'Snake is delirious,' he announced. 'He doesn't know what's what. He wants to know who won the last round.'

'Yellow as a buttercup,' snorted Uncle. 'Who needs him, anyway. If the worst comes to the worst, we will find our own way to Lickey Top. All this fuss about a few weasels. What's so special about weasels, I'd like to know? Weasels are only slim scraps of skin and bone. They can be choked easily enough, if we put our minds to it. That snake doesn't deserve such a pleasant pool. We can leave the burying of Snake to Cousin, for he is a kinder creature than most folk think.'

'I would be glad to perform that last duty,' said Cousin humbly. 'Goodbye then, and thank you for dropping in. It's been a pleasure meeting you all.'

But Snake was stirring and attempting to rise. He was a dreadful sight. His mid-section was covered with angry-looking weals and lumps.

'I must admit he's game, for a sucker,' said Cousin. 'But need we bother with the final round? I don't think he'll survive my boomerang chuck somehow.'

'It is only that a draw . . .' began Little Brother.

'A draw it is,' announced Pentecost.

'I say!' protested Cousin. Suddenly, he had an idea. Calling Pentecost aside, he whispered in the mouse's ear. A lot of nodding went on. The rest of the expedition and Snake watched curiously. After a while, Cousin and Pentecost approached Snake.

'Cousin has just made a very generous offer,' he said to Snake. 'He is prepared to share the pool with you. And looking around, you must agree it's a very roomy pool. Why not take up Cousin's offer and live happily ever after?'

Cousin switched on the charm. He could be very charming and gracious when he wished. All professional swindlers have this in common. 'The fact is, I'm becoming quite fond of that snake,' he said. 'I'm sure that, in time, we could become inseparable chums. And, I must admit, I'm growing tired of all these wild parties. So, if my injured relative agrees...?'

Snake replied. He could only speak in a whisper, for his lips were badly swollen. 'I'll agree, on condition all chores are equally shared,' he said faintly. 'And no more wild parties.'

'I agree to your terms, from the bottom of my heart,' said Cousin. 'Let's bury our differences and try to make a go of it.'

Snake brightened. 'And we'll clean up all the mess and make it a pool to be proud of? Like it was in Father's day?'

'It'll be a little paradise before we're through,' said Cousin. 'For we must respect the memory of my dear uncle, who left the pool to me in his only will. And we'll play puzzles and dive and float and blow bubbles... oh, life will be so good.'

'I still can't understand why Father left the pool to you,' said Snake, still bewildered.

'Never mind about that,' said Cousin hurriedly. 'It's all in the past. Let's forget it and begin our new life together.'

165

'In a way, I'm glad you're my cousin,' said Snake. 'It'll be as if Father is still here, for you remind me of him a little.' Uncle groaned aloud, but Pentecost quickly shut him up. 'You may call me "cousin", if you wish,' said Snake. 'I think I'd like that.'

'I was hoping you would say that . . . Cousin,' said Cousin, a sob in his throat.

Uncle could stand no more of this. 'You've called him an impostor every step of the journey from Pentecost Farm. That sweet-talking cousin is making a fool of you. How come he's suddenly your long-lost relative? Ask him to prove it.'

'He's no need to prove anything to me,' said Snake. 'He has the family look about the eyes.'

'All snakes have cunning lemon-flecked eyes,' scoffed the old mouse. 'That's no proof at all.'

Cousin was watching Snake uneasily. He was searching for signs of doubt. There were none.

'I won't have a word said about my cousin,' said Snake sharply. 'So just keep your mouth shut, old mouse.'

'Shut your trap, Uncle,' cried the little ones. 'Leave the two cousins to get on with their clearing up and puzzling.'

Pentecost was contented. Things had turned out all right after all. 'That's that then,' he said. 'Now that everything is settled and our part of the bargain has been kept, we can resume our journey. Are you ready to travel, Snake?'

'I've done all the travelling I need,' said Snake. 'My cousin and I have a lot to do. And we also wish to get to know each other better. So, if you know what's good for you, I'd advise you mice to clear off.'

'But you promised,' said Pentecost desperately. 'You wouldn't go back on it, would you, Snake?'

'You just watch me,' was the reply. 'I've learned a lot,

these past few days, and one lesson stands out above the others. Never give a sucker an even break.'

Cousin looked at him admiringly. 'That's the way to talk,' he said. 'And now, let's see how fast mice can run.' Together, the snakes advanced on the stricken family. The mice turned and fled in terror. Little Brother would have stood and fought, but he realised how hopeless it would be against such odds. Helplessly, he turned and followed after the nice.

'I never doubted your identity for a moment,' Snake was saying, as he and Cousin lounged comfortably along their log.

'You are so trusting,' Cousin replied.

'It was all a great big misunderstanding,' said Snake. 'It could have happened to anyone.'

'How true,' was the reply.

'Just think, our fathers must have been brothers.'

'And a closer pair of brothers you'd never find, I'll bet,' Cousin said.

'As fond of each other as we are,' said Snake dreamily.

'Come here a moment,' said Cousin suddenly. 'I want to show you something.' Puzzled, Snake slid closer. He was immediately seized in a vice-like grip. 'I never did show you my boomerang chuck, did I?' shouted Cousin gleefully. He began to whirl Snake about his head. 'Might as well start as we mean to go on,' Cousin grunted. He released Snake, who spun through the air, resembling remarkably a boomerang in flight. 'My round, I think,' said Cousin happily. 'And now, I'll just look up a few old friends. I just feel like a wild party tonight. See you later ... sucker.'

14 The Weasel Woods

Later, it would be recalled how easily Uncle kept pace with the fleeing expedition, in spite of his paw condition. Perhaps fear had spurred him on. Whatever the case, it would be remembered how effortlessly he had outstripped many of the faster runners. He would deny it, of course, quickly changing the subject when his sprinting talents were discussed. But, at this particular moment, the mice were too dispirited and tired to comment upon such things.

The mice had fled without sense of direction. To escape the two snakes had been their only concern. Yet luck had intervened, even in that flight from danger. As the cockle-snorkle, winging above, remarked to himself, 'Bang on course. These mice are quite remarkable, you know. An uncanny sense of direction. If they're not careful, they'll reach Lickey Top, quite unaided.'

But it wasn't like that at all. Pentecost and the family couldn't have cared less where their panic-filled dash led them. Yet here they were, slumped in exhaustion in the shadow of a great steep hill. Pentecost, even by craning his head, could barely make out the summit. But for the steps cut into its side, there was no way the mice could have climbed it.

Pentecost's ponderings were interrupted by the arrival of the cockle-snorkle. The bug alighted nearby and began to commiserate with the mouse. 'Fancy Snake doing a dirty trick like that,' he said. 'But, never mind, at least you are all still in the land of the living. And, to cheer you up, I've a bit

168

of good news for you. I've had a word with Owl and he said he's delighted that soon he will be welcoming his new neighbours. He's preparing a little house-warming party for you. Who's pleased as Punch, then?'

'Well, it's something,' said Pentecost tiredly. 'But I hope you aren't still playing both ends against the middle. I couldn't bear that, after all we've been through.'

The bug looked hurt. 'As if I would. I've been putting in a good word for you. At least be a little grateful.'

'I am, I truly am,' said the mouse. 'But you will understand how the family and I are feeling at the moment.'

'You're feeling betrayed and deserted,' said the treacherous bug kindly. 'But, never mind, the feeling will pass. I have the notion your journey will be plain sailing from now on.'

At this point, a shocking thing happened. Pentecost, the brave leader and the hope of the family, buried his head in his paws and wept. The tears (a few for himself, for that he couldn't help) were for the trusting group about him. And they backed away, not unkindly, but in fear, for his strength was theirs and now there was none.

'Hop it,' said a firm voice. It was addressed to the circling bug. Fox loped past the huddle of mice, to sink upon his belly beside the distressed Pentecost. Gently, he nudged with his nose the small heaving form. 'And where has my brave friend gone?' he said kindly. 'The one with the name all to himself? The "through thick or thin" buddy who rescued this no-good fox from the trap? Where's the Pentecost mouse who will dry his tears, grab this expedition by the scruff of the neck and, with a little help from a friend, lead it through the Weasel Woods to a happy ending? I can't see him around. I wonder where he's got to?'

'I am he,' said Pentecost, raising his head. He scrubbed at the tears. 'I am not worthy, Fox. I knew deep down, Snake

169

would betray us. And he has, and I have failed. And please don't mock me, for who could befriend a mouse who doesn't deserve the title Pentecost? If I am left alone with my shame, it is all I deserve.'

'Is this a shamed mouse?' thundered Fox. He glared about at the onlookers.

'Never!' cried the family.

'It is only, never,' echoed Little Brother.

'Or a matter of opinion,' said the crushed and sulking bug. He sat on a twig, dulled and angered by Fox's brusque manner.

Uncle had moved away, pretending to occupy himself with his sore paws. But there was no denying the fact that his 'never' had been the loudest of all.

'Up on those determined paws then,' said Fox grimly. 'You are outvoted. Up the steps, across the plateau and we'll worry about the weasels later.'

Pentecost rose. He looked at the rock-hewn steps that soared upwards, blurring with distance as they levelled out on to the high plateau. Then his eyes returned to the first one.

'One hundred,' said Fox, reading his thoughts. He grinned. 'And I'll be right behind you all the way.'

Pentecost was smiling now. The family, too, were smiling. Everyone was hugely relieved. The steps, seemingly so formidable, were climbed easily and with light heart.

'Fox,' said Pentecost, as they lay on the flower-strewn, twilight-dimmed plateau. 'I'm sorry.'

'For doubting me?' Fox asked. 'I'm not in the least hurt. And not another word.'

Curious, the mouse continued, 'By the way, where were you during the battle of Snake's pool? Business, I suppose?'

'A battle, you say?' Fox pretended surprise. Then he was serious. 'But, now you mention it – business, I mean. I won't be long.' He made a few lame excuses and slipped away into the night.

'Each to his own,' called Pentecost forgivingly. 'One's points can't be all good, after all. And thank you, once again.'

'More crimes against rabbits, I suppose,' said Uncle grimacing. Before settling for the night, he busied himself. Carefully he unbound the healing herbs from his paws, fresh ones newly picked at his side. 'Now, perhaps, I shall get a little rest from the constant pain,' he said piteously. 'But no doubt the throbbing will wake me in the night. When will the suffering end for this old mouse?'

'Soon, Uncle,' yawned Pentecost sleepily. 'Quite soon now.'

'I wasn't talking to you,' retorted the old mouse. 'It was a private conversation.'

The wind howled as the expedition sat gazing into the dark woods. The weather had changed drastically from the warm sunshine of the previous day. Gales had been raging since first light. Now, an hour or so later, they had whipped themselves into a fury as the skies blackened and the first drops of rain began to fall. The patter became a downpour and soon the party was soaked and shivering. Hastily, they took shelter beneath a pine tree at the edge of the Weasel Woods.

Not even the shrieking of the wind could drown the threats of the enemy, waiting impatiently and concealed inside the trees. 'Drive 'em down dark 'oles and do for 'em.' The voices, high-pitched and snarling, were filled with hatred and a terrible blood-lust. 'Rip 'em to pieces down the black, blind, squealing tunnels of hell. Rip out their throats and suck at the sweet life-blood, flowing, flowing, red and bright ... ahhhh. Kill! Kill! Death to all who dare cross the Weasel line!'

172

The mice shivered and huddled close to each other. The smell of rotting vegetation and decaying flesh was heavy and sweet in their nostrils. And the rain lashed down, soaking through the canopy of leaves, trickling down the trunks of the oaks and the moss-stained pines.

Fox sat out in the open, his fur slicked and sodden, the rain pouring in a steady stream from his nose. He was deep in thought. From time to time a gust of wind would tug at his brush, as if angered that anything could stay so calm, so unruffled before its fury. The mice, watching from the bole of the tree, saw his eyes flicker, brighten and, disappointingly, dull again. They were waiting for the miracle their red friend would surely work. Their trust in him was absolute, for without his help, they knew that to venture into those woods would result in the death of them all. But Fox was no miracle worker. For one brief moment, he considered calling the whole thing off. All he need do was to turn and go. Angered at himself for thinking such a thing, he threw back his head and howled.

'If you wish to desert us we won't hold it against you, Fox,' said Pentecost. 'We just won't respect you so much in future.'

'Be quiet! I'm thinking,' snapped Fox. 'Just leave me alone.'

At that moment the cockle-snorkle arrived. He had received a tremendous buffeting from the wind to get here and, for a time, he just hung beneath a pine-cone, panting and recovering his breath. After a while he spoke. 'What's the hold-up?' he asked. 'And what's Fox doing, sitting on his backside in the pouring rain?'

'He's thinking,' said Pentecost.

'When's he going to stop thinking and do something positive? We're all rooting for you, Owl and I, that is.'

'I find that hard to believe,' said Fox. 'But we'll let it go for now. At the moment, we've more important things to

173

consider. We'll find out what you and Owl are up to, afterwards.'

'What's that supposed to mean?' said the indignant bug. 'I'll have you know, I'm a friend of this expedition.'

'And we all know Owl is waiting to give us a big welcome,' said the little mice. 'All we need to do is to get through the Weasel Woods and all our troubles will be over.'

'Or just starting,' murmured Fox quietly. Suddenly his eyes lit up. Then they narrowed. Then they lit up again. 'Of course,' he said. 'Why didn't I think of that before?'

'Is the plan dawning, Fox?' asked Pentecost.

'It was just a question of time,' Fox replied. 'I knew I'd think of something, sooner or later.'

'You reckon you can get the expedition safely through the woods?' said the bug, suddenly interested.

'I do,' said Fox.

'Is that official?' insisted the bug. 'Can I inform Owl, that we can leave everything in your capable paws?'

'You can tell him what you like,' Fox replied. 'As no doubt you will.'

'Will do,' said the bug briskly. He relaxed his hold on the pine-cone and was whirled away by a gust of wind.

But Pentecost wasn't easily fooled. Hadn't the bug confessed that he was playing 'both ends against the middle'? The mouse was only now beginning to understand what that phrase meant. It meant the bug was deliberately stirring things up, lulling the fears of the mice, while, at the same time, enraging Owl the more with lies about them. But now was hardly the time to be worrying about that. The confrontation would have to wait. First, the mice had to get safely through the Weasel Woods.

The rain had stopped, but the winds continued unabated. Fox stood up, his red tail dry now and streaming in the wind.

He was a magnificent sight. The little mice stared enviously at that beautiful brush.

'Now listen carefully,' Fox said. He indicated a small bush, a few yards away. 'I want you all to hide beneath that bush there. At the moment, you are in clear view of the enemy and that won't do at all. Once beneath the bush, I want you all to pick a large leaf apiece and then settle down to wait.'

'Wait for what?' asked Pentecost.

'For my return,' said Fox patiently.

'You mean, for your "maybe" return,' said Uncle. 'Anxious to be away, are you?'

'Uncle says he's sorry,' said Pentecost quickly.

'Apology accepted,' Fox said. 'And now, may I continue? If you do exactly as I say, things should turn out okay. Just shut up for a moment and I'll explain my plan. When I return, I'll be in a hurry. And as likely as not, I won't be alone. Don't be surprised if I don't stop to say hello. You'll see what I mean, later. Have you got all that?'

'We stay underneath the bush, a large picked leaf apiece and wait for your return, not alone and not bothering to say hello,' repeated Pentecost. 'And then what, Fox?'

'I shall dash straight into the woods, followed by ... but we won't go into that for the moment,' Fox said. 'But my dashing into the woods will be your cue ...'

'Cue?' said Pentecost.

'Your cue to go into action,' Fox went on. 'There's a path through the woods. See it? Well anyway, that's where it starts.'

'You mean that narrow pine-needled one?' said Pentecost, pointing.

'Yes. It leads directly to Lickey Top.' Rapidly Fox sketched in the rest of his plan. 'There's a small ditch running alongside that path. I want you to travel along it. In that way, with a bit of luck, you shouldn't be seen. Keep to the side where the ferns grow thickly. Stop for nothing, until you reach the other side of the wood. You may hear a lot of noise and crashing about, but don't let that distract you. Just press on and leave the worrying to me.'

'Haven't you forgotten something?' said Uncle. 'You do remember about the leaves? Or is all this leaf-picking just something to occupy our bored paws while we're waiting?'

'The leaves,' said Fox, 'are a precaution, in case things go wrong. If you think you are in danger of being discovered, you can all crowd together and pretend to be a beautiful little bush. Good idea, eh?'

'And, with a bit of luck, we may even take root,' said Uncle sourly.

'It's all a bit confusing, Fox, but we'll do as you say,' said Pentecost. He turned to the family. 'Okay, everyone under the bush, leaf-picking and waiting for Fox's return and the cue.'

Fox watched approvingly, as the mice dashed for the bush. He followed after them and poked his nose into the thick foliage.

'Now don't forget all I've told you. I'll be back as soon as I can.'

'We won't forget, and thank you for helping us,' said Pentecost.

'Thank me when you reach Lickey Top,' said Fox. Suddenly he was gone.

The rain had started again as Fox raced through the grasses and flowers of the plateau. In no time at all, he had reached the top of the One Hundred Steps and was bounding down them, three, four, five at a time. On sped Fox, his breath coming in great gasps as the gales lashed about his nostrils. Soon Snake's pool was in sight. He swerved to avoid the branch that spanned the water and stuck out over the path. He was just in time to see Snake go sailing through the air, to hear his despairing cries and the loud laughter of the cousin. 'Serves you right,' thought Fox, as he flashed by. 'What kind of a break did you give the mice?'

Now he was flying down World's End Hill. Two rabbits ceased their nibbling to watch his progress. 'Repent, you red fiend!' they cried.

'Can't stop,' called Fox over his shoulder. 'I'm on a mission of mercy.'

'One day the world will end for you!' Their cries of damnation followed him down the hill. At the bottom, Fox turned sharp right. He was fond of making sudden changes of direction. He liked particularly making complete about-turns for no reason at all. But now the rest of his journey lay directly before him.

He had a following wind for the remainder of the way. Sporadic gusts puffed up the fur along his back as he belted across the fields, the tip of his tail swishing through the tender young wheat. Then, suddenly, his destination was in sight. His pace slowed to a wary trot. The last hundred yards or so he covered on his stomach. Quietly he sank into the drainage ditch that ran parallel to the steel mesh fence. For a while, he lay very still, recovering his breath and thinking out his next move. Cautiously, he raised his head to peer through the wire. He noted the three dogs slumped about the farmyard: Spot, Flannel-ears and Fat Billy.

Spot was a mean-looking brute; half Alsatian, half bull-terrier, he had inherited the savagery of the first and the obstinacy of the latter. As he lay there, his slavering jaws displayed the long curved fangs of the killer. Buffeting winds whipped the saliva that dripped from his lolling tongue back into his face.

In contrast, Flannel-ears was a long-eared dog, with the

soft velvet coat of the spaniel. An amiable pup, he lived for the jubilation of the chase. He had never felt hatred for Fox. Hunt days, for him, were a glorious romp, with Fox as 'it'. In the field, he would yelp his delight, his wind-blown ears streaming like banners behind.

A few chickens were strutting round the dogs on the beaten earth, pecking at the scattering of wheat and scratching for the odd worm. Fox sighed with relief. So far, so good. He licked his chops and decided to put the first phase of his plan into effect immediately.

He was out of the ditch and over the fence in a twinkling. So quickly did he move, that the dogs just stared unmoving, their faces frozen in surprise. They continued to watch in amazement, as Fox snatched up a chicken, expertly broke its neck and went sailing back over the fence again.

Seconds later, all hell broke loose. The chickens stampeded across the yard, colliding with each other in their fear and confusion. The dogs, shocked from their dream-like state, began to bark at Fox, who, instead of fleeing, remained grinning from his side of the fence. It was then the farmer wrenched open the farmhouse door, shot-gun in hand, scanning the area for something to shoot at. He saw Fox beyond the wire, raised the gun to his shoulder and fired. Fox ducked, as the pellets whistled about his head. It was time to leave, and fast. Pausing only to snatch up his prize, he was soon heading for home as fast as he could go.

Fat Billy thought the whole affair a nuisance. He had been having a quiet snooze, when Fox came along to spoil it all. But he had obeyed his master's command to 'go get the varmint', as he always had, as he always would do. His mood was one of surly irritability. Someone would pay for disturbing his day and that someone, he thought grimly, would be Fox. Already Spot and Flannel-ears had leapt the fence and were off in hot pursuit, leaving Fat Billy straddled half-over and scrambling to free himself. The humiliation only served to fuel his anger. A helping shove up the rump from his master and he, too, was away on the enemy's trail.

It was a dangerous game Fox was playing, but the success of his twin projects demanded risk. First, he intended to do his duty as father and provider. Afterwards, he would do what he could for the mice. All depended upon him reaching his lair in good time, so as to be away again before he was spotted.

Things worked out just right. Quickly, he stuffed the chicken into the den and proceeded to dash about in ever-widening circles, before setting out for a distant outcrop of rock. And there he sat, silhouetted against the cloudy sky, waiting.

Fox's mate was quite used to these unexpected homecomings. She dragged the chicken further into the den and began to dole it out to the delighted youngsters. It was at that moment Spot arrived. From his vantage point, Fox watched anxiously, as the dog snuffled around the entrance to his den. Then Flannel-ears came panting up and immediately began to race about in Fox's circular trail. Spot withdrew his nose from the den and joined him. Fat Billy was late, but he was smart. The eldest of the three dogs, he knew the wiles of Fox well. He paid no heed to his companions, as they nosed about the puzzling trail. Instead he gazed expectantly towards the distant rock. It was just as he thought. It was also what Fox had hoped for. Fat Billy bayed triumphantly and rolled off in Fox's direction. To his disgust, he was easily overtaken by the fleeter dogs. But Fat Billy was a stayer. Slow and over-weight he might be, but he possessed a streak of grim determination and, if the end of Fox came, he would be in on it, of this he was sure.

As the dogs approached, Fox felt that old familiar twinge of fear. His heart thumped, his paws tingled, and his muscles tensed in anticipation. He leapt from his rocky perch, only just in time. As he turned to run, so he felt Spot's teeth clip the end of his tail. Then began the long wild-goose chase back into the hills.

Fox made sure not to outdistance his pursuers. He could easily have done so, but he had no wish to dispirit them. He wanted them to believe that their slightly-lengthened stride would seal his fate for ever. He even adopted a limp, thus spurring the dogs to greater effort. Up and over World's End Hill he raced, the harsh panting of Spot ever in his ears. Always he enticed them on, adding a laboured roll to the limp, as if he were tiring. And all the while he grinned, enjoying his mastery over them.

And now he had reached Snake's pool. The two snakes, their quarrel for the moment forgotten, plunged into the water and watched in astonishment, as the pursued and the pursuers charged by. Now Fox was running smoothly, his limp discarded, his stride lengthening, as he sighted the small bush and the woods beyond. 'Now!' he yelled, dashing past the astonished mice and into the trees. He and the snapping dogs were instantly swallowed up in the denseness of the woods.

'The cue!' cried Pentecost. 'Don't forget your leaves. Follow me and keep close together.' He crawled from beneath the bush and hurried for the tree line, followed closely by

180

Little Brother and the excited family. Soon, they were pushing through the ferns that grew along the side of the path, their leaves above their heads as added protection.

Fox was crashing about in the undergrowth and howling for all he was worth. In and out of the trees he raced, the dogs hard on his heels and making enough noise to awaken the dead. His carefully thought-out plan had the desired effect. The Weasels, shocked and terrified, slid beneath tree roots, dived for the safety of their holes and scrambled into the branches of the pines, in a frenzied attempt to escape the fury of the dogs. All thoughts of mouse for lunch were forgotten as each sought to preserve his miserable hide. Not all escaped. Scarcely pausing in his maddened attempt to close with Fox, Spot snapped up a fear-crazed weasel, crushed its spine and flung its twitching corpse into the undergrowth. A good half-dozen more died in similar manner. If the blood of Fox was to be denied them, Spot and Fat Billy were determined to slake their lust on something.

In the meantime, the mice were making good progress. At last, they could see a glimmer of light through the trees ahead. Even as they hurried along the side of the path, the black rain clouds above the woods were scudding away to the south. They emerged from that forbidding place into a new world of bright sunshine.

Lickey Top gleamed beneath the freed sun. All its beauty lay revealed before them, in sharp washed colour. The flower-strewn slopes of their promised land seemed to beckon them. For a long time, the mice just stared about them. Some wept quietly. It was as if they had emerged from the black tunnel of nightmare into the most soothing of dreams. And that dream was one of the most satisfying sort, of home. Pentecost watched the family shyly exploring their future haven and on an impulse, quite alone, he offered up thanks for their deliverance.

182

Much had happened to Fox, during that time. His plan had been to shake off the dogs, as soon as he thought the mice safely through the woods. But the dogs, Spot in particular, were in no mood to be shaken. So began another long chase back down to the lowlands.

Now Fox was really tired, the dogs too. But they had tasted blood in the Weasel Woods and they yearned for more. Fox realized that, if he didn't do something quickly, he would soon be dead. Much as he hated the idea, he came to the conclusion that his den was the only safe refuge left to him. He made for it.

Fox, his mate and fearful cubs eyed the opposition. They could see Spot, Flannel-ears and Fat Billy, sitting on their haunches outside, their sides heaving from the exhausting chase. Spot growled from time to time, as he spied the foxes' eyes glittering from the darkness of the den.

Fat Billy had played this waiting game before. He knew the chances of coming to grips with Fox now were remote. He was bored. He longed for his quiet nook in the corner of the barn, back home. His mouth watered as he pictured the bone and biscuits, temptingly arranged in his favourite blue bowl. His alarm rose as he imagined the two new pups, their own meals scoffed, starting with relish on his. The thought was too much to bear. For the last time, he launched his tubby body at the hole, wriggling and squeezing, in a vain attempt to gain entry. But it was no use. He was just wasting energy. So, tired, disgruntled and hungry, he turned for home. Spot, appreciating the wisdom of the elder dog, reluctantly tagged on behind.

Now only Flannel-ears remained. For a while, he sat gazing fondly at Fox. Then, suddenly, the little mongrel dashed forward, slipping easily inside the den and chasing the foxes along the winding passage to the dead end. It was there Fox turned, prepared to sell his life dearly in defence of

his family. But, to his complete surprise and embarrassment, Flannel-ears leaned forward, gave him an affectionate lick and departed, never to return. 'It' had been caught, and the lick was a reward for an exciting chase.

It was a bemused fox who settled down to sleep the sleep of the exhausted. But, before he closed his eyes, his last thoughts were for the mice. How had they fared, he wondered? Had they managed to get safely through the Weasel Woods? And, if so, what would Owl do upon seeing Lickey Top invaded? All these questions surged about in his mind, before he finally fell asleep. Tomorrow he would go up there and find out for himself. But, in the meantime, he desperately needed sleep. His cubs curled close beside him, he drifted off . . .

15 Owl of Lickey Top

Two friends parted. But, hopefully, they would meet again soon. As the family explored their new home, Pentecost, who sat apart, deep in private thought, was joined by Little Brother.

'It is only that I yearn to peep over the brow of Lickey Top,' he said hesitantly. 'The apple core tree must look beautiful with the sun shining so.'

His broad hints weren't lost on Pentecost. 'But if you need me further?' continued Little Brother. He was dancing with impatience. Pentecost hadn't the heart to burden him with the problems that were worrying him.

'Go, Little Brother,' he said. He looked into his friend's

eyes. 'And may you find your heart's desire, for you have had unhappiness enough, in the past. But come and see us soon. And, who knows, you may see two eyes . . .'

'Bright, and regarding me with approval,' finished Little Brother. 'It is only that one day, hopefully . . .'

'Sons may trail behind,' finished Pentecost. 'And may God swim by your side for ever. Goodbye, my friend.'

'And may the Pentecost mouse learn to play again, for his burden is too heavy for one so young. Farewell.'

They parted, one light of heart, the other deeply troubled.

The joy upon the faces of the family disturbed Pentecost. Though he pretended to share their happiness, his thoughts ranged farther ahead. True, they had arrived. But he knew their troubles weren't over yet. Whilst they brought him tales of freshly-discovered beauties, he sat alone watching the world below.

It was at that moment the inner mouse, so long a counsel and comfort for the old Pentecost, spoke to him. As the sun fell upon the hill, the voice offered advice. 'And will you share them now?' it asked. 'These troubles? For you have borne them alone for far too long.'

'But, see their happiness,' replied Pentecost. 'Already, they forget their past sorrows. Already, they are at home and find peace. But Owl of Lickey Top has not yet spoken. This hill, this view, the grassy slopes the family play upon, they are all his. And I fear he will not wish to share.'

'Then you must tell them,' the voice urged. 'Before these delights become loves and all the dearer for the parting.'

And Pentecost called them. Reluctantly they gathered, for they were happy and the clouded expression upon their leader's face troubled them.

'The time has come to tell you of my fears,' he began. 'I

186

wouldn't mention them before, for I could see no point in upsetting you, whilst we were making such good progress. But now we have arrived, I'm forced to warn you that Owl might prove difficult in accepting us as neighbours. It was something the cockle-snorkle said that first aroused my suspicions.'

'Why do you speak this way?' shouted Uncle. 'Don't you wish us to be happy? Why do you pour cold water on our new home?'

'Because the bug has been playing both ends against the middle,' cried Pentecost. 'He happens to be a double agent.'

'So,' said an accusing voice, from near at hand. 'The Pentecost mouse has broken my cover, eh? I never thought he'd turn out to be a sneak.'

The mice turned about, just in time to see the bug change from a drab bit of mould on a blade of grass to a bright orange spy.

Uncle looked puzzled. 'What is a double agent, by the way?'

'A spy,' said Pentecost. 'A plain and simple spy.'

'A rare and complicated spy,' said the bug quickly. 'There's nothing plain and simple about me. What are you doing here, anyway?' he continued. 'This is Owl's property. You can't go trampling over other folk's property, without permission. Owl will have a fit when he finds out.'

'Do you mean to say he doesn't know we're here?' asked Pentecost. 'I'd have thought you'd have told him by now, you being the kind of bug you are.'

'I've told him the Weasels have got you,' said the bug, hugging himself gleefully. 'As far as he's concerned, the invasion has been thwarted.'

'You wicked little liar,' said Pentecost. 'Well, I intend to tell Owl about your double life when we meet.'

'I'll deny it,' the bug replied. 'The old fool believes

187

everything I say. I'm in charge up here, regardless of what Owl believes.'

'Such treachery,' said Pentecost. 'Can't you be true to anyone? Haven't you the tiniest spark of decency in you, at all?'

'Not a flicker,' replied the bug proudly. 'But come on, let's go surprise Owl. Oh glory me, how beautifully this plot is thickening. By the way, did I tell you Fox was torn to bits by the dogs?'

'Fox dead?' repeated Pentecost, aghast at the thought.

'Well, he would be, wouldn't he?' said the bug. 'Being ripped to little bits and all?'

'Fox dead?' repeated Pentecost, aghast at the thought.

The bug showed signs of irritation. 'Must you keep repeating yourself? I've told you, yes. And now you're all alone and friendless in the world. What do you think about that?'

'We'll face whatever comes,' said Pentecost. 'There's no going back for us, now. We owe it to the memory of Fox to see this thing through to the end.'

'There's a courageous mouse,' said the bug kindly. 'And I hope things work out all right for you all.'

Pentecost was suddenly angry. 'But how can you say that, when you are plotting against us?'

'Steady on,' protested the bug. 'I'm plotting against Owl, as well. I can't go against my nature. I'm just a born plotter. I am what I am, for better or worse.'

Pentecost glanced anxiously at the sky. It was almost dark now and, meanwhile, precious time was being wasted. He wanted desperately to come to some agreement with Owl, before complete darkness fell. He intended to throw himself upon the bird's mercy, and hope that he possessed a spark of decency in his heart. The confrontation could not be put off any longer. Silently, the family, Pentecost leading, filed off in the direction of the lone oak, stark and brooding against the sky.

The bug had flown up to perch on the edge of the hole in the tree. He appeared to be having a whispered conversation with the occupant within. Ever curious, the mice craned their ears to catch what was being said. They caught the word 'Fox' and the phrase 'impudent invaders', but the rest was a meaningless jumble.

'He'll be telling Owl how bravely Fox died, I expect,' said Uncle. 'And the impudent invaders must be some other expedition. It goes on all the time, you know, invading.' The rest of the party thought all this most unlikely. They were all, by now, well aware to whom Owl was referring.

'Owl's coming out to deal with you in a few moments,' called the bug. 'He said to line up in two tidy rows, at the foot of his tree.'

The mice shuffled about uneasily. 'When Owl appears, would he mind if we gave him three hearty cheers?' said Pentecost. 'And afterwards, I would like to discuss the letting of a small section of his pretty property, if it's convenient.'

'Owl says you can cheer all you wish, as soon as you're off his land,' was the reply. 'And he's hanging on to all his pretty sections for the moment.'

Just then, something appeared from the hole. It was a pair of filthy clawed feet. They scrabbled about in the air for a while, before disappearing again. There came some muffled grunts and groans from inside, followed by a loud thud. The sound of cursing filled the air. Suddenly, a weird apparition framed the entrance of the dark hole. It was a large head, tousled and with clumps of feathers sticking out at crazy angles. Two bloodshot eyes, as large and as round as lily pads, glared down at the petrified mice. A cruelly-curved beak snapped out a final oath, as Owl, with a great deal of squeezing, emerged from his home.

189

'Let me introduce, in person, the one and only Owl, the Wise,' sang the cockle-snorkle.

Owl waddled on to his perch and surveyed the mice contemptuously. He was very fat. To make things worse, he fluffed himself up until he was twice his normal size, inciting nervous giggles from some of the mice.

It was Pentecost who broke the awkward silence. Somehow, he had to bring about a change of heart in Owl. Everything depended upon it. The journey, the sad loss of their comrades, all would have been in vain, if Pentecost failed to move Owl's heart. The family, with the exception of Uncle, seemed to sense this. They waited silently for their leader to save the situation, their paws crossed behind their backs.

'As leader of the family, I would like to say how happy...'

Owl ignored him and whispered to the bug. The insect flew into action.

'Right, look sharp,' he said. 'Owl wants you all in neat rows. Shortest at the front, tallest at the rear. Move.'

'... and we would take it as a great kindness, for we would need the smallest of plots,' Pentecost was saying. He might as well have been talking to himself, for all the good it was doing. But still he persisted, trying to make himself heard over the general hubbub.

'They're not used to dicipline I'm afraid,' said the bug. 'Every time I get 'em tidy, they start fidgeting around, Owl.'

'What is that ugly mouse rambling on about?' said Owl softly.

'... small neat homes,' Pentecost continued, 'and not at all an eyesore, as Snake would have you believe, but tastefully woven by the Great Aunts, who are experts at such things...'

'It's the Pentecost mouse, Owl,' said the bug. 'He's trying to melt your heart with sob-stories.'

190

'Well, tell him to be quiet,' Owl rapped.

'. . . and a few seasonal festivals, very hushed affairs and not in the least abandoned. And a little light dancing and singing, when the joy becomes too much to bear . . .'

'Quiet,' yelled the cockle-snorkle.

'. . . and now I would like to call for three cheers, for Owl of Lickey Top,' ended Pentecost. 'Hip, hip . . .'

Uncle had heard quite enough. Fuming with rage, he opened his mouth and neatly put his paw in it. In loud ringing tones he said exactly what was on his mind. 'Owl of Lickey Top is a bully,' he shouted. 'And he'll get no cheers from me.' There was a deathly hush. The mice, in their neat rows, began to tremble. This time, Uncle had gone too far.

'Who is the old crippled mouse, who dares to insult me?' asked Owl ominously.

The flustered bug was about to reply, but Uncle got in first. '"The crippled old mouse" is me, Uncle, the true leader of this expedition,' he said, drawing himself up proudly. 'And I would like to know who you are, ordering us all to stand in rows? I've never stood in a neat row in all my life and I don't intend to start now.'

Owl listened with mounting fury. He gripped the perching stump, his claws sinking deep into the wood, as he imagined them rending the old mouse apart. Fierce hissing sounds escaped from the side of his curved beak and his eyes were fixed balefully on the object of his hatred.

Despite all these warning signs, Uncle continued. He still had a few more things to say upon the subject of Owl. 'All this begging for a small section,' he scoffed. 'Don't you realise this Owl is a tyrant? I have long thought Pentecost planned to sacrifice us elderly mice, in exchange for a small section. It all makes sense now. Have you noticed how Owl smiles secretly at our leader, when he thinks no-one is watching?'

191

'You're wrong there,' said the bug quickly. 'Owl never smiles at anyone.'

'Well, he winked then,' Uncle argued. 'It's the same thing. He winked smilingly.'

Again the bug interrupted. 'It isn't a wink, it's Owl's nervous tic. And, if you watch closely, you'll notice how he jerks his head for no reason at all. And, never once in our long friendship, have I ever known him to sponge his claws. That's guilt, that is.'

'We noticed the filthy claws immediately,' sniffed the Great Aunts. 'A proud bird would have done something about them long ago. Water is free enough, after all.'

'Owl can't bear to look at his claws,' explained the bug. 'It's because of the terrible deed they committed when he was a chick. As far as he's concerned, they belong to some other bird, not him.'

At long last, the cockle-snorkle accused the bird directly. He had been longing to do so for a long time. The effect of those words was sad to behold. Owl gave a strangled cry. It was a sound full of regret and deep mourning. He made to move, but was unable to. Instead, he toppled forward from the perch, his claws still deeply embedded in the stump. Like a trapeze-artist, he performed a graceful half-loop, before being brought to an abrupt halt by the trunk of his tree. The sickening thud, as his head struck, caused the mice to wince. And there he hung, suspended upside-down and quite unconscious.

'I hope he isn't dead,' said Pentecost. 'Only we haven't discussed the small section, yet.'

'Owl, dead?' said the bug, with a chuckle. 'The very idea.' Why, Owl is merely doing his exercises. He likes to keep in trim, does Owl. A few swings around his perch keep him as fit as a fiddle. Feeling more supple now, Owl?' But the bug's assurances didn't sound at all convincing.

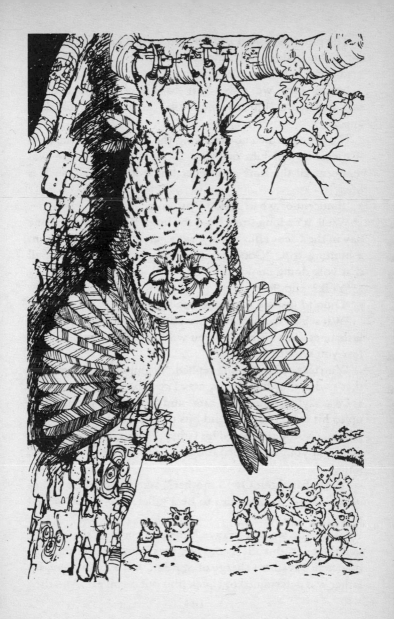

The moon was high and full and bathed Lickey Top in its soft light. It also bathed the gently-swinging owl, who was beginning to look deader with each passing minute.

'It's a pity we never got to know him properly,' said Pentecost. 'I'm sure he wasn't as bad as he liked to appear.'

'To think he died not knowing the truth,' sighed the bug. 'I meant to tell him one day. Now it's too late. He was innocent all the time and never knew it. Oh well, such is life.'

'Innocent of what?' asked Pentecost.

'Well, it's a long story,' said the bug. 'But it all started one day in the Clent Hills when Owl's parents came home from a hunting trip. "Good gracious," they cried. "What is all that yolk doing on our son's claws?"'

'Yolk?' said Pentecost.

'Didn't I just say that?' the bug snapped.

'What had the parents been out hunting for?' asked the little ones. 'We are hoping you will reply hazel-nuts, but we fear you won't.'

'You fear right,' the bug replied. 'A plump Harvest mouse, that's what they had. Now, may I continue my story? Well, as I was saying, home they came and there stood young Owl, up to his ankles in yolk, and bits of smashed brother everywhere. "Murderer," cried his father. "Fancy jumping up and down on your unhatched brother." Oh, he was in a terrible state.'

'But what about Owl's mother?' asked a horrified Pentecost. 'Did she believe him to be a killer, too? Without real proof?'

'Well, she wanted to give him the benefit of the doubt,' said the bug. 'But all he could do was splutter. Spluttering is no defence against a charge of murder, you see. Anyway, his father was determined to chuck him out on his ear. And then

194

it was all too late. It was about that time he met me and here we are, living as recluses.'

'What a sad story,' breathed Pentecost. 'I feel almost sorry for him. And did he splutter for a long time afterwards. Trying to sort things out in his confused mind?'

'For ages,' admitted the bug. 'But my companionship helped him to pick up the threads of his shattered life.'

'But wait a moment,' said Pentecost slowly. 'If I remember correctly, you mentioned the word "innocent" a while ago. Didn't you say he died never knowing that he was innocent of the crime?'

'And so he was,' said the bug sadly. 'You see, just before his parents' return, Owl had been polishing his brother's eggshell, lovingly ...'

'Polishing?' said Pentecost.

'You're doing it again,' snapped the bug. 'Must you repeat everything I say?'

'He does that, because he can't think of words of his own,' said Uncle nastily.

'Let me explain,' the bug went on. 'It so happened that Owl loved his brother's egg dearly. He couldn't wait for it to hatch out, so that they could play clawing each other and other owlish games. As I said, Owl was polishing his brother's egg when ...'

'When what?' asked the leader mouse quickly.

'The poor little mite slipped and fell. It was an accident, of course. Murder never entered his head.'

'But why didn't he explain to his parents?' said Pentecost. 'Surely they would have understood and forgiven him?'

'That's the sad part about it,' was the reply. 'He tried, but they wouldn't listen. And what with all the tears and accusations, he became more and more convinced that he really had committed that dreadful crime. That's why he eventually came here to Lickey Top. To atone for his misdeeds, I

195

suppose. To deliberately deprive himself of the company of his own kind.'

'But there's one thing I don't understand,' said Pentecost, a perplexed frown on his face. 'How do you know he is innocent . . . was innocent, God rest his soul?'

'Because I was there and saw it all,' was the flippant reply.

At last, the terrible truth was beginning to dawn. The bug had been there? He had watched the awful event occur. And . . . 'But why didn't you say what you saw? Why didn't you clear Owl's name?' Pentecost was flabbergasted. 'You knew what really happened, yet you said nothing?'

The bug shrugged. 'It was none of my business. We rare cockle-snorkles don't go in for the "help thy neighbour" rubbish. As far as I was concerned, it was a strictly private, family affair.'

'But a word from you, and Owl would have been a different bird,' the mouse could hardly believe his ears. 'All this time you've allowed him to think himself a killer. You callous little bug!'

'I've always tried to cheer him up,' the bug protested. 'What are you getting all steamed up about? What has Owl ever done for you, except stand you in neat rows?'

'That isn't the point,' said Pentecost. 'There's such a thing as Christian charity. No matter what Owl had done to me, I wouldn't ruin his life as you have done.'

'Who's too good to live then?' sneered the bug. 'Anyway, why should you care now? Lickey Top is vacant. It's yours. Just thank your lucky stars Owl's gone. Did you really think he'd let you have a small section?'

'He might have done, eventually,' said Pentecost. 'I was only just beginning to plead the case of the family, when Owl toppled dead from his perch.'

'Well, you can get ready to start pleading again,' said Uncle, tugging at his leader's fur. 'For, if I'm not mistaken,

196

Owl will be swinging back into action quite soon. I just saw his beak move.'

Still very annoyed, Pentecost looked upwards. To his amazement the 'dead' bird was beginning to stir in a most life-like way.

'Who moved my perching stump?' mumbled Owl, blinking rapidly. 'Green sky? Whoever saw a green sky? And where have all the stars gone?'

'You're looking at the grass, Owl,' said Pentecost, hurrying to assist in some way. 'And the stars are above your toes. The truth of the matter is, you're the wrong way up.'

Owl swung heavily back on to his perch. The bug fussed about him, pretending to be concerned. He was a worried insect. Thinking Owl to be dead, he had 'spilled the beans'. Now he was furiously thinking of a way to keep the mice from telling Owl what they had heard. But he need not have feared. Owl was in no mood to listen, despite Pentecost's pleas.

'But, Owl,' said the mouse. 'If you'll just listen for one moment? I have some news that will make you jump up and down on your perch for joy . . .'

'Owl's done quite enough jumping about for one day,' interrupted the bug sternly. 'What are you trying to do, make him injure himself again? Now, in my opinion, that insolent old mouse is to blame for your crack on the head, Owl. I suggest we make an example of him.'

Owl clicked his sharp beak angrily. The sound struck terror into the hearts of the simple Harvest mice. Pentecost realized that, at this moment, Owl was in no mood to be trifled with. He decided to go along with Owl, obey his instructions, and hope that at some time he would be allowed to speak. He realized that the bug would do everything in his power to prevent this. He could only wait for an opportunity and hope that the bug would drop his guard.

Owl and the bug were whispering again. After much nodding, the bug drew away and spoke. 'Listen carefully, for Owl is about to speak,' he said in a loud voice.

'The example will take one pace forward,' said Owl softly.

'One pace forward . . . step,' echoed the bug.

Uncle stayed where he was. 'I can't,' he said airily. The others gasped at such boldness.

'Can't, or won't?' asked Owl. 'Perhaps you would like me to make up your mind.' He teetered on his perch.

'And perhaps you would like another bang on the head?' replied Uncle. 'Don't forget what happened last time. The truth of the matter is, I can't. As you see, the little ones are cluttering up the front row. I happen to be in the back row. I can't pace through a solid wall of mouse, can I?'

'The small mice will part in the middle,' said the bug. 'In that way, the example can pass through their ranks.'

Owl watched approvingly, as the little ones obeyed. 'I was just going to suggest that myself,' he said. 'It's the obvious solution.'

Uncle stepped forward, his snout grim and set as he waited to hear his punishment.

'Your impudence will earn you imprisonment for life,' rasped Owl. 'The rest of you rabble will be gone from my property by morning, is that clear?'

'There's a problem, Owl,' said the bug. 'No prison, I'm afraid.'

'Then we'll build one,' said Owl, irritated that he hadn't thought before he'd spoken. 'Harvest mice weave, don't they? Well, they can weave a prison. Where's the problem?'

'Neatly solved, Owl,' said the admiring bug. 'Now listen, you lot. All the expert weavers, step forward.'

The Great Aunts, wringing their paws with worry, hurried forward. Even so, throughout the troubles they had continued to spin their grasses together, it having a soothing effect upon their minds. But they felt terribly afraid to be singled out by the terrifying owl. Numb with fear, they stood at the foot of the tree and stared upwards with tear-filled eyes.

'Now,' said Owl. 'I want this prison to be absolutely escape-proof. I want the inside lined with wickedly-pointed thorns and stinging nettles. I want that old mouse to suffer, is that clear?'

'Wicked thorns and stinging nettles,' said a Great Aunt faintly.

'Hedgehog quills are quite painful, so I believe,' said another. 'And there are a few lying about, I notice.'

'Whose side are you on?' yelled Uncle. 'How about a few brambles, as well?'

The good ladies began to scurry about, selecting the most vicious-looking materials they could find. Uncle watched morosely, as his prison began to take shape before his eyes. 'The Great Aunts always did hate me,' he said sadly. 'That's why they are making such a good job of it. They've never forgiven me for remaining a bachelor and refusing to marry one of them.'

The Great Aunts certainly were producing a work of art. They chose only the strongest grasses for their task. In no time at all Uncle's prison was completed. Cleverly, they had woven a tiny grass-barred grille into one side, so that Uncle could peer out at the free world. A few final touches and they stood back to admire their handiwork. 'A stronger prison, you'll never find,' said one proudly. 'We used a special cross-ply, so that Uncle cannot break out.'

Uncle walked around it a couple of times. He was enjoying his last free moments on earth. Pentecost and the mice bowed their heads, unable to meet his accusing stare. 'Throw the old mouse inside and bind up the entrance,' commanded

199

Owl. Uncle was shoved inside by the Great Aunts, who proceeded to secure the tiny door shut.

'Let that be a warning to you all,' sang the bug. 'Don't forget, first thing in the morning, off Owl's sections. And where you got the idea that Owl would ever let you have one, I can't imagine. If you had any ideas that Owl was good and kind, you can forget 'em.'

'I already have,' shouted Uncle. 'You should be the one chased packing. Is no-one going to tell Owl the truth about that traitor?'

Owl frowned and looked questioningly at the bug. 'What is he on about?' he asked.

'It'll be his mind wandering, I expect,' the bug said quickly. 'Being locked up has that effect on some.'

'But what's going on?' Owl persisted. 'What do they know that I don't? Is there some secret being kept from me?'

'If there were, you'd soon get to the bottom of it,' said the bug. 'There's not much folk can keep from you, Owl.'

But this time, the bug's flattery didn't work. He could sense trouble brewing. He desperately wanted the mice off Lickey Top, as soon as possible. He watched Pentecost carefully, ready to interrupt, if the mouse so much as opened his mouth.

Owl was still looking very strangely at the bug. 'What did the Pentecost mouse mean, about you being a traitor?'

Pentecost seized his opportunity. 'It wasn't I who said it, Owl. It was Uncle, who's in prison. But I can tell you what he meant. It was while you were hanging upside-down. The bug told us the truth about the egg business ...'

'I did no such thing,' declared the cockle-snorkle. 'Don't listen to him, he's lying.'

'You protest too much,' snapped Owl. 'Perhaps I will listen to what the mouse has to say.'

'Thank you, Owl' said Pentecost. 'You see, the bug thought he was safe when you were dead ...'

Owl interrupted. 'When I was dead? Whatever are you on about?'

'They're all mad, Owl,' pleaded the bug. The bird shushed him and motioned Pentecost to continue.

'You were hanging upside-down and we all thought you were dead,' went on the mouse. 'Of course, we were wrong, I can see that now. But what I want to tell you is, you never murdered your brother's egg, at all. Think, Owl, cast your mind back ...'

Owl closed his eyes and thought deeply. 'I was ... I was standing ... and they came home and ... killer they said ...'

'Before that,' urged Pentecost. 'Before they came home. Try and remember. You were ... come on ... you were ... polish ... polishing ...'

201

'. . . my dear brother's eggshell!' shouted Owl. 'I wasn't jumping up and down on it, I was polishing the bits of fluff off it. It's all coming back now . . .'

'That's what I was afraid of,' muttered the bug. 'Now I'm for it.'

'You certainly are, Cockle-snorkle!' cried Pentecost. 'For you saw the whole thing. Don't deny it.'

'Is this true?' breathed Owl softly. 'You saw the whole thing. You knew it was an accident, that I slipped.'

'It depends upon how you look at it,' said the bug lamely. 'I could have sworn that it was a deliberate murder. Oh dear, I'm getting all confused. What I mean is . . .'

'What you mean is, you are a liar,' said Pentecost. 'You told us it was an accident, pure and simple. The game's up, Cockle-snorkle. You used Owl's grief and confusion to further your own ends. Own up, do something good, for once in your life.'

Owl and the mice waited, as the miserable bug tussled with his conscience. Uncle stared impassively through the bars of his cell. All attention was switched from his plight, to the drab and tongue-tied insect, who had gone to ground behind his slip of bark.

'I'm saying nothing until I get advice,' he said sullenly.

'Come out, you skulking bug,' cried the little ones. 'Tell Owl the truth.'

'I'm saying nothing, on the grounds that it might incriminate me,' was the muffled reply.

'Perhaps if you said you were sorry, for starters?' encouraged Pentecost. 'And then, perhaps, a full confession would follow naturally?'

'I don't know about that,' the bug replied. 'We cockle-snorkles being so rare and all. We rarely say we're sorry. It's our code, you see.'

'Nevertheless, you look sorry,' went on the mouse. 'I've

never seen you looking so dull. So are you prepared to bare your soul and save all this unpleasantness?'

'I am,' said the bug, in a small voice. 'It's true I was there when your accident happened Owl. Believe me, when I say my heart went out to you on that terrible day. Even now, I can see you trying to shovel the smashed egg back together with your beak. I meant to tell you one day, truly I did. It just kept slipping my mind.'

Meanwhile, Pentecost had been studying Owl. He couldn't help but notice the change that had come over the bird. Gone was the nervous twitching. Gone was the haunted red-rimmed stare. Owl now wore an aura of serenity. He paced confidently along his perch, a jaunty spring to his heels.

'I must say you're looking chipper, Owl,' said the bug, trying to worm his way back into the bird's affections. 'That cock-sure strut suits you, I must say.'

'Yes, I do feel like a new bird, no thanks to you,' replied Owl. He heaved a great sigh, a sigh filled with regret and sadness, yet tinged with an inner peace. 'When I think of all the wasted time,' he whispered. 'All the things I could have done . . .'

'Ah yes,' echoed the cunning bug. 'The old enemy time, eh, Owl?' A pale lemon glow now illuminated the underside of his bark shelter, a glimmer of hope, no less.

'I might have done great things, had my chickhood been different . . .' Owl's voice trailed away.

The bug pressed home his stealthy attack. 'Surprising how it flies, eh, Owl? Time I mean. One minute, the world's your timeless oyster; the next, it's slammed shut in your face.'

'Yet the one who could have proved my innocence stood by and did nothing,' Owl went on, disbelief in his voice. 'He fed me lies while pretending to be my friend.'

'They say, if you're going to tell a lie, tell a whopper,' said the bug uneasily. The glow behind the slip of bark wavered. 'I had that on good authority, Owl.'

Pentecost interrupted. 'Don't you feel any remorse at all?' he said. 'After what you've done to this poor Owl's mind?'

The bug was silent for a few moments, as he considered this. 'I feel like I'm out on a limb,' he said. 'It isn't a pleasant feeling. Would that count as remorse?'

'It certainly wouldn't,' said the mouse. 'You're just thinking of yourself. Open up your heart, Cockle-snorkle, and tell us what you see.'

'I can see my world crashing down about my rare ears,' was the gloomy reply. 'And it's all thanks to you interfering mice. I should have known better, than to tell you the true story of Owl's chickhood. I'll think twice next time, before divulging top secret information. And never to a Harvest mouse, for they can't keep their mouths shut.'

'There are some secrets too terrible to keep,' replied Pentecost. 'Your world began to totter when you began to play both ends against the middle. Didn't you realise that, one day, the ends would meet and spell your own ruin?'

'They never did before,' sighed the bug. 'I should have examined Owl more closely for signs of life. But I didn't. I mean, he looked so dead, didn't he? But he wasn't and now I'm in a proper pickle.'

'And still you won't admit that you caused Owl's life to be worth less than a fig,' said the mouse. 'It's a wonder he hasn't tried to end it all before now. And I suppose you're banking on Owl's forgiveness? Kind as he is, I doubt if he could ever forget what you've done.'

'If I hadn't heard that with my own ears!' cried Uncle. 'Owl, kind? So he kindly put me in prison, did he? And he's given the family their marching orders from the goodness of his soul, eh? What kind of a mouse are you, to believe such claptrap?'

'The kind of mouse with the welfare of his family at heart,' replied Pentecost.

'Stooping even to crawling?' said Uncle, contempt in his voice.

'If necessary, yes,' was the reply. 'The lives of these little ones are more important than my personal honour. But then, you would never understand that, Uncle.'

'But I would,' said the grey old Pentecost, from the family group. 'Leadership requires many sacrifices. I have a worthy successor in that odd-eyed mouse. But I have said too much already. I will only add that the destiny of the family is in safe paws.'

'So speaks my brother from the shelter of obscurity,' spat Uncle. 'He wouldn't be so mealy-mouthed from the shelter of this prison.'

'Release the old mouse,' ordered Owl. The Great Aunts hurried forward to obey. Soon the door of the prison swung open and Uncle, with a superb bit of acting, lurched forward to fling himself into a dried-up puddle.

'Water, for pity's sake,' he gasped, raising his mud-smeared snout appealingly.

'Don't be silly,' said Pentecost. 'You can't be any thirstier than the rest of us. Be patient. We'll all have a good supper, when Owl has straightened out his problems.'

The mice looked up at the great bird. Owl cleared his throat and began to speak. 'Perhaps I've been a little hasty,' he said. 'I realise now the bug is to blame for our troubles, yours and mine. And so,' Owl continued, 'provided you keep the place neat and tidy and so long as you keep the noise of your festivals to a minimum, I am going to allow you to settle on a small section of Lickey Top . . .'

205

The rest of his words were drowned in cheers.

'A truly magnificent gesture, Owl,' said the bug. 'And please forgive me for not venturing out, but I'm in fear for my life. You do intend to settle accounts, I suppose?'

'You can rely on it,' said Owl grimly. 'I can't begin to describe what I feel for you. Words fail me.'

'That's nothing new,' said the defiant bug. 'I was always the brains of the outfit. It was I who fed you all your so-called flashes of genius. Admit it, Owl, you wouldn't recognize a good idea if you fell over one. And now I'm to be punished for being too bright for my own good. But I must warn you, I belong to an extremely rare species. The world will point an accusing finger, if you endanger us cockle-snorkles still further.'

'Your punishment is not for being too bright, but for ruining my life,' snapped the bird.

'But he's got something, Owl,' said Pentecost. 'All life, however wicked, is sacred.'

'I'm thinking forgiveness should be the order of the day, Owl,' said the bug hopefully. 'But, I've just realized, I've insulted you again. I never learn, do I?'

'You don't,' said Owl grimly. 'And now, a punishment to fit the crime. What shall we do with this bug, I wonder?'

'We could tear his legs off,' suggested Uncle. 'Or isn't that cruel enough?'

'You needn't bother,' said the bug. 'I intend to punish myself. I shall fly into the city and dance up and down the window-pane of a certain professor. You know the one I mean, Owl? Always poking about in the bushes with that net of his. In search of me, of course. Well, I shall go to him, this time. I shall give myself up. I won't last long in the pickling jar. In short, I will be popped, pickled, pulled out and pinned on pretty pink paper, prior to my preparation

206

for proper periodic perusal in the practical place provided. In short, I expect I shall end up in the Birmingham Museum, for folk to gawp at on rainy days.'

To his complete surprise, he could hear some of the mice sobbing. Curiosity caused him to poke his head from beneath his hide to see Owl's reaction to his words. To his astonishment, Owl had two large tears standing out from his eyes. 'Am I the cause of all this emotion?' thought the bug. Amazingly, it seemed he was. Never one to let advantage slip away, the bug piled on the agony.

'Of course, I wouldn't die straight away,' he said. 'It could take as long as a week. Pickling is a lengthy business, so they say. But then, my death throes are none of your concern. Oh well, I won't keep you mice from your celebrations any longer. I expect you are eager to begin dancing and singing in honour of Owl's change of heart? As for me, I will go and surrender immediately.' He rose into the night sky, his glow an unhealthy shade of lemon.

'Wait!' said Owl.

The bug hovered uncertainly overhead. Respectfully, carefully hiding his jubilation, he said, 'What is it, Owl? Isn't the punishment harsh enough? Do you wish to torture me, before I buzz off to be pickled? I wouldn't blame you in the least.'

'I can't do it,' said Owl brokenly. 'Regardless of what you've done, I can't bear to think of you in that jar.'

'I'll only gurgle desperately for a week or so,' consoled the bug. 'You think of yourself, Owl, and your new and happy life.' Despite the sadness in his voice, the bug's glow was becoming brighter.

'Anyone can fall into bad ways,' ventured Pentecost. 'Perhaps you could see your way clear to giving him another chance, Owl?'

The bug's light positively bloomed. 'What would you say

to three days banishment from my sight?' asked Owl. 'Would you accept that as your punishment?'

'Certainly not,' replied the bug. 'To be parted from you, for so long, would be sheer hell for me. No, I'd sooner be pickled.'

'Just as you wish,' said Owl sadly.

The bug leapt in quickly. 'No, Owl,' he said. 'Orders are orders. I will take my punishment, as a rare cockle-snorkle should. Three terrible days of banishment it is.'

Owl controlled his emotion enough to spell out the terms of the punishment. 'You will remain beneath your slip of bark for three days. During that time, you will make no attempt to communicate with anyone. You will use those three days to reflect upon your misdeeds. The sentence starts as from now.'

'How truly forgiving you are,' murmured the bug. 'I don't deserve it. In fact, I refuse such leniency. No, I shall go and give myself up.' Once more, he prepared for flight, but only going through the motions, this time. He was expecting to be recalled at any moment.

'Don't overdo it, Cockle-snorkle,' warned Pentecost. 'Owl's patience can only be strained so much.'

'If you really feel you must go, we won't try to stop you,' said Owl. 'But my offer still stands.'

'It's no good,' said the bug, at last. 'I can't go against my friend's wishes. I will remain and begin my sentence. By the way, Owl, will it be all right if I take a short flyabout, from time to time? You know how cramped one's wings get.'

'I don't see why not,' replied the bird.

'And I would need to speak to folk, from time to time. You know, to tell them how much I'm suffering and how much I miss you, Owl. Would that be too much to ask?'

'Contact within reason will be permitted,' said Owl. 'Never let it be . . .'

'And would it be possible to start my banishment tomorrow?' said the bug quickly. 'Only I'm so excited, having new neighbours and everything. I doubt if I could control my happiness. I'd be constantly breaking the rules and flying about and chattering. That would never do, would it, Owl?'

'Tomorrow it is,' said Owl solemnly. 'Or perhaps next Wednesday. I really don't mind. So long as you remember that the sentence must be served, I don't really care when you start it.'

'I'll start next year, promise,' said the bug happily. His brilliance, by now, equalled the stars in the sky.

'That's the cleverest bit of unbanishing I've ever seen,' said Uncle admiringly. 'That's what I call an expert bit of hoodwinking. The bug was right, he was the brains of the outfit.'

Owl glared at him through those huge eyes. Pentecost hastened to repair the damage. 'You really must learn to control your tongue,' he said. 'You've been in prison once, Uncle. I doubt if you'd survive a longer stretch. Be warned. And now, if Owl will excuse us, we will rustle ourselves a bit of supper and then settle down for the night. It's been a long day and we're all very tired.'

'I quite understand,' Owl replied. 'For myself, I think I'll have a fly around. I want to be alone for a while.' He slipped clumsily from his perch and wobbled off into the night, a ghostly grey shape, soon swallowed up in the gloom.

'Good mousing, Owl,' called the bug.

'What do you mean,' retorted Uncle. 'Owl wants to be alone. What have mice to do with lonely thinking?'

'Quite a lot, when one feels peckish,' grinned the bug.

'We believe Owl has gone to gather hazel-nuts,' said the little ones. 'But we're rarely correct.' They were hustled off by old Mother and the tut-tutting Great Aunts.

For a while, the bug, warm and safe beneath his scrap of

209

bark, watched the mice going about their tasks. Pentecost supervised the gathering of sweet roots, while the Great Aunts erected temporary shelters for the night. In the morning, they would begin their labour of love, the building of the new homes. These would be strong, weather-proof and lined throughout with the softest mosses. But, for this one night, the family would have to make do with something more rough and ready.

Already the bug was bored again. The excitement of the day had worn off. Even now, he was plotting new mischiefs. Various schemes were being sifted through his computer-like mind. What he needed was a good intrigue to occupy his busy mind. 'I say there,' he called. 'Yes, you, the Pentecost mouse.'

Pentecost stopped what he was doing and approached the tree. 'Now what?' he said. 'More lies, I suppose?'

'It depends' replied the bug. 'What if I was lying all the time? What if I really did see Owl jumping up and down on his brother's egg?'

'Not again,' sighed Pentecost.

'But what if Owl really is a killer?' insisted the bug.

'If he was, he'd never know the truth,' the mouse replied.

'Oh, and why not?'

'Because he could never be sure whether you weren't playing both ends against the middle again. He may forgive you in time, but he'll never completely trust you.'

'To tell you the truth, I can't stand the new Owl,' sighed the bug. 'I liked him when he was full of woe and hate. I hope he isn't going to turn out prissy and holier-than-thou.'

'He's at peace with the world, leave him be,' said the mouse.

'Yes, well you have to say that, don't you?' said the bug. 'After all, you've got a new home out of this. It's in your interest to keep him sweet.'

210

'The trouble with you is, you don't know when you're beaten, Cockle-snorkle.'

'Me, beaten?' laughed the bug. 'Just you watch me.'

'That's exactly what I intend doing,' was the reply. 'You aren't the only clever one on Lickey Top now, Cockle-snorkle. Didn't I win a new home for the family?' His voice dropped. 'My only regret is, that Fox never lived to see it.'

'There's an old saying, kill a fox in one spot and he'll pop up in another,' grinned the bug.

'What does that mean?' asked the mouse.

'It means I've said enough for one night,' was the reply. 'And now, will you agree to a truce? Not a permanent one. I mean, just for the time being?'

'A truce it is,' replied Pentecost.

'See you in the morning then?' said the bug.

'Bright and early,' replied Pentecost.' We've a lot to do tomorrow.'

'So it's all's well that ends well, eh?' said the bug.

Pentecost thought about this. 'I wouldn't say that,' he replied. 'Members of my family died, that the rest of us might reach Lickey Top in safety.'

'I realize that,' said the bug. 'But so did Fox. Die, I mean. Or have you forgotten about him? Didn't he lay down his life in the Weasel Woods for you lot?'

'I haven't forgotten,' replied Pentecost soberly. 'I would give anything to see him rolling up Lickey Top, his red brush streaming in the wind.'

'Anything?' enquired the bug. 'Or is that just big talk? Would you, for instance, swop places with him? Would you have sacrificed your life for him, say?'

'I would,' said the mouse firmly. 'For he was a good and true friend.'

The bug looked bemused. 'I really believe you would, at that.'

211

'But all this talk is silly,' said Pentecost. 'Didn't you yourself see Fox torn to pieces by the dogs?'

'I do remember saying that,' grinned the bug. 'But I've a feeling, don't ask me what it is. If we all keep our spare legs crossed, who knows what might happen?'

'More double agent work?' sighed the mouse. 'And what are you cooking up this time, Cockle-snorkle?'

'Never you mind,' said the bug. 'But, in a strange world, unexpected things happen. That's what makes life so exciting, don't you think?'

'I prefer the quiet life,' said Pentecost. 'And now my work is over, I intend to settle down and watch the world from Lickey Top.'

'So all your troubles are over, eh?'

'I hope so, with all my heart,' replied Pentecost.

'You mice,' sighed the bug. 'So naive. Never stopping to wonder what's just around the next bend. It'll be the death of you one day, mark my words. And now, goodnight to you, young mouse.'

'And you too, Cockle-snorkle.'

The bug crawled beneath his slip of bark, to savour the secret only he knew. Fox of Furrowfield was alive and kicking. He couldn't wait to see the faces of the mice, when Fox came rolling upon Lickey Top, for he surely would, being the curious creature he was.

That night Pentecost spent a lot of time gazing at the moon, thinking of what had gone before and grieving the loss of his good friend, Fox.

16 In Country Sleep

The next day was a proud, but sad, one for a mouse called Pentecost. He sat quite alone on the highest tip of Lickey Top and thought of all that had gone before. He smiled to himself, as he wondered how Snake was getting on with the crafty Cousin. He felt a surge of pity, as he imagined the lying frog, sitting on his dustbin-lid, crying out for company and compassion. He felt happiness, that Owl's terrible burden of guilt had been lifted from him. As for the cockle-snorkle, he could only frown and wonder how such beauty could mask so much malice. Only the thought of Little Brother cleared his brow and he smiled wistfully. Again, he saw the anticipation upon his friend's face, the excitement as he scurried over the hill to Wending Way Stream. And here, from his high vantage point, he watched his family hurrying about below, intent upon building a new and peaceful life.

Pride indeed. But sadness too. For lastly, and most of all, he thought about and grieved for Fox.

Suddenly, as if in answer to a prayer, Pentecost saw a flash of red emerging from the Weasel Woods, far below. For a while he watched, hardly daring to hope, as the speck of red grew larger, as it began to roll in a familiar way up Lickey Top. And then, there was no doubt.

'Fox!' cried Pentecost. He rose to his paws, his happiness complete. He began to run down the hill, impatient to narrow the distance between him and his friend. The family, work for the moment forgotten, stopped to watch their leader race by. Then they too saw.

'It's Fox!' shouted Pentecost. His heart thudded, sang. That great open thing, enwrapped in so ridiculously small a frame, fluttered, exuding love and joy enough to comfort the whole wide and wicked world. Two friends, one feared for dead, the other dying, neared.

The boys stepped from the trees; one, air-rifle held to shoulder, the second impassively watching.

'CRACK!' Instinctively, Fox ducked. The mean, hot, singing shot whistled over his head, burying itself into the hill and through the breast of a mouse called Pentecost.

'It's only a mouse,' the voice, in disgust, a foot nudging the small lifeless creature.

'Straight through the heart,' the second voice, not sad, for fear it would give its own heart away.

The boys turned and left. For a long time there was quiet. Then suddenly the sleeping countryside seemed to stir in noisy tumult. And the four winds, their tusslings for that captured moment stilled, sighed as one.

Fox sat motionless upon the hill. And, as the moon rose, he threw back his head and howled, expressing for all the loss, the sheer wanton waste, the loneliness.

One by one, the stars appeared. And then, great burdening clouds built up to blot them out. There, in that funereal darkness, the body of Pentecost of Lickey Top was laid to rest. And there were flowers there.

Uncle, his face as dark as the night, stood alone, his thoughts unspoken. No need to say what was on every mind. The bug and Owl sat silently upon their perch, the insect in his drab attire to suit the sad occasion.

And then it was all over.

Some time later, Fox paused just inside the Weasel Woods and, looking up, saw the clouds part. A solitary star winked once, winked twice, before vanishing behind more cloud. It was at that moment he heard the voice. It was chanting in a strange and haunting monotone.

'The family sleep,
And though tomorrow they may laugh or weep,
Still life goes on . . .'

Surprised, Fox spun around. It was then he saw. 'And what is a small mouse like you doing, rhyming in a wood so far from home?' he asked kindly.

The mouse stepped from the shadows. Fox noticed the misshapen ears, the earnest expression.

'I like to be alone sometimes. Especially now,' the mouse replied. 'Ever since my hearing was impaired in Woodpecker Wood, I've tended to keep myself to myself. I find rhyming a great comfort, don't you, Fox?'

Fox grinned. 'However did you guess?'

'I suppose I'm gifted that way,' the mouse replied. He twisted shyly.

Fox sobered. 'I'm so very sorry about your loss. In a way, I feel responsible. If only . . .'

'It was meant to be,' was the reply.

'I still can't believe he's gone. He was my friend, you see. The only friend I'd ever known.'

'And still have,' the mouse replied.

Fox looked puzzled.

'You'll come and see us again soon?' the mouse continued. 'You are always welcome on Lickey Top, you know that, Fox.'

Fox nodded. Then he grinned again. 'And who shall I ask for, when I come a-calling and a-rhyming?'

'Just ask for Pentecost,' came the reply. With that, the mouse vanished into the tall grasses.

For a long time, Fox just sat there. Then gradually, the

sights and sounds of the night began to intrude upon his deep thoughts. He listened to the breeze rustling amongst the leaves, picked up the sound of running water, heard a nightingale warbling in a thicket. All around he could hear it . . . the song.

Once more the clouds parted to reveal that twinkling star. And Fox, grinning, winked right back. Happy now, he set off for home, secure in his understanding. Before he vanished into the trees, some impulse caused him to kick up his rear paws in a most unfoxlike way. The night closed around him. And the song spun on, a word to a note, a note to a word unendingly . . .

A Selected List of Fiction from Mammoth

While every effort is made to keep prices low, it is sometimes necessary to increase prices at short notice. Mandarin Paperbacks reserves the right to show new retail prices on covers which may differ from those previously advertised in the text or elsewhere.

The prices shown below were correct at the time of going to press.

☐	7497 0978 2	**Trial of Anna Cotman**	Vivien Alcock	£2.50
☐	7497 0712 7	**Under the Enchanter**	Nina Beachcroft	£2.50
☐	7497 0106 4	**Rescuing Gloria**	Gillian Cross	£2.50
☐	7497 0035 1	**The Animals of Farthing Wood**	Colin Dann	£3.50
☐	7497 0613 9	**The Cuckoo Plant**	Adam Ford	£3.50
☐	7497 0443 8	**Fast From the Gate**	Michael Hardcastle	£1.99
☐	7497 0136 6	**I Am David**	Anne Holm	£2.99
☐	7497 0295 8	**First Term**	Mary Hooper	£2.99
☐	7497 0033 5	**Lives of Christopher Chant**	Diana Wynne Jones	£2.99
☐	7497 0601 5	**The Revenge of Samuel Stokes**	Penelope Lively	£2.99
☐	7497 0344 X	**The Haunting**	Margaret Mahy	£2.99
☐	7497 0537 X	**Why The Whales Came**	Michael Morpurgo	£2.99
☐	7497 0831 X	**The Snow Spider**	Jenny Nimmo	£2.99
☐	7497 0992 8	**My Friend Flicka**	Mary O'Hara	£2.99
☐	7497 0525 6	**The Message**	Judith O'Neill	£2.99
☐	7497 0410 1	**Space Demons**	Gillian Rubinstein	£2.50
☐	7497 0151 X	**The Flawed Glass**	Ian Strachan	£2.99

All these books are available at your bookshop or newsagent, or can be ordered direct from the publisher. Just tick the titles you want and fill in the form below.

Mandarin Paperbacks, Cash Sales Department, PO Box 11, Falmouth, Cornwall TR10 9EN.

Please send cheque or postal order, no currency, for purchase price quoted and allow the following for postage and packing:

UK including BFPO — £1.00 for the first book, 50p for the second and 30p for each additional book ordered to a maximum charge of £3.00.

Overseas including Eire — £2 for the first book, £1.00 for the second and 50p for each additional book thereafter.

NAME (Block letters) ....

ADDRESS ....

....

☐ I enclose my remittance for ....

☐ I wish to pay by Access/Visa Card Number ☐☐☐☐☐☐☐☐☐☐☐☐☐☐☐☐

Expiry Date ☐☐☐☐